JASMINE ZUMIDEH NEEDS A WIN

JASMINE ZUMIDEH NEEDS A WIN

SUSAN AZIM BOYER

WEDNESDAY BOOKS
NEW YORK

First published in the United States by Wednesday Books, an imprint of St. Martin's Publishing Group

JASMINE ZUMIDEH NEEDS A WIN. Copyright © 2022 by Susan Azim Boyer. All rights reserved. Printed in the United States of America. For information, address St. Martin's Publishing Group, 120 Broadway, New York, NY 10271.

www.wednesdaybooks.com

Designed by Devan Norman
Case stamp art © Shutterstock.com

Library of Congress Cataloging-in-Publication Data

Names: Boyer, Susan Azim, author.
Title: Jasmine Zumideh needs a win / Susan Azim Boyer.
Description: First edition. | New York : Wednesday Books, 2022. | Audience: Ages 12–18.
Identifiers: LCCN 2022021560 | ISBN 9781250833686 (hardcover) | ISBN 9781250833693 (ebook)
Subjects: LCSH: Iranian Americans—Fiction. | CYAC: Iranian Americans—Fiction. | Identity—Fiction. | High schools—Fiction. | Schools—Fiction. | Student government—Fiction. | LCGFT: Novels.
Classification: LCC PZ7.1.B6955 Jas 2022 | DDC [Fic]—dc23
LC record available at https://lccn.loc.gov/2022021560

Our books may be purchased in bulk for promotional, educational, or business use. Please contact your local bookseller or the Macmillan Corporate and Premium Sales Department at 1-800-221-7945, extension 5442, or by email at MacmillanSpecialMarkets@macmillan.com.

First Edition: 2022

10 9 8 7 6 5 4 3 2 1

To my knight in shining armor,
the man who has literally made all of my dreams come true,
who has never lost faith in me (even as I lost faith in myself):
my husband and best friend, Wayne.
I would not be here, on these pages, without you.

JASMINE ZUMIDEH NEEDS A WIN

CHAPTER ONE

SOMETHING EXTRA

When I'm on the tour bus interviewing Chrissie Hynde of the Pretenders and she hands me a bottle of Jack Daniel's, I'm taking a swig. It would be rude to refuse. The last thing I'd want to do is piss Chrissie off.

My import single of "Stop Your Sobbing" is already warped from listening to it over and over. And over. I'll be first in line at Tower Records when their debut album comes out in January. All I have to do is convince the editor of the school newspaper to let me be one of the first college reporters to interview Chrissie when they tour next fall. *If* I get into NYU.

I have to get into NYU.

I grab my notebook and pen from my nightstand and start jotting down notes.

Chrissie Hynde, leather-clad lead singer for the Pretenders, is surrounded by male bandmates. "A sausage-fest," she calls it. The bus reeks of clove cigarettes and Jack Daniel's.

Leather-clad. Ugh. Too cliché. And who even knows if she smokes clove cigarettes?

Chrissie's face is etched with defiance: lip semi-snarled, eyes underlined in black—a bid for attention belied by the curtain of fringe that obscures them.

Curtain of fringe. Mr. Ramos would like that metaphor.

"Jasmine-joon, you are helping me with the rice?" Auntie Minah calls from the kitchen.

"Coming," I answer sharply. I'm *right* in the middle of my interview.

"They're all men." Chrissie gestures to her bandmates and crew. "Nobody to talk to about sex or commiserate with when you're on the rag." She upends the now half-drunk bottle. "That's why it's so nice to have someone like you here to interview me, Jasmine."

She hands me the bottle.

"You are coming, Jasmine-joon?" Auntie Minah calls again from the kitchen.

My editor would probably strike through the last paragraph. Rock chicks never get to talk about their periods.

Male journalists write about gawking at groupies or plaster-casting their penises with Mick Jagger all the time.

New York University. My one-way ticket out of Bumfuck, California, and into the New York music scene to write for *Creem*, the only rock magazine that cares about artists with integrity like Chrissie Hynde and Elvis Costello. The LA scene is deader than Jim Morrison (and a two-hour crawl from our house to the Sunset Strip). Your reign is over, Aerosmith. It's 1979: fossilize the dinosaurs of rock already.

Mr. Ramos says I'm one of his first students with a real shot at acceptance. I have "a voice" and "a point of view," and I'm "dogged," which doesn't sound like a compliment but is.

The Heidi and Ruthie dolls Mom got for my first Christmas stare at me with feigned indifference from their perch on my pink scalloped shelves. I can't take them with me. East Coast girls are way more mature. They wear pearls and blazers and go to private schools with names like the Covington Academy.

"*Joonam*," Auntie calls with more urgency.

I stuff the notebook into my nightstand and run downstairs to help Auntie Minah with the rice.

|||||||||||||

Making Persian rice is a whole production. First, you rinse the basmati—it has to be basmati rice from the Persian market—then soak it in salt water overnight. Rinse again and transfer to a pot to parboil, which Auntie Minah says means to cook halfway.

She quizzes me. "What is next, joonam?"

I said we didn't need Auntie Minah to babysit us while Mom's in Kansas with Grandma Jean and Dad has to travel for work—I mean, I'm almost eighteen—but nobody listened.

"Drain the parboiled rice and add oil to the pot, Auntie," I say, sliding on Mom's hideous, moss-green oven mitts, which match the flocked wallpaper and hanging ferns.

"*Amme* Minah, Jasmine-joon," she huffs. "Why your father never teach you the Farsi?"

I pick up the pot and dump the steamed rice into a colander in the kitchen sink. "He was too busy trying to be American to teach us how to be Iranian."

"I teach you," Auntie says, brushing her thick auburn hair away from her face.

Maybe she'll teach me how to do a henna rinse, too. We're two days into our crash course in All Things Iranian. Somehow, Dad was able to coax her out of her apartment in San Francisco. To her, Los Angeles is nothing but one big five-lane freeway. She's not wrong. Everyone thinks Southern California is all bikinis and beaches, but we're more than an hour inland, a blur of recurring tract homes and mini malls inhabited by the same combination of a nail salon, 7-Eleven, Winchell's Donuts, and "ethnic" restaurant.

Dad says we're probably the only Iranians within a twenty-five-mile radius.

"If your father marry an Iranian woman, he would never be divorced. You would speak the Farsi," she declares.

I turn the heat up under the pot and add a layer of corn oil, then grab a couple pieces of lavash flatbread from the package on the kitchen counter. "They're not divorced yet. Not totally." Legally separated. They *could* still reconcile. They have every other time.

Although, Mom has never left before.

Auntie raises a hand. "No, Jasmine-joon. Wait. The oil is not hot enough."

I reach for the November issue of *Creem* magazine on top of the pile of mail on the kitchen counter. Why is Jimmy Page on the cover when Zeppelin is so played out—

Oh my God! The letter I've been waiting for, it's right here under my magazine. No one even told me. My notification from the Aspiring Young Journalists Award Committee: after my grades and my writing samples, the finishing touch for my application. Finally.

"Now, joonam." Auntie motions to the pot. "Layer in the lavash. Oil is popping."

"Wait, Auntie, let me look at this—"

"*Now.*"

I put the letter aside and quickly layer the flatbread on the bottom of the pot, then dump in the rice, grabbing a wooden spoon to make wells with the handle end. I pour in more corn oil so the crunchy bottom layer of tahdig will taste like movie popcorn, only better.

While the rice cooks, I snatch the envelope and open it. Did I get first place, second, or third? Even an honorable mention will do.

"Dear Miss Zumideh," the letter reads. "Thank you for your interest in the Aspiring Young Journalists Award. Unfortunately . . ."

Unfortunately?

Unfortunately.

My chest collapses in on my stomach. It's not possible. I didn't even *place* in this competition. Mr. Ramos told me not to write about David Bowie, how he's the only artist reinventing himself—he's cycled through three musical personas in the last decade alone: Ziggy Stardust, Aladdin Sane, and the Thin White Duke—while the Eagles and Led Zeppelin are still suspended in the resin of the 1970s like prehistoric insects. The 70s basically *ended* in '77 with the Sex Pistols.

Write a straight news article about a town council ordinance or mayoral malfeasance, Mr. Ramos said. Why didn't I listen?

"Something wrong, joonam?" Auntie asks.

"No, Auntie." My voice cracks. "I mean, Amme."

Nothing, except the something extra for my application just went up in smoke. I can practically smell it burning.

"Oh no, joonam," Auntie cries. "The rice. You turn the oil up too high."

Auntie performs a rescue operation on the rice while I

toss the rejection letter in the trash. Now I've got absolutely nothing for my something extra.

"Dinner ready?" Dad emerges from his office cocoon.

"Jasmine burned the rice," Ali says, bounding down the stairs. "I could smell it all the way upstairs."

"How do you know? Your room smells like a wet dog—and we don't have a dog."

"It's okay, it's okay," Auntie says. She skims the unburnt portion from the pot. "Go. Sit."

We take our places around the dining room table. No reruns in front of the TV with Auntie, which means Dad, Ali, and I have to engage in idle chitchat. I'm not telling them about the contest. Dad's too wrapped up in his business trip, and it's not like I'd get any sympathy from Ali. We're certainly not going to talk about Mom.

"Um, what time is your flight?" I ask, tearing off a piece of lavash bread Auntie has set on the table along with the sabzi: raw onion, herbs, and, inexplicably, radishes.

"Five a.m.," Dad says with a sigh.

He looks so tired. His tan skin is sallow, his dark hair is thinning at the temples. Ten cities in four weeks to introduce a new fighter jet to the other engineers at his defense contracting firm. He'll be even more exhausted by the time he gets back.

Ali grabs a piece of lavash. "Did you get a window or an aisle seat?"

"Window," Dad says as Auntie carries in the platter of rice with tomato and eggplant stew. "Kheili mamnoon, Minah-joon," he says. "Khoresht-e baademjoon. My favorite."

"Khaahesh mikonam, you're welcome," says Auntie. She takes Dad's plate and piles it high.

"Aisle's better," Ali says. Now that he's a junior, he thinks he knows everything.

"Window is way better," I say, handing her mine. "You can see the clouds and the cities all stretching out below."

"You can stretch your *legs* in the aisle," Ali says, popping a radish in his mouth.

"Window's still better."

"No, it's not."

"Yes, it is."

"*Guys,*" Dad nearly shouts.

We get quiet.

"None of this while I'm gone, understood?"

We nod. But asking us not to argue is about as realistic as asking the same of him and Mom. By now, I've lost my appetite. All I want to do is go upstairs and figure out a plan B for my application. I make crazy eights with my fork to make it look like I'm eating so Auntie won't be offended. "It's delicious, Auntie," I say. "Thank you."

Her face crumples. "Daadash, why you never teach them the Farsi?"

"I got them that Learning Language series," Dad says, mixing his rice and stew together.

Thirty cassettes to learn a language. Ali listened to every . . . single . . . one.

The only way you'd know he's Iranian is his full-on *Starsky & Hutch* 'stache and wild, puffy hair. He got Mom's green eyes and slender, Irish American nose. But Ali is the one who learned the language, follows the politics. I got Dad's "sleepy" brown eyes and "strong" nose. And Auntie's figure. "Zaftig," Grandma Jean calls it.

"Anyway, we're never going to Iran now that the ayatollah took over," Ali says with his mouth full.

"Ali," I hiss at him. Talk like this upsets Auntie.

Auntie's eyes well. "Your grandmother says protesters are still in the streets every day."

As a half 'n' half, I never paid much attention to what was going on in Iran, a faraway place we would visit "one day." As long as Grandma Zumideh was safe. Now we get updates on the Iranian Revolution that overthrew the king daily.

"But she's okay, right?" I ask.

"She's fine," Dad says. "And I guarantee, the CIA will run some covert operation to put the shah back in power."

Auntie frowns. "The shah was a very bad man, daadash. There is no freedom under Reza Shah. Nobody wants the shah back."

"He was better for *us*," Dad says. He soaks up the rest of his stew with the flatbread.

"Who is 'us'?" Auntie asks with the arch of one perfectly threaded brow.

"You know what I mean," he says. "Listen, you kids be good for your aunt."

"We will," Ali and I say in unison. He means Ali. I'm pretty much an adult.

"I'll be back in time for Thanksgiving." He stands up, gives Auntie a kiss on each cheek. "Kheili mamnoon, Minahjoon. Back to work. Early flight." He gives me a quick kiss on the forehead and Ali a pat on the shoulder.

Just as he heads back to his office, the phone rings. Ali jumps up to answer. I hope it's not for me.

I have to figure out what to do about my application. I should have fought harder to be editor of the paper this year, but I would have had to wrestle Gerald to the ground for it. And who wants to edit articles about the cafeteria menu or the big game when I thought I had this contest in the bag? I don't want to talk to anyone.

"Jasmine." Ali hands me the phone. "It's Mom."

Except for Mom. "I'll take it upstairs." I pull the phone from the hallway into my room so Auntie won't hear if Mom says anything bad about Dad. "Hi, Mom." I force a cheery tone.

"Hi, honey," she says, inhaling the Eve Menthol she must have retrieved from her sequined cigarette case. "Ali said you and your aunt made dinner together."

"I helped make the rice is all." I sit cross-legged on my bed with a half-eaten bag of Skittles I grab from my dresser. Little yellowed pieces of Scotch tape litter my walls from years of putting up and taking down posters. Cheap Trick has to come down. Elvis Costello can stay up. "How are you feeling, Mom?"

"Better. I saw a therapist today." A big exhale. "She gave me an emotional checklist of symptoms to watch for when the divorce is final. Like uncontrolled rage."

Sometimes, she overshares.

They've threatened it so many times before. They've always gotten back together.

The last time, in fifth grade, I locked myself in my room and listened to *Goodbye Yellow Brick Road* for two days straight. The double album had just come out. The title track and "Candle in the Wind" and "Bennie and the Jets" were all about love and loss and letting go, and it felt like Elton John was right there with me in just as much pain.

I fish an orange Skittle out of the bag. "Do you . . . know when you're coming back?"

No answer. She's already been gone for two weeks.

"Mom?"

She exhales again. "Jasmine, I've been talking to your grandmother about maybe staying. Here. In Kansas."

I nearly choke on the Skittle. "*Staying?* Like, forever?"

"I could go back to school here, get my teaching degree."

"What about me and Ali?" I cry.

"You can finish out the school year there and come here in the summer. You're going off to college in the fall."

"Mom, if I don't get into NYU . . ."

I'm not moving to Manhattan, Kansas. Imagine saying

you're from Manhattan and then having to say, "No. The other one." If I don't get into NYU, I'll stay with Dad and go to Cal State.

God. I can't choose between Mom and Dad. Plus, Cal State doesn't even have a proper journalism department. Kansas State does, but what band has ever come out of Kansas except . . . Kansas?

"We'll talk about it another time," she says abruptly. "Forget I brought it up."

As if I could. We hang up. I flop back on my bed. An hour ago, I was on the tour bus with Chrissie Hynde. Now it's driving away, belching a big black cloud of smoke in my face.

And she's serious this time. They could *actually* get a divorce. Split our family apart. Mom and Dad would fight over custody of Ali. Sit on opposite sides of the auditorium at my graduation. Refuse to talk to each other at my wedding.

Dad better have a good apology ready for Mom when she comes home—and maybe those emerald earrings she's always wanted.

|||||||||||||

"You don't want the sangak with feta and walnut for breakfast?" Auntie asks as I breeze by.

"Uh . . ." I stall.

I'm on a mission to get to school before first period and meet with our guidance counselor to find that "something extra" for my application.

Her shoulders droop. For her, an uneaten meal is like unrequited love.

Ali is at the kitchen table devouring Auntie's sangak along with the *New York Times* Dad left behind. Poor Ali, trapped in Kansas with Mom and Grandma Jean: Grandma badgering him to cut his hair or bursting in on him at inopportune moments, like when he's secretly browsing through Mom's *Cosmo*.

I pause at the back door. "You want a ride to school?"

"Got one," he says, turning to the sports section.

Just as well. I've got to get to the counselor's office.

Outside, a warm, acrid wind—the Santa Anas, whirling up from Orange County—covers Mom's lemon-yellow Toyota Corolla in an even thicker layer of dust. Somehow, Ali has resisted writing "Wash Me" on the back window. The fake strawberry air freshener hanging from the rearview reminds me of Mom, blasting her Janis Joplin cassettes, singing along to "Me and Bobby McGee." I like Janis. She's wild and raw like Chrissie.

Another week or two at Grandma Jean's, and Mom will be ready to come back as her old self. Or a new, improved one. As long as she comes back.

The Eisenhower High parking lot is nearly full when I pull in: the stoners and skaters, the jocks and soon-to-be dropouts sneaking one last cigarette before class. Our campus must have seemed super-modern when it was built in the 1950s. Lots of concrete and low, boxy buildings painted pale sage green with a lone oak tree in the middle of the quad.

I head toward the Admin building and our counselor, Mr. Buchanan's, office. He's rocking a radical comb-over and sporting his plaid, bad sportscaster sports coat when I show up in his doorway. A portrait of former president Richard M. Nixon hangs on the wall opposite his desk. Everyone knows Mr. Buchanan is obsessed with him.

"It wasn't so much the crime as the cover-up," I say as I sit across from him, the only thing I remember about the whole Nixon Watergate scandal from when it was on television 24/7.

"I agree. Nixon should have done a much better job covering it up. Now, Miss Azumski—"

"Zumideh," I correct him. Everyone gets intimidated by all the vowels.

He dons his reading glasses and peers at my transcript. "So, you need something extra, something that makes you stand out from the crowd. Apart from your name."

"Yes. I'm on the school paper, taking honors classes. I was a student reporter for the—"

"Oh, Miss Zip-uh-dee-ay," he says, not even coming close, "*everyone* applying to NYU is taking honors classes and interned at their local paper." He leans back in his chair. "You know, East Coast schools are out of reach for most Californians. You're not the country club set. You're all barefoot at the beach, toking on marijuana cigarettes. Rutgers man, myself."

"Actually, I don't smoke."

"Were you a Girl Scout?" He removes his reading glasses. "Did you get that Gold Award?"

"Uh, no." Not even a Brownie.

"A camp counselor?"

No. I wasted the summer on soap operas because I thought I would win the Young Journalists Award. And I would have, if the judges knew anything about music.

I should have known they wouldn't.

"Do you speak a second language?"

Dammit. Why didn't I listen to those cassettes?

"Mr. Buchanan, I need that something extra *now*. The application deadline is December first. It's already October twenty-eighth."

He sticks his finger in his ear while he thinks, as if tuning to a certain frequency. "What about a service project? Volunteering at the hospital or an old folks' home."

Great. Barf or bedpans.

He exhales, straining the center button on his jacket. "You and that other fella, putting all your eggs in the NYU basket, you may end up with yolk on your face when we have several fine universities right here: USC, UCLA. Cal State."

USC and UCLA are filled with stuck-up sorority girls. "I'm applying to State as a fallback, but—wait, what 'other fella'?"

"Oh, you know. Gene, or is it . . . Joe? Anyway, Miss Zum-buh-dum, take heart." I lean forward with anticipation.

"No one from Eisenhower High has ever actually gotten into NYU. You won't have to feel bad if you fail."

I'm not going to fail. I'm going to be the first college reporter to interview Chrissie Hynde.

I gather my purse and folder. "Thanks for your, um, guidance, sir," I say. "And by the way," I add on my way out, "it's pronounced 'Zoom-ee-day.'"

CHAPTER TWO

SHIT-TALKERS AND SNAKES

Barf or bedpans. At least I've got two options. Volunteer time will have to fit around my shifts at Hot Dog on a Stick. I should have made out with the assistant manager in the breakroom since he does the schedule. But his breath smelled like bong water and—

"Ah!" I yelp, nearly colliding, head-on, with Curtis.

Wait. I forgot. I'm not ever saying His name again. I had managed to avoid Him by taking long, circuitous routes to first period. I hate Him. I hate that my heart still jumps for Him.

"Jasmine," Bridget calls out from across the quad.

Good. I can hurry by and pretend I don't see Him.

Bridget O'Connell walking through the quad is like Moses parting the Red Sea. All the guys pause and turn. Maybe because she's a cheerleader. Or because of her heart-shaped face, which *Seventeen* magazine says is the best. Let's be honest: it's probably her heart-shaped ass in her saddleback jeans. Standing next to her is like a magic trick. Abracadabra and . . . poof. You disappear. I will never look like her in a million years—even if Dad *would* pay for a nose job. It's not her fault her looks are the currency by which the guys value the girls around here.

She falls into step beside me.

"I almost steamrolled over Him," I say.

Our strides naturally sync up like we're in a chewing gum commercial.

Her face puckers. "Who cares about Him? You're way too good for Him anyway."

Exactly the exaggeration expected of a best friend. And she's right. Forget about Him. Anyway, East Coast guys value brains over beauty—so I've heard.

"Guess what?" I say glumly. "We might move to Manhattan."

She turns to me, wide-eyed. "The whole family? If you get into NYU?"

"No. The other one. Manhattan, Kansas. If my mom stays there with my grandma."

Without hesitation, she says, "Then you could come live with us."

All the times Mom and Dad fought when we were little, I hid out at her house. If her dad had been drinking, we would pull down the frothy pink netting around her four-poster bed and pretend we were princesses, safe in our castle with her golden retriever, Elsie, there to protect us, instead of two scared, little girls.

"Thanks," I say, with a grateful smile, but I don't want to move in with Bridget. I want to get into NYU.

We get to our spot on the quad. Kyle, Patty, and Malia are already there.

"Hey, babe." Bridget drapes herself across Kyle's lap.

After she broke up with her last boyfriend—right around the time He broke up with me—Bridget said we'd all be single girls senior year, find some cute boys for prom. Everyone would be jealous.

Kyle ruined everything.

I plop down next to Patty and Malia. "Guess what? We might have to move to Manhattan."

"Really? My cousins live near Central Park," Malia says, riffling through her purse.

"The other one. Manhattan, *Kansas*."

"Kansas? Like *The Wizard of Oz*? Why?" Patty squints up at me, her nose all crinkled and sunburnt—a side effect of being on the Fast-Pitch All-Stars three years in a row. Her dirty-blond hair must be three shades lighter from all that time in the sun.

I lean back on my hands. "If my mom stays there with my grandma and I don't get into NYU."

"I said she could come live with me," Bridget says with a proud smile.

"You'll get in," says Malia. She dabs her lips with some

Pot o' Gloss. "Did you figure out your something extra? I'm going to say I was a Sunday school teacher on my 'SC application even though I only did it a few times. If I book something before I get in, though . . ."

I don't know how she's going to break it to her mom—an English professor at USC—that she'd rather be a model. Her instructors at the Barbizon Modeling School think she has a real shot at success, between her almond-shaped green eyes and warm, brown skin that never, ever gets even one stray zit.

"Cal Poly offered me a full softball scholarship," Patty boasts.

"That's great," I say over a soundtrack of sad trombones.

Patty's got a scholarship. Malia's got her mom. Kyle is a legacy at Notre Dame. Meanwhile, I've got nothing. No leg up on admissions. I'll be stuck at State with Bridget—that's *if* she gets her application in once I help her figure out her major and help write her college essay.

"Mr. Buchanan says I should candy-stripe or volunteer at the old folks' home."

"Be a TA. Take roll, grade a few papers. Terrorize the freshmen." Kyle chuckles.

"It's too late to be a TA, Kyle," I reflexively disagree.

Kyle van Camp is a chocolate cherry cordial. Appealing on the outside—blue eyes and jet-black hair—but on the inside: ick. A snake is slithering around there somewhere, I know it. The permanent smirk gives him away. He must wink at himself in the mirror every morning.

"Babe, she can't terrorize the freshmen," Bridget says with a mock pout.

Kyle might be right, though. Maybe I should ask Mr. Ramos about being a TA. And grading freshmen comp papers would be easier than tending to sick people or senior citizens.

Mr. Ramos glances up from his newspaper when I hover near his desk. "Hey, Jasmine. What's news?"

I love his journalism in-jokes. Perfectly feathered hair grazes his shoulders. He's like the cool young detective on a gritty cop show. I had such a crush on him in ninth grade. He wrote about the Chicano movement for that Spanish-language newspaper, *La Opinión,* and runs our school paper, the *Eisenhower General,* like a real newsroom, with our desks arranged in a semicircle and everything.

I bite my lip. "I know it's late notice, but I'd like to be your TA this semester."

"Oh man. Wish you had asked sooner. I already promised Gerald."

Of course. Gerald Thomas is one of those seniors who looks—and acts—like he's forty. The human equivalent of mashed potatoes: lumpy, bland, and pale. Ratted me out once in kindergarten for taking an extra Entenmann's during snack time.

And he's the one who made me realize being Iranian didn't make us special, it made us weird. When Grandma Zumideh visited our class in third grade, he said she smelled weird. "She talks weird, too." It's his fault I never listened to those cassettes.

We've said maybe ten words to each other in all the years we've gone to school together, even though our dads work for the same defense contractor. He didn't even thank me when I ceded editor to him. Probably thinks he won it on the merits.

"But I—I need an extracurricular activity or award for that section of my application," I plead.

"I understand." He closes his newspaper. "But I'm only allowed one TA per semester."

"Could you . . . make an exception?"

Mr. Ramos rises, gives me one of those exasperated smiles sitcom dads give their daughters when they break curfew. "I can't." He's such a stickler for ethics and integrity.

Looks like it's barf or bedpans for me. I slouch over to my seat as everyone files in. Flynn slips into the seat next to me. He has bulging eyes and a shock of red hair and only *just* got over his Kennedy assassination obsession. Seriously, there is *no* evidence John F. Kennedy's assassination was actually an alien abduction.

"What about that Young Journalists contest?" Mr. Ramos asks. "You hear anything back?"

"I didn't even place." I sound like Eeyore.

His head bobs sympathetically.

"I got third place for my article about municipal fiscal mismanagement," Gerald boasts.

No wonder he strutted in as if he had just won a Pulitzer. I would have fallen asleep reading the first *sentence* of Gerald's article. It's such bullshit.

"Okay, people." Mr. Ramos claps his hands and wades into the semicircle. "Let's talk senior projects: your major investigative pieces due by semester's end." He turns to me. "Jasmine, your senior project is not about a government abuse of power or misdeed."

Mr. Ramos wants everyone to write about government abuses of power, which is so tedious since the government is always abusing its power.

He smiles. "But why don't you read us your lede?"

I clear my throat and flip my feathers out of my face.

"If you have an extra X chromosome, wade into the mosh pit at your own risk: a writhing sea of sweaty male bodies whose only impulse is to shove the person next to or in front of them. Punk is all about the boys—Joey Ramone, Johnny Rotten, Darby Crash. The list goes on. But where are all the punk chicks? Don't say Debbie Harry of Blondie when 'Heart of Glass' is borderline disco. Or the Runaways, a girl group dreamt up by a bunch of horny record execs who might as well have called them Jailbait. Punk is muscular. Visceral. If country music is nothing but 'three chords and the truth,' punk is three chords and a burst of testosterone. It's angry. Furious, even. Are there any female artists willing and able to channel this fury?"

"Great job, Jasmine," Mr. Ramos says. "Keep it up."

Take that, Young Journalists Award Committee.

"I'm doing mine on Three Mile Island," says Flynn. "The fallout. All that nuclear waste, people are glowing, turning *bionic* and shit. The government's covering it all up."

Everything in Flynn's mind sounds like it came out of a comic book.

Mr. Ramos calls on Gerald next.

"I'll be looking at the inner workings of a successful senior class presidential campaign," he says proudly. "Mine. Should put me over the top with NYU."

NYU? "*You're* applying to NYU?" I don't mean to shout.

"Of course. The journalism program. I'm editor of the paper, after all." His chin juts out. "I'm going to write for the *National Review.*"

Oh no. He's the "other fella" Mr. Buchanan mentioned. Editor of the school paper *and* a Young Journalists Award recipient. A *definite* leg up on me.

Just then, Mr. Ramos glances over our heads at the door. "There he is. We have a new reporter joining our ranks."

I turn. The hallway light haloes this super-cute guy. He has shorter, sandy brown hair and glasses. And good posture. Most guys skulk around here with their hands in their pockets, but his shoulders are back, his chin is up. He looks like a narc; a super-cute, undercover narc to Mr. Ramos's cool young detective.

"This is Mike Wagner. He just transferred here from Germany."

"Do. You. Speak. English?" Flynn shouts.

"My dad's in the military, Air Force," Mike says with the practiced smile of a military brat.

That explains the posture.

"My mom majored in journalism. Thought I'd give it a try."

Flynn scooches his desk over to make room. Mike is only one desk away from me.

Not that I care. My focus is on NYU.

"We're talking about senior projects, Mike," says Mr. Ramos. "Major investigative pieces to be completed by semester's end. And we're reading *All the President's Men*, greatest treatise on a free press versus a corrupt campaign in modern history. Pick up a copy in the library. So, Gerald. You were saying?"

"My senior project will track my successful candidacy for senior class president."

We have two elections—in the fall and spring—to give everyone a chance at public service. No self-respecting senior wants to be on campus spring semester let alone serve in student government. It's like being on *Dick Clark's New Year's Rockin' Eve* after the ball-drop in Times Square. No one cares by then, not even Dick Clark. Classic Gerald.

But wait a minute . . . senior class president. Sounds

impressive, *way* easier than volunteering. All I'd have to do is attend a few cabinet meetings. It connotes authority. Leadership ability.

"When is the election?" I ask.

"November twenty-first, the day before Thanksgiving," says Gerald.

Less than a month away. I could run and win before my college application is even due.

"I'm also running for senior class president," I blurt.

Gerald's mouth half-opens.

A little smile plays at Mike's lips, as if he could tell this was spur-of-the-moment.

Gerald's brows settle into a determined V-shape. "Well then, may the best man win."

"I'm his campaign manager," says Gerald's best friend, Ellory, whose chunky, black glasses dwarf his face.

"Right on," says Mr. Ramos, pacing back and forth, stroking his chin. "Ask not what your school can do for you and all that." (He's never gotten over his Kennedy obsession, either.) "What are your platforms?"

Platform? Well, winning. And getting into NYU.

Before I can answer, Gerald says, "Mine is restoring order and patriotism after two decades of hippie degradation: dress code, Pledge of Allegiance, that sort of thing."

Gerald was also hall monitor in middle school, busting kids left and right for overlong bathroom breaks. "Restoring order" sounds like the silliest platform ever, which fills me with a wave of confidence.

Mr. Ramos looks at me with anticipation.

"I'll, uh, identify my principles and platform during the campaign kickoff," I say, which sounds very presidential without actually saying anything meaningful.

The rest of the class is a haze. When the bell rings, I quickly gather up my books. I can't wait to tell everyone I'm running for senior class president.

"Jasmine, can I talk to you for a second?" Mr. Ramos says, leaning against his desk.

"Uh, sure," I say. Uh-oh. Is this about my lack of a concrete campaign platform?

He waits for everyone to clear out.

I shift nervously from side to side.

After everyone is gone, he says, "You're applying early decision, right?"

I've never heard of it. "What is that?"

"This new thing. Dartmouth and Amherst started it. You get your application in and commit to NYU. Should give you an advantage. Could make the difference, in fact."

My own leg up!

"I am," I say, breathless. "Committed. *Totally.*"

I'm not even applying anywhere else. Except for Cal State. But only as a fallback. Whoever is up there—Mom's Protestant God, Bridget's Catholic God, or Grandma Zumideh's

Muslim God—I don't want to confuse Him. If my prayer is answered, make it the one about NYU.

Mr. Ramos glances around. "Listen, they're not likely to admit two applicants from the same school. Gerald is a good guy. Serious. Disciplined. But like I said, you have a voice. If you're applying early decision, I'll write your letter of rec right away."

"I am, I will." I practically pogo. "Oh, thank you, Mr. Ramos, for your faith in me. I won't let you down."

I run back to the quad at lunch, hopscotching over two punk dudes—one with a Mohawk and the other with a safety pin earring—to make my official announcement. Everyone's in their usual spots.

"I'm running for spring semester senior class president against Gerald Thomas for my something extra," I announce. "Ellory is Gerald's campaign manager, his platform is totally out-of-touch, I think I can beat him."

I drop down next to Bridget. She picks apart the peanut butter and honey sandwich her mom made. "Gerald? That dorky guy who went to Jefferson Elementary with us?"

"I know him. It's going to be hard to beat him," says Kyle.

Patty's face turns red. "Gerald Thomas is the *asshole* junior G.I. Joe who got my brother expelled senior year for smoking weed behind the gym."

Oh, right. Gerald is also ROTC.

"Why would he beat Jasmine?" Patty demands, biting into her burrito.

"Because"—Kyle shrugs—"he seems more presidential."

"You're only saying that because he's a guy," Malia says, nibbling the ration of grapes her instructors at the Barbizon School have allowed.

"Exactly," says Kyle. "My dad says a woman will never be elected president. Besides, Jasmine just said Gerald already has a platform and positions. And a campaign manager. If you're going to run, you need a strategy and positioning."

"No duh, Kyle," I say, with no idea what a "positioning" is.

Patty says, "How would you know, Kyle? You've never won anything."

"Patty," Kyle says with his perma-smirk, "I helped my dad walk precincts for the Republican gubernatorial campaign to defeat the 'rock star' Governor Brown."

He's such a know-it-all. David Bowie is a rock star. Governor Brown is not a "rock star," no matter what *Time* magazine says. He wears his hair in a side part for God's sake. Still, I can literally see my wave of confidence receding from the shore.

Somewhere in there, Mike, of all people, shows up with a sack lunch and sits next to Kyle. No way I'm eating my boiled egg in front of him. It might stink. Not that I care.

"This is Mike Wagner," says Kyle. "Just transferred here. Dad's in the military."

"Are you the one on varsity golf with Kyle?" Bridget asks.

"Yeah. My dad says that's the first thing they build on any military base, before they run out of money." He chuckles about this. To himself. As if it's enough *he* thinks it's funny. He turns to me. "Women can run governments. Look at Margaret Thatcher and Golda Meir."

I bet everyone calls him a "brainiac," too.

"Who?" Patty says with a scrunch of her perpetually sunburnt nose.

I say, "Prime ministers of England and Israel," and I can tell Mike is impressed.

"I'll help you beat Gerald," Patty says, popping the last bit of burrito in her mouth. "I'll help you *beat* his ass."

Patty is super tough. Her dad—who is Scottish—always said of her five brothers, "Nothing this lot can do that you can't do, too." From the first minute she came to Roosevelt Junior High, no one messed with her and she didn't allow anyone to mess with me or Bridget.

But the main thing about Patty Hamilton is, she hates to lose. And rarely does.

"Patty, you don't know anything about politics or the finer points of polling," says Kyle.

"I was a Fast-Pitch All-Star three years in a row, Kyle. I know how to win."

Suddenly, a lightbulb goes off in my head. If Kyle knows the finer points of polling and Patty knows how to win— "Could you do it together?"

Kyle looks to Bridget, who glances at Patty. She's making some sort of internal calculation, I can tell. I throw her a pleading look.

Finally, she says, "Babe, help her. For me. Please?"

Kyle strokes his chin and smiles. "My dad would *shit* if I got a girl elected."

Patty crumples her burrito wrapper and lobs it at the trash. Just misses. "*My* dad would shit if we beat Gerald's ass. He ruined my brother's whole future."

"I'd vote for you," says Mike.

"Okay. I'll do it," says Kyle.

Yes! It's official. I'm running for senior class president. I have almost four weeks to convince the five hundred other seniors at Eisenhower High to vote for me instead of an over-zealous hall monitor with a totally dorky platform. Should be a cinch.

CHAPTER THREE

THE EAGLE HAS LANDED

I have to finish this article about the Clash before my presidential campaign begins on Monday. Their album comes out next month. Rodney Bingenheimer has already begun playing the title track on KROQ.

I like to be the first to tell everyone about a new artist or record. The moment of discovery, where it's just me and, say, the Specials, is even better when we're in this little bubble together.

I'm almost done with my lede:

> Who knows what the rest of the record will sound like, but the single "London Calling" is a symphony compared to previous releases. "I'm So Bored with the U.S.A" was predictably punk: threadbare, chaotic, anarchic. If the entire double album lives up to the title track, the Clash promise to take their place in the—

What is that sound?

It's coming from downstairs.

It's like . . . a cat . . . playing . . . a violin. I have to make it stop.

I put aside my pen and notebook and rush downstairs. Halfway down, it becomes clear: Auntie and her friends are dancing and drinking tea, listening to Persian music.

Dad says the vocals, instrumentation, and even the time signatures of Persian music are different from what we're used to in the United States, which is why it sounds odd to our ears. I can't say anything now; it would only hurt Auntie's feelings.

She's been here for two weeks and has already discovered more Persians than Dad has in a decade. Her friend Shahrazad is here with her daughter, Firuzeh. Shahrazad is shorter and rounder than Auntie, with a prominent beauty mark on her left cheek. Which only makes her daughter's height more conspicuous. Firuzeh is taller than Malia. Her eyes are so big and brown, they're nearly bovine. She's the Persian Bridget, the most popular girl at Lincoln High. She must have turned down a hundred dates to accompany her mother here on a Saturday night.

Auntie and Shahrazad pop sugar cubes into their gold-rimmed demitasse cups while Firuzeh belly dances. Her hips undulate; her hands and arms are so graceful. "Hi, Jasmine," she says without missing a beat. "How are you?"

Of course, she's sweeter than the platter of honey-soaked pastries her mother has brought from the Persian market.

"Great," I say, as I wonder whose superpowers are stronger: Bridget's or Firuzeh's?

"Haal-et chetowr-e, Jasmine-joon?" Shahrazad says.

"I told you, Shahrazad-joon," Auntie says with a sip of her tea. "She doesn't speak the Farsi. Remember, her mother is American."

"Oh," Shahrazad sympathizes, as if Auntie had said I was an orphan.

"H-hey." Ali stumbles in from the kitchen, completely under Firuzeh's spell, and immediately begins speaking Farsi.

Show-off.

For a moment, I take it all in, what it might be like if we were surrounded by Persian friends and relatives. If I spoke Farsi. If we listened to Persian music all the time.

It might be nice.

After the moment passes, I turn around to head back upstairs.

"Joonam, you don't want some tea and pastry?" Auntie asks.

"I have homework, Auntie. Thank you."

They'll all be speaking Farsi.

"Nice to see you," I say to Shahrazad and Firuzeh and get back to the Clash.

‖‖‖‖‖‖‖‖‖‖‖

"Tick-tock, do, do, do, do, do." I would never listen to the Steve Miller Band in front of another living, breathing human being, but I'm alone in my car on the way to school and have gotten all nostalgic senior year.

"Fly Like an Eagle." That's me and Bridget having a sleepover in the pool, lounging on Mom and Dad's chaise floaties, sipping root beer floats, smelling of Coppertone. The perfect song can evoke a memory like nothing else.

What I remember most is, we didn't have one chaise floatie sleepover this past summer because of Kyle.

If he's going to be my campaign manager, though, I better get over my grudge.

Our main goal for today is to figure out my strategy and positioning. And Kyle said something about a slogan, a simple sentence that conveys my campaign platform.

We're meeting in the north hall before class. Patty and Malia are already there. Patty has poster board spread out on a folding table. She holds up one of the posters, which says, VOTE FOR JASMINE ZUMIDEH—THE BEST SENIOR CLASS PRESIDENT in big black marker. Her penmanship is atrocious. She's a lefty.

"Well, it's simple," I say, "and direct."

She beams. "I figured it was better than 'Beat the Narc'— hey, watch it," she snaps at our mascot, who's wearing the Eisenhower Hawk costume, when he accidentally bumps into her on his way to the gym.

"Sorry, man," comes a muffled voice from inside the hawk.

"Patty, he didn't mean to bump into you," Malia says with an eye roll.

In fairness, it is hard to see out of the costume since the eye holes are so small.

Just then, Kyle and Bridget approach from the west end of the north hall. "All right. You need a platform. And a slogan," Kyle says. He frowns at Patty's poster. "Something catchy that conveys your campaign theme. Like how President Ford said he was 'a Ford, not a Lincoln' when he ran against Carter."

"But . . . Ford lost," I say.

"That's not the point." He motions to all the students streaming around us. "The point is, these voters need something they can latch on to."

"Well, I want to uphold democratic ideals and protect the freedoms we all cherish," I say. "In Iran, where my dad is from, they had a whole revolution because the king wouldn't allow freedom of speech or thought. Meanwhile, Gerald wants to turn the school into a fascist state."

"Jasmine. Something *meaningful*." Patty tsks. "And don't use the word 'fascist.'"

"Like what?"

As we all contemplate a more viable campaign platform, Mike arrives. There's something about the way his hair parts on the side—a *side part*—that looks good on him.

"Hey," he says to me. To *me*.

"Hey," I say.

Oh God. My cheeks are growing warm. I've been looking at him too long. Who cares if he has nice hair and good posture?

"I've got it," Kyle says. "No tardies for seniors if they're late to first period."

Malia cocks her head. "She can't promise that, can she?"

"She can promise anything," Kyle says with a sly smile. "She doesn't know what she can *deliver* till she's president."

"You guys are overthinking everything," I argue. "Gerald wants a *dress code*. Why would anyone vote for him?"

"Exactly," says Bridget. "I agree." She's always been my cheerleader.

"Okay, so you're against the dress code," says Kyle. "What are you *for*?"

"I don't have to be *for* anything if I'm against that, right?" I look to Bridget and Malia for backup.

"Right," Bridget says with confidence.

"*Wrong*," Patty says, equally emphatic.

"How do you know?" Bridget shoots back.

"You guys," I shush them.

Their squabbling has gotten worse since the start of senior year. I mean, I'm not happy Bridget abandoned us for Kyle, either. But like Bridget says, Patty all but disappears during softball season.

"I don't know about the tardies thing," Mike says with a thoughtful shake of his head. "My dad says people can smell a fake promise from a phony politician a mile away."

"Ha. Your dad is wrong." Kyle snorts.

I restrain myself from saying, *no he's not,* since I've never met Mike's dad.

"*I've* been thinking," says Patty. "We need to change our mascot."

"Patty. Seriously," Malia clucks. "He didn't mean to bump into you."

"That's not why." Patty throws her hands up. "It's on every uniform. Look at it. It's ugly." She gestures to the giant mosaic of the Eisenhower Hawk on the far wall.

We all turn.

"Oh my God, you're right," Malia says, with her hand over her mouth. "Its eyes are beady and mean."

"What if your platform is to change it to something better or cuter?" Patty suggests. "Like a tiger or a dolphin?"

While she's talking, the same refrain keeps running through my brain, the opening of "Fly Like an Eagle": *Ticktock, do, do, do, do, do.*

"What about an eagle? An American eagle?" I say in a flash of inspiration.

Kyle and Mike nod vigorously.

"How about, Fly Like an Eagle with Jasmine Zumideh, or something like that?" I add.

"I love it," Bridget pronounces.

"Totally all-American," says Kyle.

"Bring the cassette," says Patty. "We'll play it during the campaign kickoff rally."

Perfect. My slogan is all set. Poor Gerald. I bet he thought he had already won.

||||||||||||||

There will be some "undecideds" right up until Election Day, Kyle says, but most of the seniors will have made up their minds about me and Gerald within the next two weeks. Of the five hundred, about a third will vote, and I need the majority of them to win. That's about ninety seniors. There are probably thirty (give or take) I can count on to vote for me over Gerald, which leaves another sixty to be persuaded.

Kyle has segmented everyone into "voting blocs." I've put aside my geometry homework on perpendicular lines in the Cartesian coordinate system to strategize how to win them over while listening to the *My Fair Lady* soundtrack in my room. Mom listens to Broadway soundtrack albums all the time—*Camelot, Oklahoma!*—and her favorite, *Fiddler on the Roof*, so it's strangely comforting to hear Rex Harrison bemoan the fact that women are not more like men.

And the reason, Mr. Harrison, is because *we're* ruled by what rests between our shoulders instead of between our legs.

I skim over the list Kyle's given me: AV Club, marching band, the jocks, the brainiacs. Skaters, surfers, stoners, and more. I can't see why any of them—except maybe the jocks— would care about a new mascot. I do love my slogan, though: Fly Like an Eagle with Jasmine Zumideh. Very inspiring.

Maybe it can mean more than a mascot. Maybe it *can* mean upholding the democratic ideals and freedoms we all cherish like I originally intended. I mean, look what happened in Iran when people weren't free. I'll promise Patty I won't use the word "fascist."

We all meet at the green lunch table behind the gym the next morning before first period to map out the campaign.

"I'll be conducting a snapshot poll every day over the next twenty-three days, from now till the election," Kyle says, referring to his clipboard. He has to make everything sound so official. "Week one is to introduce you as a candidate. Week two is persuasion. The final week is GOTV—Get Out the Vote. You should carry the surfers and the skaters. Maybe the jocks. You have a shot at AV Club and marching band. But we've got work to do if you want the stoners. They don't even know there's an election."

"The jocks will vote for a new mascot." Patty grabs Kyle's clipboard out of his hands. She checks off the box next to "Jocks" and hands it back to him with a confident smile.

"About that," I say, squirming.

She's going to be so disappointed.

"I want Fly Like an Eagle with Jasmine Zumideh to be about freedom. Freedom of speech and thought, freedom of expression, to wear what you want to wear. As opposed to Gerald, who's a total fascist."

"No one even knows what that means," Patty insists.

I hold up my right hand. "I won't use that word, I swear.

But you should see what it's like in other countries where they're not free."

Patty's face falls. "You don't like the new mascot?"

"It's not that I don't like it, it's just . . . I'd rather my campaign be about something more."

"Listen." Kyle holds up his hand. "We haven't poll-tested anything yet. We have no idea what will work."

"Let me *try* it my way." I gesture to a band of rockers in their tattered concert T-shirts sitting under the old oak tree. "I speak their language."

Jimmy from Algebra II is sitting with them. We hung out at a Queen concert in ninth grade.

I lead the way over with an ebullient smile, as if I'm about to present one of those big oversized checks to a contest prize winner. "Hey, guys. Jimmy."

Kyle and Patty hang back a few feet. Her body language screams "skeptic."

"Hey, Jasmine." Jimmy nods. "You going to see KISS at the Forum?"

"Oh, um, probably."

. . . not. Unless U2 is the opening act. Guys get super attached to bands like KISS in the same way young girls get attached to horses and unicorns.

"I, um, I'm running for senior class president against Gerald Thomas and I'd like your vote."

"Why should we vote for *you*?" one of the rocker dudes demands.

"Because." I lean forward. "Gerald is running to reinstate a *dress code* and the Pledge of Allegiance."

"Right on, I'll wear a bow tie and suspenders," another says, hooking his thumbs under a pair of imaginary suspenders.

They all laugh. Like it's a joke. Patty throws me a "toldja" look.

I've got to win them over.

"No, you don't understand," I say, my head ping-ponging back and forth. I point to a rocker with shaggy, blond hair. "You won't be able to wear that *Highway to Hell* T-shirt. Or *any* T-shirt. I've seen it in other countries. Like Iran. It starts with crackdowns on speech and dress; next thing you know, you have to recite the Pledge of Allegiance every morning. Like, standing up with your hand over your heart and everything."

They exchange worried glances.

"And listen to the National Anthem every day—not even the good one by Jimi Hendrix."

Now I've got their attention. I'm on a roll. I lean in and tap my temple. "It's thought control, just like Pink Floyd is warning about."

They're playing that single, "Another Brick in the Wall," nonstop on KMET.

"Whoa," Jimmy says, his eyes wide with horror.

"If you don't want that, then fly like an eagle with me, Jasmine Zumideh."

"Fly like an eagle, Steve Miller Band. Right on." Jimmy raises his fist in the air.

The other rockers do the same, as if I'm on my third encore.

"Can I count on your vote, then?"

They all look to Jimmy.

"Yeah. For sure," he says.

"Yeah, right on," they all chime in.

"Thanks, guys."

I spin on my heels and saunter back toward Kyle and Patty. "I didn't mention the mascot or use the word 'fascist' once."

She gives me a grudging nod.

After I tell a group of skaters they'll have to cut their hair and warn the brainiacs the library will no longer carry copies of *1984* if Gerald is elected, they all promise to vote for me.

Patty and Kyle are finally sold on my strategy. I'm cruising to victory.

CHAPTER FOUR

LITTLE WHITE LIE

Between the campaign and my shift at Hot Dog on a Stick—where I had to clean the fryer *and* balance the register—I'm beat. Then Bridget calls with a campaign of her own. "Like Mike, like Mike! We could all double-date and go to prom together."

Her life is one big Harlequin romance. I pull the hallway phone into my room and close the door. "He said he'd vote for me, not go to prom with me."

Not that I would turn him down.

While we talk, I take out my application to check on that early submission thing Mr. Ramos mentioned. I'm not sure whether to type "*spring semester* senior class president" or "*second semester* senior class president" into the Extracurric-ular/Awards/Honor field of my application if I win. When I win. I *have* to win.

"What if he likes *you*?"

Nothing on the first page about early submission.

"Let him like Patty." Honestly, she doesn't seem like his type, but still. "I have to concentrate on college."

"Why would he like Patty?" Her tone has suddenly curdled. "You know she talks about me behind my back."

"That's just her shit talk from being on the Fast-Pitch All-Stars," I say distractedly. "They chatter at the batters from the dugout all the time. It doesn't mean anything."

Nothing on pages two or three about early submission, either.

"Kyle could be your campaign manager on his own." Bridget sniffs. "He said Patty doesn't know anything about politics or polling."

"But she was first to volunteer. And she's super competitive." I turn the application over. "Kyle will take the lead. He'll come up with our strategy and positioning and—"

Oh no.

Oh *no*.

Oh NO!

The *regular* decision deadline is not till December first, but the *early* decision deadline is *November* first—only two days away. The date is hidden at the bottom of the last page in microscopic, six-point type we wouldn't even use for classified ads in the paper. I should have looked this over sooner.

"Bridget, I gotta go, I'll call you later."

I hang up and start chewing my nail like a bunny nibbling a carrot. Mr. Ramos made it sound like submitting early decision could be the difference between acceptance and rejection, especially if I'm up against Gerald. Forget the election, I couldn't candy-stripe or help old folks in two days if I *wanted* to.

I'm not going to be a commuter at Cal State. I want to be on the East Coast, wearing burgundy knit caps and oversized spectacles in a stately library that reeks of first editions while the fall leaves turn, and interviewing Chrissie Hynde for the *Washington Square News*.

And Mr. Ramos said I *have* to be on the East Coast if I want to write for *Creem* or any other music magazine. That's where the industry and internships are. Right when I get a leg up, it gets knocked down. The closest I'll ever get to Chrissie Hynde is this "Stop Your Sobbing" single.

I pick it up and turn it over. What would Chrissie do? She looks so determined. Chin up, mouth set in a straight line.

She'd never give up, that's what. Break the rules if she had to.

Oh my God. That's exactly what she'd do. *Accelerate* the truth. Say she won the election. It's not a *total* lie, I'm going to win. Gerald's platform is super dorky.

Maybe it *is* a lie, but a little white lie that will soon be true anyway. As long as it says "senior class president" on my spring 1980 transcript, it'll be okay.

Instead of "spring" or "second-semester" senior class president, I'll write "senior class president–*elect*" in the Extracurricular/Awards/Honor field. My hand shakes as I type it. I accidentally leave out the *o* in senior, have to Wite-Out the whole field, and retype it.

I stare at my now-complete application. Am I really going to do this?

Before I can change my mind, I pull the application out of my typewriter, sign it, and seal my fate along with that large manila envelope, which I'll have to send Federal Express first thing tomorrow since it absolutely, positively has to get there overnight.

ıııııııııııııı

This Halloween morning, I awoke with two thoughts. The first was crap, I don't have a costume. I spent ten minutes scrounging around my closet and found a black leotard and a long, flowy Stevie Nicks skirt. You could be almost anything with a black leotard and a flowy Stevie Nicks skirt: a kitty cat or a witch or a vampire. Even Stevie Nicks. I drew a little circle around the tip of my nose and whiskers on my cheeks.

Plus, we had no Halloween candy. Auntie's going to hand out gaz, this Persian pistachio nougat. It'll be a miracle if our house doesn't get egged.

My second thought was about my second thoughts. As I stand here in the middle of the Federal Express depot— which stinks of stale cigarettes—clutching my Federal Express envelope, I'm seized with them.

What was I thinking? I can't lie on my application. If I get caught, I could go to prison for fraud, I think. I move on from nibbling my index finger to my middle finger.

It's not a *total* lie, though. A *total* lie would be if I said I had won that Aspiring Young Journalists Award or gotten my pilot's license. I may not be senior class president–elect yet, but I will be. Gerald is running to *reinstate the dress code.*

What if I lose, though? How would I explain that to the admissions department? "Uh, hello, Admissions? You know how I said I was senior class president–elect on my application? I may have been . . . mistaken." My acceptance would immediately be rescinded.

My grades are good. My SAT score is solid. Mr. Ramos said my writing samples are outstanding. Who cares if I was never a youth pastor or a Junior Olympian?

If I send in my application now and don't win the election, I'll have to admit I lied. On the other hand, if I miss the early decision deadline and *don't* get in—and Gerald does— I'll never forgive myself.

"You ready?" an impatient businessman with a beat-up briefcase barks at me.

"Oh, no, sorry," I say, moving aside.

Chrissie Hynde would do this without so much as a *single* second thought. I take a deep breath and step back in line.

"This is my university application." I thrust my envelope at the Federal Express guy with the big white handlebar mustache.

He glances at the delivery address. "Eh, I went to the school of hard knocks. That'll be eight fifty-three."

"It will absolutely, positively get there by tomorrow?" I fish a ten out of my wallet.

"Absotively." He hands me my change and throws my envelope on the conveyer.

That's it. It's done. No turning back now.

Oh, God. There's no turning back now.

That envelope absolutely, positively must get there overnight, and now I absolutely, positively must win this election.

||||||||||||

The parking lot is clogged with Luke Skywalkers and Wonder Women when I pull up. Assorted members of KISS. The shark from *Jaws*. I'm one of a litter of kitties. We're all meeting in the quad to compare costumes.

I have to keep my little white lie to myself. It won't change anything.

Malia has on a black leotard and tights with leopard print cat ears and whiskers. "We'll be Josie and the Pussycats," she says as soon as she sees my costume. "I'll be Josie."

"Which one am I?"

"Does it matter?"

Patty's wearing one of her brother's football uniforms with black shoe polish under her eyes.

Bridget and Kyle are coming across the quad. She's wearing a formal gown. He's got a bedsheet twisted around his body.

Patty wrinkles her nose. "What are you supposed to be?"

"Antony and Cleopatra," Bridget says with a wide smile.

Kyle's cheeks flush at this admission.

Bridget's gown is one of her mom's formals, a long white column dress with a metallic gold belt. Her eyes are rimmed with thick, black liner, her hair swept up in a bun.

"We're Josie and the Pussycats." Malia smushes her face next to mine. "I'm Josie."

"I'm . . . one of the other ones," I say.

Mike shows up in jeans and a white T-shirt with rolled-up sleeves and slicked-back hair. I did *not* picture him as Fonzie.

"*Happy Days*?" I ask with a look of horror.

"No," he says, all affronted. "Ponyboy."

Wow. I've never met a guy who laughs at his own jokes, knows *two* female prime ministers, and has read *The Outsiders*. With good posture.

Don't stare, don't stare. *Look away.*

"Could you ever just wear, like, a *regular* costume?" Patty fake-laughs at Bridget. "You always have to pretend to be a movie star."

It's true. You would never catch her as, like, the Hamburglar to Kyle's Ronald McDonald.

"Could you ever *not* wear one of your brother's uniforms?" Bridget shoots back.

Uh-oh. Here we go.

"No, because it's not a fashion show." Patty harrumphs.

"You *guys*," I groan.

Bridget should never have told Patty to dye her hair blonder and wear teal shimmer shadow so she would look "more girly" right when she was emerging from the chrysalis of her junior high school self and trying on makeup for the first time. Patty's never gotten past it.

Besides, they're fighting over childish things like Halloween costumes when I may have committed a felony. "I've got to get to first period," I say, and head for the bungalows.

My FedEx envelope must be east of the Rockies by now. It's too late to retrieve it, even if I wanted to. I'll just have to—

"Mr. Buchanan!" I squawk like he had jumped out from behind a bush instead of simply rounding the corner.

"Miss Zuh-pay-duh." He's sporting a houndstooth cap and carrying a large pipe.

"Sherlock Holmes?"

"Elementary, my dear," he says with a puff on his fake pipe. "Did you decide on that extracurricular?"

"Oh, yes, sir. I'm running for senior class president."

At least I've been spared the barf or bedpans.

"Well then, good luck at the kickoff assembly Monday," he says, just as the bell rings. "I worked for the Nixon campaign myself back in 1960. I remember the whole debate *debacle*."

I've heard all about it, the first nationally televised presidential debate between Richard Nixon and John F. Kennedy. I've got to get to first period, but I don't want to interrupt him.

"Nixon had been in the hospital, so he was a little . . . pale on TV in comparison to Jack Kennedy, who must have been out *bronzing* himself on his yacht in Hyannis."

Evidently, *no one* has gotten over their Kennedy obsession.

"And, well, that debate just went to show you, in politics, appearances are everything."

"Appearances are everything. I'll remember that," I say, rushing off to first period.

"All right, Miss Zuh-pay-duh."

Honestly, it's not exactly phonetic, but if people would just sound it out.

"Remember to turn in a copy of your application when it's complete," he calls after me.

I come to a dead stop. Of *course* I'll have to turn in a copy of my application to him. Whereupon my little white lie will be laid bare.

Dammit. I should have thought of that. The next three weeks better go by quickly—and without a hitch.

CHAPTER FIVE

TAKE COVER

The only homework I had this weekend was baking banana bread for home ec, so I've been working on my campaign kickoff speech, muscling in several quotes about democracy from Alexis de Tocqueville (I restrain myself from saying Gerald's election would usher in a "reign of terror") when Bridget calls.

I hop on the new cordless we just got because Dad gets all the latest gadgets first. It's awesome as long as you point the antenna in the exact right direction. I lie down on the bed with my head hanging over the side. "Bridget?"

Not the right direction. I sit up. "Bridget?"

"I *said*, is your mom going to stay in Kansas? Like, for good?"

I exhale. "I don't know. She hasn't mentioned it again. I don't want to ask."

"If you had to move, you could always stay with me," she says. It almost sounds like a plea.

Suddenly, I'm filled with a happy, warm feeling in my chest that makes me want to cry. "Remember when your mom used to read us bedtime stories whenever I would sleep over? Until we were *way* too old for them."

"She did all the voices for *Charlotte's Web*," she says wistfully.

It's like we can both feel our childhood slipping away.

Before things get too melancholy, Bridget brightens. "Anyway, what about our double date?"

I'm not getting sidetracked by Mike. He's not even my usual type: long-haired rocker dude with attitude. Like Him—a Neanderthal. Mike's much more . . . evolved, but—

"Oh no! No! Oh my God!" All of a sudden, Auntie Minah is shouting from the living room.

Is she hurt? Did she fall?

"Bridget, I—something's wrong. I have to go." I jam the antenna down on the cordless phone without waiting for her reply.

When I get to the living room, Auntie and Ali are glued to the TV, stunned looks on their faces, speaking rapid-fire Farsi.

"What happened?" I ask, out of breath.

"The Iranian student, they take Americans hostage!" Auntie Minah gestures dramatically.

"What?"

Ali keeps running his fingers through his hair. "Iranian students seized the US Embassy in Tehran. They're holding everybody hostage, all the Americans."

This makes no sense. Iranian students took *American* hostages? "But, but . . . why?"

"Because. The United States let the shah in," Auntie says with her hand to her mouth.

The house isn't rumbling, but it feels like an earthquake, everything tossed off-kilter. I turn to the TV.

Ali says, "He was exiled in Mexico, but he wanted to come here for cancer treatment. President Carter let him in. Now the Iranian students say the US is harboring a dictator."

He quickly flips through all the channels—two, four, and seven. On every channel, a news anchor narrates footage of the US Embassy overrun with angry Iranian students. We settle on CBS and Ed Bradley. He says the Iranian religious leader, Ayatollah Khomeini, told the students to seize the US Embassy in retaliation for President Carter letting the shah come to America for medical treatment. They're holding all the American employees of the embassy hostage until we kick the shah out.

It looks bad. Really bad. A feeling of dread, like cowering under the bed, waiting for the walls to come crumbling down, envelops me. "What about Grandma Zumideh? Is she okay?"

"We can't get through to her," Ali says grimly.

Auntie looks like she's going to faint. "Here, Auntie, sit down." I guide her to the recliner.

We continue watching what looks like the same news footage of the hostages over and over in silence. "Is it as bad as it looks?" I finally ask Ali under my breath.

Just then, the phone rings. Ali runs to the kitchen to answer it. "Dad," he says, breathless. "Yes. We've been watching the whole thing on TV."

I hurry over and Ali hands me the phone. "Dad, how is Grandma Zumideh? Is she okay?"

"She's okay," he says. "The demonstrations are in Tehran. She's outside the city."

I glance back at the television, at the deep furrow of concern across Ed Bradley's brow. "What does it all mean?"

"Well, it's not good," he says, stating the obvious. "But they're just kids. The media always exaggerates everything. As soon as these students realize they've riled up the US military, they'll let the hostages go."

This is supposed to be reassuring. And, yes. The shaking has stopped. But that only means it's time to brace for the aftershocks.

I hand the phone to Auntie Minah. Thankfully, Dad is able to calm her down.

It's almost ten o'clock before I call Bridget back.

"We saw it, too," she says. "What does it mean? Is your grandma okay?"

My stomach is still in knots. "My dad says she's okay, the media is exaggerating everything. It'll be over soon."

The knots loosen. Until I remember Dad said "everything

is fine" right before he and Mom announced their separation. Ali believed him. I did, too—until Mom took her cigarettes out of hiding. The smoke curling up to the ceiling from the tips of her Eve Menthols was a signal: everything was not fine. In fact, everything was about to fall apart.

||||||||||||||

Bridget counseled me to wear my tightest, high-waisted jeans for the campaign kickoff, but I could barely get the top button buttoned. I slept in them so they would stretch out.

Sleeping in tight jeans is hard enough, but I kept tossing and turning, thinking about the hostages. They did stretch a little, though. At least my hair is feathering perfectly.

When I get downstairs, Auntie Minah is asleep on the living room couch. She must have watched the news all night.

Ali is in the kitchen frying an egg. "Oh, man," he says with a manic smile, "those Iranian students are so radical."

"*Radical?* Ali, they're holding American citizens *hostage*," I snap at him.

"I know. It's payback." He flips his egg in the skillet. "The CIA overthrew that prime minister, Mossadegh, in the fifties and propped up the shah for the oil. Remember? Dad taught us all this stuff."

Dad did teach us about Russia and Britain interfering with Iran for the oil since the late 1800s—and America, too—but I say, "No, I don't remember. And anyway, that doesn't justify taking Americans hostage."

He slides his egg onto a plate with burnt toast. "People should know the whole story before everyone goes around making Iranian students out to be the bad guys."

I snatch my keys and folder. "'Everyone' is not doing anything, Ali. No one cares about Iran." At least, they never did.

"You should care," he yells at me on my way out the door. "This is our heritage."

Tick-tock, do, do, do, do, do. I climb in Mom's car and immediately pop in the Steve Miller Band cassette to try and forget about Ali and the hostages.

Radical. What is he thinking? And no one cares about Iran.

But as I park and make my way through the lot, there's a strange buzz, snippets of animated conversation and random words like "I-rain-ians" and "hostages." I pull my folder closer to my chest.

Everyone is still buzzing when I get to homeroom. Gerald is holding a newspaper with a banner headline that reads: AMERICAN HOSTAGES SEIZED!

"Did you hear about what happened in I-ran?" he asks. "It was on all the networks."

I want to tell him it's pronounced *Ee-ron* but don't.

The homeroom teacher, a substitute, tries to take roll. "What are you squawking about?"

"Didn't you hear?" Gerald holds up the paper. "I-rain-ians seized the US Embassy. They're holding everyone hostage." He puts the paper down and turns to his ROTC buddies.

"My dad said it's an 'act of war.' Like Pearl Harbor. That we should bomb the living crap out of the entire Middle East so we don't end up with another Vietnam."

This sounds like a gargantuan overstatement, but still, I say nothing. Part of me wants to defend the Iranian students, like Ali, part of me is mortified by them.

"Pipe down while I call roll," says the sub, an older woman with a sky-high bouffant.

Gerald quietly resumes his discussion with the junior G.I. Joes. The first one says, "I heard those I-rain-ians are religious fanatics." The second one says, "Yeah, they're mausoleum, or something."

"*Muslim,*" I finally say, but nobody hears me.

Gerald makes a circling motion around his head. "The women, they all wear sheets around their faces."

I can't help it. "It's called a chador and they wear it for modesty's sake."

Of course, right then, the sub calls my name. "Jasmine, uh, Zum-ba-duh . . . Zum-ba-day." She throws her hands up as if she can't be expected to keep trying.

"Zumideh." My stomach roils.

Gerald looks at me, suspicious. "*You're* I-rain-ian, aren't you?"

It's suddenly 1973 again, the last time Grandma and Grandpa Zumideh visited, before Grandpa died, when Gerald told everyone we were weird.

That was only the beginning. Bridget walked by their

room once while Grandma and Grandpa were chanting and praying on their prayer rugs and asked, "What are they doing?" with that look of confusion and disgust you get after a shot of Jägermeister. When I told her they were praying, she said, "They're supposed to be in church." I was too embarrassed to tell her Muslims pray in mosques.

Even Grandma Jean used to refer to Ali and me as her "little brown babies," as if we were spoiled fruit. Unlike our cousins, who are Wonder Bread white. My cheeks would burn with embarrassment. But when people ask, "What are you?" I've always said, "Iranian."

While Gerald stares at me, my brain performs an instant series of calculations and spits out the following: "I'm Persian."

Does he know Persian and Iranian are basically the same thing?

He doesn't. My stomach relaxes. A little.

⸻

I make it to the quad with a few minutes left before the kick-off assembly. Kyle is working his way toward me, stopping to talk to a bunch of seniors before delivering his morning briefing.

Patty grabs my shoulder from behind. "I'm so glad I caught you," she says. "Here." She thrusts an Eisenhower High basketball jersey at me.

"Patty, I thought we agreed. Fly Like an Eagle is not about a new mascot."

"I know," she says. "But of everyone *I've* talked to, no one cares about 'fascism.'"

"I *know*," I say, handing it back. "That's why I won't say it."

God. This must be why Patty is a Fast-Pitch All-Star. She's relentless.

"Take it, just in case," she says, and pushes it on me when Kyle finally arrives.

"Looking good," he says. "Dress code polling poorly. So is the pledge."

I can't help flashing Patty a "told you" look.

As we make our way to the auditorium, Kyle reminds me, "Remember, in your kickoff today, it's all about the American way: Fly Like an Eagle with Jasmine Zumideh."

I nod. "Fly like an eagle. Got it. It's all in my speech."

Right when he opens the double door, he says, "Especially now that our country is under attack by the I-rain-ians."

Um . . . there's nothing in my speech about that.

CHAPTER SIX

GET UP, STAND UP

've never been comfortable onstage. I'm not a natural-born performer like Ali. We were both in dance class when we were little. He was the star tapper. He didn't care if the other boys thought it was weird. He devoured the spotlight. Meanwhile, my pink leotard and tutu were too tight, and everyone laughed when the announcer made a big show of mispronouncing our last name. For me, being in front of an audience is like being on a boat, fighting that feeling of seasickness.

I've got to sell seniors on my platform without tripping or hiccupping, which I do when I get super nervous, like when I interviewed for my job at Hot Dog on a Stick, and the manager asked why I wanted to work there, and I couldn't think of anything other than "the free food." I was trying so hard to keep from hiccupping.

The spotlight glares in my face as I sit onstage with the other candidates. I can barely see Bridget, Patty, Malia, Kyle, and Mike in the front row. Ali is a few rows behind the punks and the jocks.

Gerald is at the podium. "My campaign is all about restoring order: reinstituting the dress code and bringing back the Pledge of Allegiance," he says.

Gerald was also a Safety Guard in sixth grade, which is like Special Assistant to the Crossing Guard. He wielded that stop sign with such relish.

The punks—and Ali and pretty much everyone else—fidget.

"My dad fought in World War II, came back a hero." Gerald's face puckers. "When my brother came back from Vietnam wounded, a *wounded* veteran, the hippies spit on him."

Wow. I've known Gerald forever and didn't know that. How awful. One super sympathetic detail in a speech otherwise meant for an audience of retirees won't convince enough seniors to vote for him, though.

Oh, God. I'm next. Picture everyone in their underwear. Their underwear.

Great. Now I'm picturing Mike in his underwear. Does he wear boxers or tighty whities? Tighty whities, probably, since he's from a military family.

"Especially in light of what's happening in I-ran," Gerald says in closing. "We have to restore order and curb student radicals here and abroad."

In light of what's happening in *I-ran*? Iran has literally nothing to do with this election.

The junior G.I. Joes—I mean, the ROTC guys—cheer. The punks boo. In a loud voice, Ali says, "What is this fascist clown even talking about?"

I glare at Ali as hard as I can, but he doesn't see me. I will drown him in the bathtub or tell everyone he masturbates to reruns of *Gilligan's Island* if he does anything to embarrass me.

Principal Crankovitch—which sounds totally made up, but really is his last name—takes the podium as Gerald sits next to me. "Thank you, Gerald. Quite an impressive speech."

"Impressive how?" Ali shouts. "He doesn't know what he's talking about."

Drowning is too difficult, but I will get the word out about *Gilligan's Island*.

Principal Crankovitch introduces me next. "Now we have Jasmine, uh, Zoom-uh-die."

I want to die but force myself to stand up and stride toward the podium, cheered on by Bridget, Kyle, Malia, and Mike. Patty must be in the bathroom.

Before I make it all the way to the podium, Ali jumps up and raises his fist. "Don't blame the 'student radicals' for seizing the embassy, man!"

I freeze midstride. Principal Crankovitch scrambles back toward the podium.

Ali stabs the air with his finger and points at Gerald. "You're totally ignorant, man. The US has been interfering with Iran for the oil since before the World Wars. Both of 'em."

At which point the punk with the Mohawk jumps up. "He's *punk,* man. All right."

And now the boat is capsizing in slow motion. The gym teacher, Mr. Jackson—a burly ex-Marine—makes a beeline for Ali.

"Order, everyone! Order," Principal Crankovitch shouts.

As Mr. Jackson closes in on Ali, Mr. Ramos stands up. "Hey, hey. Let him speak. He has a right to free speech."

The punk with a safety pin through his ear shouts, "He does. It's the Twelfth Amendment."

I start hiccupping like crazy and grab onto the podium to steady myself.

Ali moves toward the center of the aisle, ready for Mr. Jackson to drag him away like a political prisoner. "The students seized the embassy because the king of Iran was a brutal dictator. His family lived in a gold palace while everyone else starved."

Gerald stands up and starts booing. The junior G.I. Joes do the same.

"Mr. Thomas, *sit down,*" Principal Crankovitch says forcefully.

He does.

Then Mike, of all people, stands up. "Mr. Ramos is right. He has a right to speak." He glances around at Kyle, Bridget, and Malia as if he expects them to join him.

They don't.

I don't know whether to be more embarrassed for him or for me.

Usually, when I gulp air and swallow hard, it stops the hiccups. Not this time.

Mr. Jackson has Ali collared. As he starts to drag him away, Ali shouts, "The CIA propped up the corrupt shah. Don't make the Iranian students out to be the bad guys."

Gerald stands up again and raises *his* fist. "Well, *I* say, before we get dragged into another Vietnam, with thousands of soldiers going off to die or get disfigured, we oughtta bomb Iran." Then he starts chanting, "Bomb. Iran. Bomb. Iran."

The junior G.I. Joes stand up for Gerald, while the punks follow Ali out the door.

Right before Principal Crankovitch can intervene, Ali says, "Ask Jasmine. She'll tell you."

The double doors to the auditorium slam shut. In an instant, it's dead quiet. All eyes are on me, including the principal's. My mind is totally blank. I hiccup again.

I can't do this. What am I supposed to say? Do I acknowledge Ali? The hostages?

No. Stick to the speech. Don't let him or Gerald derail me.

One last, big gulp—a gamble since I could belch right into the microphone—does the trick.

"Uh . . . Principal Crankovitch, distinguished faculty, fellow seniors. It would be the honor of my lifetime to serve as the first senior class president of the new decade." My voice is shaking. "The 1980s promise to be an era of newfound freedom. This election is a choice between—"

"What about the hostages?" a junior G.I. Joe calls out from the middle of the crowd.

Don't let him derail me.

"—between the freedoms we all cherish, which includes freedom of dress, and—"

"The hostages aren't free," another calls out.

Principal Crankovitch cranes his neck but can't tell who's catcalling from his vantage point. The usual enforcer, Mr. Jackson, has left with Ali.

But I won't let them derail me.

"Gerald would have us in button-downs and hose and heels. I promise, if I'm elected—"

"Do you want another Vietnam?" shouts a Gerald supporter.

"Oh my God," I shout, causing all this feedback on the mic. "The hostages have nothing to do with this election! Why are we even talking about them?"

A murmur ripples through the crowd. From the look on Kyle's face, this may have been the wrong answer. I'm stuck out here in a lifeboat without a paddle. I'll have to call admissions and confess my sin. I'll be stuck at Cal State and wind up like that woman at Dad's work, a copywriter who labors over corporate manuals in an airless cubicle with no window. Her skin was gray, like, *gray,* as if she were decaying from the inside.

Unless—

The mascot.

The mascot!

I scramble back to my seat, grab the jersey, and return to the podium. "If I'm elected, my first act as president will be to change the school mascot from the hawk"—I hold up the jersey—"the ugly, predatory hawk, to the soaring American eagle."

Suddenly, "Fly Like an Eagle" floods the auditorium. My head snaps around. Patty is standing next to the PA.

Kyle, Mike, Bridget, and Malia cheer. Patty wolf-whistles like a pro, which leaves the impression of a resounding response.

I cut the rest of my speech short. No way I'm mentioning Iran now.

"And you can wear whatever you want. That's why I'm asking you to fly like an eagle with me, Jasmine Zu—uh, just Jasmine, for senior class president."

Patty turns up the music. I close my eyes and exhale, ready to get the hell off this ship.

Afterward, as I make my way through the gym, a bunch of students are talking about Ali's outburst. "That guy's weird, man." "Why does he care so much about oil?"

That's all everyone seems to be talking about. Part of me wants to defend Ali, part of me wants to drown him in the bathtub.

Patty runs up toward me. "You did great. Everyone loves that song."

"Thank God you brought the jersey," I say, closing my eyes.

"I thought you might need it," she says, beaming with pride.

I lower my voice. "But Patty, should I have defended Ali? I mean, he is my brother."

She looks horrified. "What? No! He's weird. If you want to win the election, stay as far away from him as you can. Even if he is your brother."

I turn to Malia. "Do you think I should have defended Ali? What he said was true."

She puzzles over this. "My mom says to have 'pride in our people.' She also says, if anything crazy happens with Black folks on the news, keep your head down."

Appearances are everything. Keep your head down. That's what I'm hearing.

Just then, Kyle and Mike walk up.

"Good speech. Nice recovery," says Kyle. "I have a shot at that hundred bucks."

"What are you talking about?" I ask.

"Friendly campaign manager wager. I bet Ellory a hundred bucks you'd beat Gerald."

Mike, all maddeningly decent, says, "They should have let that guy talk. He's right. You should hear the stuff my dad tells me about what the US does in other countries."

That guy. I can't bring myself to admit Ali is my brother.

"Mike, nobody cares about I-ran," says Kyle.

This stings, but it's true.

He turns to me and says, "I'll start polling tomorrow, see if you got a 'bump' from your speech. If you don't start building momentum now, you'll never win."

||||||||||||||||

"Should I have defended Ali?" I whisper to Bridget in psych class. Deep down, I know the answer, but if enough people say otherwise, I can pretend I don't.

"Care to share, girls?" Our psych teacher, Mr. Maller, stands over us.

He's hopelessly stuck in the sixties with his fringed vests and bell bottoms. His sideburns look like two giant caterpillars took up residence on his face.

"No, sir," Bridget says with a sweet smile.

"All right. This unit is on human sexuality," he says, walking back to the blackboard. "If you're going to freak out, do us both a favor and drop. I don't need any angry notes from your mommies or your daddies."

We glance around. No way anyone is dropping this class.

As he starts to talk about the nature of eroticism, Bridget leans over and whispers, "Kyle said Mike thinks you're cute."

"He did not," I say, capturing the butterflies attempting to take flight in my stomach. I have to stay focused on the election.

"Yes, he did," Bridget insists.

Mike *has* spent a while in Germany. It's possible he developed an appreciation for what Mom calls "ethnic beauties" over there.

Or maybe Bridget is just desperate for us to double-date.

"I'm focused on the election," I whisper, as one persistent butterfly flutters all the way up to my chest.

꤮꤮꤮꤮꤮꤮꤮꤮꤮꤮꤮

I should've left school earlier so I could be the first to tell Auntie—and Dad if he calls—what happened during assembly today. Ali will make himself out to be a martyr.

I'll say everything happened so fast, there was no time to think. I'll say Ali got busted for disrupting the assembly. I'll say, what about how *he* embarrassed *me*?

I'm all set to say all of these things, but as soon as I walk in the door, Auntie Minah thrusts the phone at me "Here. Talk to your grandmother."

I quickly set down my stuff and wedge the cordless between my neck and shoulder. "Salaam, Maman," I say, bracing myself.

"Salaam, Jasmine-joon, chetowr-i joonam."

She says hello, asks how I am, and starts wailing, speaking too quickly for me to understand. She's been like this ever since Grandpa died. Distraught every time we talk. It's hard for her to be on her own in Iran, but she refuses to come here.

I sit down at the kitchen table. "Bale, Maman, I know.

Yes, bale, I know," I keep repeating, as if I understand half of what she's saying.

I can't believe I spoke Farsi fluently when I was little. Now it's a phantom limb whose only painful reminder is when Grandma Zumideh calls and we are hopelessly unable to communicate.

Finally, when she's exhausted herself and is ready to hang up, she says the few words in English she knows. "Doostet daaram. I love you, Jasmine dear."

"Doostet daaram. I love you, too, Maman. I love you."

We say this over and over until she hangs up.

I put the phone back in its cradle. My eyes sting. I'm seven. Her hands are clapping and her fingers are snapping while I do my best belly dance for her and Grandpa Zumideh. We're celebrating Persian New Year. Grandma makes a Haft Sin, the Altar of Seven Things that start with the letter *S* in Farsi: seeb, an apple, to symbolize health, and samanu, a wheat pudding, to symbolize bravery, and so on. She lets me decorate the eggs. I run around excitedly teaching everyone how to say Nowruz Mubaarak—"Happy New Year" in Farsi.

That seems like a lifetime ago.

"Why did the ayatollah tell the students to take hostages? Maman is so scared," Auntie says, furiously chopping vegetables for the night's stew.

I touch her shoulder. "Dad says it'll be over soon."

But what if it's not?

Suddenly, the back door slams.

Ali barges in and throws his books down on the dinette table. "Thanks for defending me, man."

I spin around. "*Defend* you? You ruined my campaign kickoff speech."

Ali tears off a piece of lavash. "You could have used your platform today to speak out. But you didn't, 'cause you're a hypocrite. At least Gerald *believes* the stupid stuff he says."

"Oh my God!" I don't mean to yell. "I'm trying to beat Gerald and get into NYU, Ali. *Please.* Can you not make a scene until after the election?"

He scoffs. "Seriously? You want to silence me and deny our heritage so you can win some stupid high school election?"

"Of course I do."

Auntie raises an eyebrow.

"I mean, just until the election is over." He's got me all flustered. I cross my arms. "I *have* to win, Ali. I'm not moving to Kansas or getting stuck here."

His face twists. "Moving to Kansas? What are you talking about?"

Shit. I shouldn't have said that.

Auntie stops chopping.

"Uh . . ." I shift from side to side to buy myself some time. Clear my throat. How to say this?

"Mom said she might stay there with Grandma," I say, as breezily as possible. "And we would go there, too."

Ali folds his arms. "I'm not going. I'll stay here with Dad."

"Why you don't like Manhattan?" Auntie asks. "They have the Radio City and Broadway."

"Not that one," Ali and I say in unison.

"Ali, if I get into NYU, you can't leave Mom all alone."

"What about Dad?"

I close my eyes. There's no easy answer. "Nothing's definite, okay?"

"Whatever," he says, and turns and runs upstairs.

I should follow him. We should really talk about Mom and Dad. I'm the big sister. We haven't had a heart-to-heart in so long. But the election is in full swing, and I've got a full day of campaigning tomorrow. That's all I can think about right now.

CHAPTER SEVEN

UN-IRANIAN

Kyle says voters want to see themselves reflected in their candidate. My job today is to make like a mirror. Campaign hard. Bring my A game. Leave nothing on the field. Which is why it's such a bummer my period started. A big zit has erupted in the middle of my forehead.

Luckily, I took two Pamprin this morning. The energy to build a house or run a marathon is kicking in. I swear, if guys knew about Pamprin, they'd be snorting it. Anyway, by the time I get to school, I'm ready to run the ball into the end zone, to round third and slide into home—or any of the other sports metaphors Patty has thrown at me.

At lunch, Kyle and Patty lead me to the AV Club room adorned with a bunch of *Star Trek* posters. A film projector sits in the middle of the room for encore screenings of sci-fi classics.

This group of about twelve AV Club guys (they're all guys)

look at me with an unsettling mixture of curiosity and disdain. I keep glancing down at the notes Kyle handed me minutes before we walked in.

"Like you," I say, "I was relieved that the doctor didn't drown at the hand of . . ." I look at my notes again. "Chancellor Goth."

I flash my most Pepsodent smile, hoping I've won over the *Doctor Who* Fan Club, all the while wondering, who is Dr. Who?

"Which is why I'm asking you to fly like an eagle with me, Jasmine Zumideh, and our new American eagle mascot." I hold up the picture of an American eagle Patty has pasted onto a piece of poster board.

The club president, who has the longest neck and largest Adam's apple I've ever seen, glances around at the other members. "Right on. Anyone have any questions?"

This guy whose braces are bound by rubber bands raises his hand. "I do. What about the students?"

"Uh, which ones?"

Kyle's notes don't mention anything about students.

"Those I-rain-ian students on the news all the time. Gerald told us he's getting together a petition against them. What about you?"

A *petition*? For who, the ayatollah? Besides, the Iranian students have nothing to do with this election. Thank God I never mentioned Iran.

I can't say I'm *in favor* of student radicals, though.

My mouth curves into a patient smile. "There's really nothing senior class president—"

"—she wants the hostages home safe like everyone else," Kyle butts in. "Thank you, thanks for your time today."

We hustle out of the AV room and head toward the gym.

"Kyle, there's nothing student council president can do about the hostages, you know that," I say. "Shouldn't we make that clear?"

"And be seen as weak on the issue?" He turns to Patty. "Take her to the next two events while I conduct my poll. We'll meet in the quad after fifth period."

Patty leads the way inside the gym, where I change into a T-shirt with big, black, iron-on letters that spell out E-S-P-N. "A new, twenty-four-hour cable channel devoted to sports? Now that's something to cheer about," I shout to the handful of off-season basketball players she's assembled. "Just like our new mascot." Once again, I hold up the picture of the eagle.

She gives me a big thumbs-up.

"Why do you want to change it anyway?" a player with sun-kissed hair that grazes his shoulders asks.

"Yeah, the hawk is cool, man," another player with a mullet chimes in. "A hawk can conquer a squirrel. A fuckin' *squirrel*! What can the eagle do?"

I draw a breath. I haven't actually *Encyclopedia Britannica*'d the American eagle.

"Well, the eagle is a . . . a symbol. Of America. And freedom," I say.

The jock with sun-kissed hair that grazes his shoulders nods, slowly at first, then gains momentum. "Freedom. Yeah, I like it."

Yes!

"Especially now, with all those hostages in I-rain-ia."

Why did I mention freedom?

"Gerald says he's getting an official petition together to send to President Carter," the jock with the mullet says. "You gonna sign it?"

An "official" petition? These seniors can't be that gullible. I have to set them straight.

"Well, no. There's nothing—"

"She'll do everything she can to make sure the hostages get home safe," Patty interjects, guiding me by the elbow to the double doors.

As soon as we get outside, I spin around. "Patty, seriously. There's *nothing* student council president can do about the hostages. It's ridiculous. You have to let me say so."

"Why can't you say you want them home safe like Gerald?"

"Because." My voice raises by about three octaves. "They don't have anything to do with this election. And I don't want it to seem like I'm copying him."

Thankfully, the stoners she's assembled under the old oak tree don't ask about the hostages. But at the end of my presentation, one pulls out a lighter emblazoned with an American flag. "That other dude gave us these," he says. "So we don't forget about the hostages."

All the air squeezes out of my stomach like an accordion. Kyle was right. This is not going to be a cinch. The hostage crisis has turned everything upside down. Gerald is convincing people he can actually do something about it. And now I'm crashing from my Pamprin high.

I barely say two words to anyone in journalism—including Mike—and drift in and out of a lecture on acute angles in geometry. As soon as the bell rings, I have to set Kyle and Patty straight: we're pushing back on the notion there's *anything* Gerald can do about the hostages.

I head for the quad after fifth period and stand near the old oak impatiently tapping my foot in 12/8 time. The minute Kyle crosses from the bungalows toward the quad, I barrel toward him. "Why can't we say there's nothing senior class president can do about the hostages when there's *nothing* senior class president can do about the hostages? Gerald is making it sound like he's personally negotiating their release."

He motions me to follow him to our usual spot on the quad where Patty is now waiting. "He's sending a petition to President Carter. That's something."

"It's actually not, Kyle. It doesn't mean anything."

Kyle and Patty stand opposite me, forming the base of an obtuse triangle, of which I am the apex.

Oh, wow. Maybe I am getting the hang of geometry.

Kyle exhales. "Listen, in politics, you have to evolve with the electorate. They're looking for hope, even if it's from a symbolic gesture like Gerald's petition. You're saying you'd rather tell seniors it's hopeless?"

I cross my arms. "I'd rather tell seniors the truth."

Patty puts her hands up to silence us. "Okay, okay. So Gerald is a better competitor than we thought, so what? All that means is we have to study his playbook, beat him at his own game."

"She's right," says Kyle. "And maybe add a few sweeteners to the platform."

"What, like, free Coke on Fridays?" I say, half-joking.

"Now you're getting the hang of it," says Kyle.

Free Coke Fridays is exactly the kind of empty campaign promise Mike's dad warned against. But now that I think of it, what senior wouldn't want free Coke?

"We're barely into the first week of campaigning; it's only, like, the third inning," Patty says.

She's right. The game has barely begun. I've got two weeks to hit the ball out of the park—or tackle Gerald to the ground before he makes it across home plate.

"And when this hostage thing is not front-page news anymore, no one will care," she adds.

She's right about that, too. Who knows? The hostage crisis could be over and the hysteria around it dying down any day now.

||||||||||||||

Hysteria around the hostage crisis is not dying down. If anything, it's snowballing.

When I show up for our editorial meeting on Thursday, everyone is still passing around the day's paper, which has pictures of burning flags and Iranian men with bushy mustaches, who all look strangely like Freddie Mercury.

"Whoa." Flynn whistles.

Mr. Ramos paces. "The media's not providing enough context. We're always sticking our nose in other countries' affairs, propping up Pinochet in Chile, supporting the coup in Argentina."

Gerald pushes his glasses up the bridge of his nose and leans forward, which he always does when he thinks he has something important to say. "My dad says we gotta get that peacenik President Carter to quit yammering about the energy crisis here at home and drop the *bomb* on I-ran. Otherwise, we're going to end up with another Vietnam. That's why my campaign is taking a strong stand against student radicals."

I want to take a stand against student radicals, too. Namely, Ali. But drop a bomb on Iran? In a really forceful voice, I say, "You and your dad don't know *anything* about Iran. A bomb would only kill innocent people like my grandmother."

Unfortunately, it's only the voice inside my head. How am I supposed to speak up when no one will listen, when the snowball is rapidly becoming an avalanche?

"Let's talk about our lead story for the next issue," says

Mr. Ramos. "I'm thinking the senior class presidential election since we have both candidates right here." He smiles at me and Gerald. "We're counting on you both to conduct yourselves with the unimpeachable integrity we need from our journalists and politicians." He turns to the rest of the class. "What was newsworthy about the campaign kickoff?"

As a candidate, I can't say my winning proposal to change the school mascot from the predatory hawk to the soaring American eagle. If Mike really likes me, maybe he'll say it.

Instead, he says, "I thought the most newsworthy thing about the assembly was that student's protest about Iran."

Oh no. The last thing I need is for Mike to give Ali—and this whole hostage thing—*more* attention. As diplomatically, but forcefully, as possible, I say, "But is that really relevant? To our readership? I mean, with the election coming up, we don't want to get sidetracked."

Flynn sees his opening. "Yeah, we really should be covering this Three Mile Island thing. People are growing extra limbs."

"I agree, Mike," Mr. Ramos says. "In fact, why don't you cover it? How this kid's freedom of speech is under assault here at Eisenhower."

"Right on," says Mike.

Great. Now I have to strategize how to keep Mike from mentioning me in any article about Ali. Or better yet, convince him not to write one.

After class, I follow him out the door. "Hey," I say.

"Hey." He lets me catch up. As Gerald passes by, he chuckles. "I heard he's sending a 'petition' to President Carter about the hostages. Like that will do anything."

"That's what I'm saying," I say, before realizing I'm not supposed to be saying anything about the hostages. "But, I mean, writing about 'that guy.' Does anyone really care? Except, you know, *us*. Of course *we* care. As journalists."

He smiles that self-satisfied smile. "That's why I'm writing it."

Strike one. I need another at-bat.

"So, um, are you going to the game Friday?"

"Yeah, probably." He nods.

"Cool," I say.

"Cool," he says.

Before the moment turns any more awkward, Patty comes racing toward us.

"See you there," Mike says and continues down the hall.

"Look what I got." Her voice drops. She pulls a spiral-bound notebook out of her gym bag. "It's Gerald's election playbook. We stole it from his locker."

"*What?*" I pull her aside. "Who stole it? How did you get it?"

"My little brother and his friends," she says with a gleeful smile. She starts turning the pages. "His lock was from, like, Pic 'N' Save. There's a bunch of stuff in it about his campaign."

I put my hand on top of hers to stop her from going any further. "Patty, Nixon got *impeached* for stealing stuff from the Democrats."

"Where do you think I got the idea?" She cackles.

I grab it from her. "We can't keep it."

She snatches it back. "Did you forget he got my brother expelled *three months* before graduation?"

I wrestle it back from her. "I know. But this has nothing to do with that."

Kyle walks up, seems to know exactly what we're talking about. "That the playbook?" He grabs it out of my hands and quickly flips through. "We're not giving up marching band or AV Club without a fight. Wonder what other secrets are in here." He looks at me. "This campaign could get dirty, you know."

For a half second, I hesitate. Of course, I don't want the campaign to "get dirty," but my application is already in the admissions office and—

No. *No.* Mr. Ramos is counting on me to conduct myself with unimpeachable integrity.

I come to my senses. "We can't. We can't use it."

"Why not?" Patty demands.

"Because." I glance around nervously. "It's not right. We don't need it."

"You don't know what you'll need till you need it," says Kyle. "Don't get caught playing defense. My dad says winning campaigns are always on offense."

Patty shifts toward Kyle. "My dad says, if you're on defense, you're losing."

"Well, *my* dad doesn't have any snappy sports analogies. But we have to put it back."

The first bell rings for fifth period.

"Okay, okay, we won't use it. For now," Kyle says and stuffs the playbook into his gym bag. "Unless we need a Hail Mary."

"If we need a Hail Mary, I'll get a rosary from Bridget," I say, turning on my heels and heading for the bungalows. We're not using Gerald's playbook.

||||||||||||

God. Iranians were never on TV before. Now they're on all the time. Images of angry Iranian students shouting "Death to America" dominate the nightly news. There's even a whole new news show on ABC opposite *The Tonight Show Starring Johnny Carson*: *The Iran Crisis—America Held Hostage: Day Fill in the Blank*. Every day, the show's title updates, e.g., *America Held Hostage: Day Six*, *America Held Hostage: Day Seven*. The worst advent calendar ever.

All the news coverage only makes Ali angrier. "You know what they don't show, they don't show our CIA training the shah's secret police," he says right before I have to leave for my shift. "They don't show the secret police torturing and imprisoning anyone critical of the shah."

"The Iranian students got everyone's attention," I say,

adjusting my hair under my bucket hat. Do my feathers look better tucked in or left out? "Why can't they let the hostages go?"

"They will." He picks up the remote and flips through the channels. "As soon as the US returns the shah to stand trial as a war criminal."

"You sound totally un-American when you say that." I'm leaving my bangs out.

"Well, you sound un-Iranian."

It's like our two halves are at war with each other. It's exhausting. I grab my keys and go.

Thank goodness for the mall. There could be a mushroom cloud outside and people would still sort through the sale rack at JCPenney in oblivious, air-conditioned comfort. I'll finally get a break from all the hostage hysteria.

When I show up for my shift, Donna, the shift leader— one of the few people who can pull off a Dorothy Hamill wedge cut other than Dorothy Hamill—looks confused. She says I'm an hour early, my shift doesn't start till five. I have forty minutes to kill.

I'm like a celebrity walking around the mall in my Hot Dog on a Stick uniform. Little kids gawk. "Do you make the fresh-squeezed lemonade yourself?" they ask with wide-eyed wonder, as if I'm Willy Wonka and we're in the Chocolate Factory. People are always asking if they can borrow our red, white, blue, and splash-of-lemonade-yellow shirts, electric blue polyester shorts, and bucket hats for Halloween. But they can't because civilians aren't allowed.

Before I spend the majority of my time at Sam Goody—it's right here in the mall and I'm contemplating the *Quadrophenia* soundtrack—I pop into Spencer Gifts.

One of the sales guys, the one who looks like a younger, cuter Burt Reynolds, wolf whistles and says "Hot legs" when he sees me in my uniform.

"Thanks," I say. I mean, they are my best asset. I approach the counter pretending to browse the "water pipes" everyone knows are bongs while making a concerted effort to ignore the adult toys—including what look like dildos, though I haven't gotten to that chapter in Mom's copy of *The Joy of Sex* yet—lining the back wall.

"Whatcha lookin' for?" younger, cuter Burt Reynolds asks.

"Just browsing," I say in a flirty, singsong voice.

Mike liking me, or Bridget telling me Mike likes me, has made me feel more attractive. I'm even thinking about asking younger, cuter Burt Reynolds to show me one of the roach clips with giant feathers I could wear in my hair when he says to another customer, "Everybody's been yapping about Middle East peace ever since I can remember. Never happens. We always have to get involved. If I ran into any of those I-rainians on the street, I would beat their asses."

The customer, a sunburnt blonde with hair the texture of straw, nods vigorously. "Yeah, that pussy Carter better be planning an invasion to rescue those guys. Or else wipe I-ran off the map."

"The whole country, just like that?"

They turn to me with their heads cocked, as if I had just said *Star Wars* sucks.

"Yeah. Like anyone would care," says younger, not-that-cute Burt Reynolds, who must not realize his thick, black hair and bushy mustache look just like the Iranian students'. "Where you going, sweetheart?" guy-who-doesn't-even-resemble Burt Reynolds calls to me while I hurry out of there as fast as I can.

Why the hell do I smile and wave at him? I'm still pissed when I walk into Sam Goody. Their selection is shitty. They have a million copies of *Tusk*—give it up after *Rumours*, Fleetwood Mac—but no Siouxsie and the Banshees or Adam and the Ants.

I should have told Fake Burt Reynolds to take one of those adult toys and shove it.

When I finally start my shift, it's hard to maintain the ultra-pleasant demeanor required of a hotdogger. "It's a hot dog dipped in *party batter*," I say with righteous indignation to a customer who dares call it a corn dog.

Donna reprimands me after he leaves. "Jasmine. It's our job to maintain a pleasant and upbeat attitude at all times."

I will the corners of my mouth up and greet the next customer with what could pass for a smile. A man with an accent orders two hot dogs and two cheeses on a stick plus lemonade for his whole family. He's grinning at me as I make his change.

I know what's coming next, and there's nothing wrong with saying I'm Persian. It's like the difference between a hot dog on a stick dipped in party batter and a corn dog. When he asks if I'm Italian or Mexican, I know exactly what I'll say.

Instead, in what is now clearly an Iranian accent, he says, "You are Iranian, yes?"

My face flushes. I glance at the customer standing behind him, the same customer with scarecrow hair who was talking to Fake Burt Reynolds.

"No," I say flatly. "I'm Italian."

And totally un-Iranian.

CHAPTER EIGHT

GENUINE IMITATION

Bridget is showing me how to apply this light-blue shimmer shadow and . . . well, it's not exactly my shade, but you can definitely see it from a distance.

She has to leave for the game in a few minutes and is also helping me pick out what to wear. She sorts through my closet while I stand in front of the mirror fluffing and unfluffing my feathers.

She pulls out my bright yellow satin bomber jacket. "Oooh, this," she says definitively.

Decision made: my satin bomber jacket over my tightest jeans, which camouflage my post-period bloat. I've been cutting out carbs and am dying for a Suzy Q: that moist devil's food cake with a heavenly cloud of imitation whipped cream.

"Don't forget to flirt with Mike," she says on her way out.

"I won't."

My mission, however, is to stop Mike from writing about

Ali, from giving him the opportunity to defend the Iranian "student radicals" or, more important, mention me.

The bleachers are half full when I get there. Swaths of green and black blanket the stands. Cliques are clustered together like little villages: marching band, freshmen, parents, and so on.

The band is failing at "We Are Family." The trumpets bleat out the melody while the drumline attempts to crisp up the beat. The stoners are under the bleachers; you can smell it. Malia is with the drill team. Bridget is huddled with the rest of her cheerleading squad.

I walk the length of the bleachers looking for Mike or Kyle or Patty. All I see is Gerald.

Campaigning.

Campaigning at a football game, glad-handing seniors throughout the stands. Once again, he's on offense while I'm on the bench.

I survey the stands. Seniors I've met over the last three years in Freshman Comp or Algebra I or AP Lit are scattered about. I plunge in, asking for their votes.

"Hey, Stacey," I greet a girl I had gym class with. "I'm running for senior class president and could really use your vote."

She looks at me blankly.

"We, um, we were in gym together sophomore year."

She blinks. Still blank.

"My platform is to change our mascot to a cool, new American eagle." I try to sound amped about it.

She studies me for what feels like forever.

"And free Coke for lunch," I blurt.

Why did I say that? Who knows if I can deliver? Maybe I shouldn't be promising—

"Whoa! That'd be bitchin'," she says.

Oh my God. It worked.

With a newfound vigor, I go from row to row, asking for votes, promising fountains of free Coke. It's all going great, when suddenly, I come to a dead stop.

It's Curtis—I mean, Him. I . . . oh, forget it. Curtis. He's with Her. They're super-glued together.

His mom and dad sit next to him on their stadium cushions, thermos full of Irish coffee between them, watching Curtis's younger brother bang together the cymbals in marching band. His dad is talking loudly to anyone who will listen. "The Arabs, the I-rain-ians, they're all tribal peoples, you know? They don't want democracy or civilization."

He stops short. His mom is looking at me with a frozen smile.

The one and only time I met her, she said, "Oh, *you're* Jasmine?" with that same look of shock we all got when we found out Prince was a guy. I must have been Curtis's only "ethnic" girlfriend. "And where are your parents *from*, dear?" she asked.

Where is Dad from. She meant Dad. When I told her, she marveled, "I've never met anyone from I-*ran*." Like I had said Mars.

"Hey, Jasmine." Curtis snorts.

I honestly thought we were going to Do It that night, even though I had always believed my first time would be with a guy I would never see again or my first True Love. And I don't know if it's because Curtis was neither, but I squirmed out from under him before it was too late. He stood up, threaded his belt back through the loops, grabbed his Wallabees, and left. Never heard from him again.

Total Neanderthal.

"H-hey." My face burns like a fireplace poker. I hurry off to find Mike, who is nowhere to be seen. It'd be so much easier to leave Curtis in the Stone Age if I hadn't bought into Bridget's fantasy double date scenario when I don't want to like Mike anyway. All I want is to get into NYU and get the hell out of here.

I hurry back toward the snack shack. I don't care about carbs. I'm getting a Snickers. I'm not a stick-thin surfer girl, so what? Manhattan (the *real* one) has to be filled with ethnic beauties. I'll fit right in.

Okay, I do care about carbs. I'll make up for the Snickers with a Tab instead of a Coke. And then I'm going home.

Mike is not even that cute, his costume was embarrassing. He did not look like Ponyboy from *The Outsiders,* he looked like Fonzie from *Happy Days* and—

"There you are."

It's Mike. I almost spill my Tab on him. I jam the Snickers in my pocket. "H-hey."

"Hey. Where are you sitting?" he asks.

I never noticed the dimple in his right cheek. My heart pitter-patters the snare/kick intro of "I Want You to Want Me."

Stop. *Stop*. Remember the mission.

"With Patty." I nod in a general direction with no idea where she actually is.

"Kyle and I are over there." He gestures to the stands.

My heart jumps. "I'll find Patty and we'll be up in a minute."

I frantically search for Patty and find her in the girls' bathroom with Ginny. They're standing at the row of cracked porcelain sinks pouring rum into their Coke from travel-size lotion bottles.

Ginny Sumpter's jet-black, stick-straight hair cascades around her shoulders like something out of a Breck commercial. Her American nickname is Ginny instead of Jin Ae. The guys call her China Doll even though her dad's American and her mom's Korean because they can't take five minutes to look at a globe. Like how everyone thinks Iran and Iraq are the same country.

I deliver my breaking news bulletin. "I just saw Mike. He invited us to come sit with him."

Patty takes a swig from her rum and Coke. "Big whoop. He knows you. Want some?"

Ginny lines up the rim of the lotion bottle with my Tab and pours.

We used to hang out with Ginny in elementary school

and junior high, but she turned into a total party girl once we got to Eisenhower.

"That's enough," I tell her.

I'm such a lightweight. I don't even smoke weed anymore. Every time I open my eyes, we're someplace new, and I'm thinking, how did we get to 7-Eleven from that keg party—but now that we're here, I could really use some Visine and Now and Laters.

Ginny heads for the party under the bleachers while Patty and I climb up to where Kyle and Mike are sitting. Patty makes her way in first and sits on the other side of Kyle. I quickly sit down next to Mike.

Kyle leans over. "I have to talk to you about Gerald."

"I already saw him campaigning," I say. "Don't worry. I was, too."

"Not that." Kyle lowers his voice. "Something else."

Mike leans forward slightly. "Can't it wait till Monday, man?"

"At halftime," Kyle says, and gets drawn into a conversation with Patty about the other team's 4–2–5 defense.

Mike takes a sip of what looks like hot chocolate.

"What are you drinking?" I ask.

"Hot chocolate."

"And?" I say with a conspiratorial smile.

"And nothing." He shakes his head. "My parents would kill me if I came home drunk."

I don't know whether to envy or pity him. I could come

home completely buzzed and Mom and Dad would barely notice.

He nods toward the field. "You like football?"

"Don't know much about it. I usually just watch Bridget and Malia."

I glance down at the field. Bridget is waving excitedly. From her vantage point, it must look like Mike, Kyle, Patty, and I are on a double date. Shoot. I should have sat between Kyle and Patty, but it would be awkward to stand up and move now.

I feign interest in the game for a couple more plays before making my move. "So, do you like journalism? Mr. Ramos?"

"It's cool, yeah, he's cool. Good class. I'm learning a lot. My mom really wanted me to go to a 'normal' high school for senior year, with regular classes, since we moved around so much. You know, go to prom and stuff."

Prom. I take a sip of rum and Tab to steady myself and stay focused. "How's your article coming along?"

"Haven't started it yet."

Should I mention Ali? I can't mention Ali, he doesn't even know we're related.

I down the rest of my rum and Tab. "Why don't you write about growing up in the military instead? That's way more interesting."

"Yeah." He laughs. "It's not."

Strike two. I need another at-bat. Maybe if I get more personal.

"Where do you want to go? After high school?" I ask.

"Air Force Academy, probably. If they don't find out my deep, dark secret." He notices my look of alarm. "Technically, I'll be four credits shy at graduation. We've moved around so many times, no one can tell. What about you?"

"NYU, early decision. And Cal State as a fallback."

"I heard about that, early decision. Good luck."

The rum is catching up to me. "That's why I *have* to win this election. What am I supposed to tell NYU if I don't?" Shit. I shouldn't have said that.

The rum is catching up to Patty, too. She's laughing loudly and hanging on Kyle. Bridget is squinting up at us. I'm a little foggy but try to calculate how pissed she'll be if I don't get between Patty and Kyle—even though she never worried about our feelings when she totally abandoned us for him.

Mr. Ramos talks a lot about biases and blind spots in investigative reporting, how they can color our perceptions and make us overlook critical facts staring us right in the face. I admit, I have a definite bias against Kyle. I'll move between him and Patty at halftime.

But right after the quarterback fumbles, Patty stands up and mumbles, "Bathroom." She stumbles past Kyle and Mike and motions me to follow her.

I do.

To my surprise, Kyle follows me.

Patty is running for the bathroom, I'm running after her, and Kyle is running after me.

"Jasmine, wait. Wait!" Kyle shouts.

I stop right in front of the girls' bathroom and spin around with my arms folded. *"What?"*

He glances around, all suspicious, like he's being followed or bugged. "You're not going to believe what I found in Gerald's notebook."

Patty's heaving inside a stall.

"Kyle, Patty's sick."

"His dad's in prison," he says with an almost maniacal grin.

"What?" My face scrunches up in confusion.

Kyle drops his voice and says it again. "His dad's in prison."

I shake my head. "Why would you say that?"

"There's an entry in the back of his playbook. 'Call Dad.' With an inmate number and a phone number. For Men's Central Jail in downtown LA. I called. It's him."

Gerald. Hall Monitor Gerald. Assistant Crossing Guard Gerald. *Gerald,* who narc'd on Patty's brother for smoking weed. *His* dad is in prison? He can't be. Dad never said anything, and they work together.

Although, what would he say?

Gerald's playbook was supposed to be some super-secret document in which he laid out his strategy to defeat me. This sounds more like a diary.

I would die if anyone found my diary.

"Kyle, I told you to put the playbook back. Anyway, I don't believe it."

"He is. I'm telling you."

I really wish I hadn't had that rum and Tab so I could think more clearly. "So what? You're not saying you want us to use it against him, are you?"

He can't be saying that.

Kyle gestures toward the bleachers. "Did you see him up there? He's gaining support because of his stance on student radicals. If they found out his dad was in prison . . ."

He *is* saying that.

Dammit. Kyle *is* a know-it-all who probably winks at himself in the mirror every morning. But he's also a savvy campaign manager who knows more about strategy and positioning than anyone else at Eisenhower High.

Ginny sticks her head out of the bathroom. "Jasmine, Patty needs you."

"I'll be there in a minute." I turn my attention back to Kyle. "No one will care. At least, they shouldn't. And anyway, if we did, he would know we stole it."

"We're not going to come out and *say* anything. We're going to start a whisper campaign."

Ew. That's so . . . sleazy. I shake my head. "No. I don't need to win that way."

Kyle closes his eyes. "Jasmine, politics is a dirty business. Sometimes, you have to be willing to get down in the mud."

I stand a little taller. "I'm not."

He snorts. "Oh, really? Want us to give the playbook back?"

I don't answer. My brain is fuzzy from the rum and Tab. "You don't think he'd do the same to you?"

Ginny pops her head out again. "Jasmine, Patty is—"

"I'm coming," I practically scream at her. "I have to drive Patty home, Kyle. Can you tell Mike?" With that, I disappear inside the girls' bathroom.

Kyle calls after me. "My dad says overconfidence kills the candidate every time."

This reverberates as I enter the stall and pull Patty's hair back toward the nape of her neck so she won't barf on it, which I've done at more parties than I can count. She can*not* drink her brothers under the table.

But it's a moot point. Kyle's integrity may be about as genuine as the imitation whipped cream oozing out of all those Suzy Q's, but mine's not.

||||||||||||||

Bridget is trying on bras—really pretty, lacy bras that fit perfectly because her boobs are unfairly symmetrical—while I sit on a hard bench in the fitting room under the harsh glare of these unflattering fluorescent lights, chin in hands, thinking about what Kyle said last night.

Every week, Bridget goes to catechism and mass with her mom. She knows about all the mortal sins, and even the major ones, so I ask, "Do you think the ends justify the means?"

"What do you mean?"

"I mean, I *have* to win this election, and the campaign could get a little . . . dirty."

She squeezes her boobs together to create epic cleavage and leans into the mirror. "What do you *mean*?"

I gaze past her torso at my own reflection. "I mean, it should have been a cinch, but then the whole hostage thing happened, and Gerald is making it seem like he'll single-handedly bring the hostages home, which is so stupid, but no matter what, I *have* to win."

Bridget meets my gaze in the mirror. "What if you don't?"

I can't look at her. I stare down at the linoleum—its blue sunbursts are littered with cigarette butts and wads of gum.

I need Bridget on my side. She's always been my cheer-leader, no matter what. From my first byline in the *General*—and every one since—she always says, "I loved your article!" When we both know she could care less about Siouxsie Sioux or the B-52's.

"I have to."

"Well, don't fight dirty," she says, looking down on me. "But *of course* you'll win. Kyle is your campaign manager." She turns to the right for a side view of her new bra. "Patty was hanging all over him last night."

I *knew* I should have sat between them. "She didn't mean it. She was drunk. She got sick."

Plus, Patty said Kyle was nothing to get a hard-on over. I can't tell Bridget that.

"Is she coming tonight? To the sleepover?" she asks with a look of distaste.

"Yes," I say with a sigh. "Unless she's hungover."

"Well, I'm not taking any shit from her," Bridget says, giving her bra one last full-frontal appraisal. "She's always bragging about her softball scholarship like she's better than everyone else." She unhooks the lacy bra to slip into her own. "Did I tell you I'm thinking of joining the Peace Corps?"

The look on my face says I need subtitles.

"After we graduate. The nuns say Ethiopia needs volunteers."

It's not like I want her to wait tables at Denny's, all the truckers fighting over her when she bats her eyelashes at them. But she is not cut out for the Peace Corps.

"You know there'll be bugs there, Bridget. Big bugs. At least apply to State."

She pulls her scoop-neck tee over her head. "Are *you* applying to State?"

I stand up. "As a fallback."

She adjusts her top and slings her purse over her shoulder with one final glance in the mirror. "All I know is, you better stick up for me if Patty starts talking shit."

CHAPTER NINE

THE WHOLE TRUTH

If Patty starts talking shit about Bridget and Bridget pushes back, it's going to boomerang back on me. Bridget will want me to take her side over Patty or vice versa. I can't. Not now. Not in the middle of this election when I need Patty and Kyle to win. Which means I better stop the shit-talking before it starts.

First, I have to get Auntie out the door. She's freaking out about leaving us alone for one night, which is kind of a joke. Mom and Dad used to leave me and Ali home alone all the time. Sometimes, they'd ask a neighbor to check on us. Half the time, they forgot.

Everyone's freaking out now about "latchkey kids" because our parents are too busy with their own lives and personal soap operas to worry about us. We're used to it.

"I make dinner for you and your friends," Auntie says, opening the refrigerator to reveal a lifetime supply of ghormeh sabzi—the lemony stew with kidney beans that tastes better than it sounds. "And the zoolbia and bamieh for dessert."

My favorite honey-soaked donuts and twisty, deep-fried pastries.

She ties a periwinkle silk scarf with a bright red-and-yellow paisley pattern around her head. "Why you don't come with me to Shahrazad's?"

"Auntie, go." I put my arm on hers and gently usher her to the door. "We'll be fine."

She's barely out the door when Patty walks in carrying an electric blanket. "The dog peed on my sleeping bag. I'll be okay as long as I'm next to an outlet." She thrusts her blanket at me and heads for the living room, where Auntie has left her Camels on the coffee table next to Mom's clunky, acrylic ashtray. "Oooh. Whose cigarettes? Can I have one?"

"We're not supposed to be in the living room."

Dad gets pissed if we spill anything on the cream-colored sectional sofa and matching dome chair or damage the glass coffee table on which rests his prized coffee-table book, *Persia: Bridge of Turquoise.* I used to spend hours poring over the photographs of Iranian architecture and landscapes, the dramatic mountainsides, and glistening tracts of desert that made Iran look like this magical, mythical place.

The harsh reality of the last week has eclipsed all that. Auntie sits in there all day now, smoking cigarette after cigarette, just like Mom did.

Patty ignores me, reaches for the pack.

"Patty, don't say anything about Gerald's playbook or you-know-what in front of Bridget or Malia, okay?"

She flicks Auntie's Bic and inhales. "What? The narc's dad is in jail?"

I wave away the smoke. "We don't know that. You can't go around saying it. Even if it is true, who cares?"

"I do. He's a total hypocrite."

I snatch the acrylic ashtray from the coffee table and head to the den. "Just don't say anything about it to Bridget or Malia, okay? I don't want them to know about the stolen notebook. And cigarettes will kill you."

Patty follows me. "Why? Because Bridget is such a Catholic goody-goody?"

I spin around. "Patty, you can't talk shit about her either, okay?"

"You always take her side," Patty says, cradling her left hand under her right to catch the falling ash from her cigarette. She pushes past me toward the walnut coffee table, where there's another ashtray.

I go after her. "What are you talking about?"

She barely makes it to the coffee table and taps her ashes. "She totally bailed on us for Kyle; you didn't say anything. Boyfriend after boyfriend, she ditches us. She thinks she's better than everyone. You *never* say anything." She stands over the ashtray, irritably tapping her ashes.

I have to admit, there is some truth to what Patty is saying. But it's a tiny grain of sand she's turning into a black pearl of hyperbole. I don't *always* take Bridget's side . . . do I?

It was just me and Bridget at Jefferson Elementary. We were neighbors, we took the bus together, hid out under her frothy pink netting. Then we got to Roosevelt Junior High. One day, Oliver Bryant was teasing us, calling us Laurel and Hardy because I was chunkier and Bridget was super skinny. Patty came out of nowhere and charged him. Pushed him so hard, the palms of his hands were black from the blacktop. From then on, we were the Three Musketeers—we spent all our time together at the mall or in the pool.

Until ninth grade, when Bridget got her braces off and sprouted her C cups, and Patty became a sports superstar. Suddenly, it seemed like they had nothing in common. Except me.

I had hoped Malia might even things out when she got to Eisenhower, but she never takes sides. Her mother counseled her not to get caught up in our "petty nonsense."

But it's senior year. I don't want to spend it fighting. I want us to stay friends after we graduate. Sure, I'll be busy with my new East Coast friends, taking the subway to all the cool clubs and concerts. But we can write. And I'll see everyone on breaks.

"Patty." I motion her toward the couch.

She sits opposite me with her knees to her chest.

I rest my elbow on the couch with my cheek on my fist.

"I'm sorry, really sorry, if you've always felt like I was on Bridget's side. I'm usually just trying to keep the peace."

Which I must do now.

"You're right." I sigh. "Bridget bailed on us. Again. But it's our senior year. Let's just enjoy the time we have together."

She shrugs, softening.

I tap her knee. "And who's on my campaign? *You*."

The truth is, I've known Bridget longer, and we are closer. But, sometimes, it's helpful to leave Patty with the subtle impression she is my best—like, best-*est*—friend.

A grin fights its way out of her mouth. "It's fun."

"And you're good at it," I say, fluffing her up.

"See?" She rearranges herself so she's sitting cross-legged. "I can do more than pitch no-hitters." She smiles. "And Kyle's not as bad as I thought. We make a good team."

"You *do*."

Whew. Disaster averted, and right when the doorbell rings.

"Come in," I call out. "Patty, hide your cigarette."

Malia's mom would have a fit if she saw Patty smoking. All of Malia's living room furniture is covered in plastic. We take our shoes off in the entryway. She won't let Malia drive past midnight and always drops her off and picks her up from sleepovers.

"Bye, Mama," Malia calls out, and I'm struck by what it must be like to have a mother who actually mothers you, even if you do have to take off your shoes.

A minute later, Bridget arrives and makes her way into the den with the Chatty Cathy sleeping bag she's had since third grade. She makes a big show of waving away Patty's cigarette smoke and plops her sleeping bag on the floor. "I saw you with Kyle last night."

"I was so wasted." Patty laughs.

"Who's hungry?" I quickly change the subject. I mean, we *just* averted a crisis.

I head for the kitchen and open the fridge. Malia, Bridget, and Patty will never eat all these Tupperware containers full of rice and ghormeh sabzi. "Want to order pizza from Milano's?"

Patty forages around the liquor cabinet behind the wet bar. "What is there to drink?" She pulls out bottle after bottle. "Crème de Menthe. Gross. Mint schnapps. Gross. Don't you have anything good? Like Jack? We could have Jack and Cokes."

We don't have any Jack Daniel's. Any Coke, either. All we have is orange Fanta and Dubonnet.

"Nothing for me," I say. I need to keep my wits about me. "I'm ordering a large pepperoni."

"Me neither," says Malia. "I have a look-see tomorrow. Mall fashion show."

Patty mixes the Fanta and Dubonnet for her and Bridget while I retrieve two Tabs for me and Malia. We all sit around the dining room table waiting for the pizza.

"Are you still moving to Manhattan?" Malia asks. "Superman was from there, you know."

"Malia, he's fictional," I say. "And no. No way."

"Kansas looks kind of nice, though. In the movie. That one with Christopher Reeves."

"*Hello-o,* ladies." Ali cruises through the dining room. "You're all looking mighty fine tonight."

Ugh. He is so embarrassing. "Be home by midnight," I shout at him on his way out the door. I mean, I am in charge.

"Why was he so mad at assembly?" Bridget asks.

It's weird. We've never talked about Iran before. Maybe I was too embarrassed. Maybe they weren't interested. But it would be nice to be able to explain things.

I take a deep breath. "He's mad because the United States has been interfering in Iran since, like, forever. He feels like the students are getting a bad rap."

Bridget's face contorts. "But they took *hostages.* With families."

"I know, but . . . there's more to it," I say.

"There's *always* more to it," Malia says with a knowing sigh. "My mom says, when people are fed up, they rise up." Her brows meet over the bridge of her nose. "Is your other grandma near where the hostage thing is happening?"

I cover my mouth to stifle a burp. "No. That's in Tehran. She's outside the city."

"She's not talking about Ali or I-ran anymore," Patty says bluntly.

I throw her a look. I mean, we're not at school.

"Guess what," Bridget says, patting the table with both

hands to get everyone's attention. She's already buzzed. "I'm joining the Peace Corps."

Patty almost spits out her Fanta and Dubonnet.

Bridget's eyes flash with fury. "Why are you laughing?"

"You don't even like *camping*," Patty says with a snicker.

Patty's dad took us camping once, and Bridget was so cold, she slept in the station wagon with the heat on. Then we had to wait for AAA the next day because the battery went dead.

"Where?" Malia asks.

The doorbell rings again.

"Ethiopia. I'll get it," says Bridget, who manages to stand up while holding her drink steady.

"No, she won't," Patty says confidently.

"You don't know that," Malia chastises her.

She hates it when they talk shit about each other.

"You guys, our delivery guy is a total stone fox," Bridget calls out.

She's done this before. We all leave our drinks at the table and head for the door.

In fact, our delivery guy is *not* a stone fox. His ears stick out from under his baseball cap. But we play along.

"What's your name?" she asks with that singsong voice only she can pull off.

"Uh, Caleb," he says, balancing the large white pizza box on his left hand.

"Do you want to come in and party with us, Caleb?" she asks brightly, knowing the answer.

"N-no. I can't," his voice cracks. "Not while I'm working."

"Oh, bummer," Bridget says with her trademark mock pout.

He hands her the large pepperoni in exchange for four five-dollar bills.

"What about the mozzarella sticks?" she asks innocently.

Malia covers her mouth to stifle a giggle. Bridget hands the pizza box to me while Patty drifts back to the living room for another cigarette.

Poor Caleb. He looks stricken. "I . . . that wasn't part of the order? Was it?"

"It was," Bridget says with eyes so wide and sad you'd think she just heard the truth about Bambi's mother.

He shifts nervously from side to side. "Wait. Let me check the truck."

I feel so bad for these delivery guys.

A minute later, he returns, holding out a brown paper bag. "H-here. I found them," he says, and hands Bridget some other customer's mozzarella sticks they'll probably deduct from his next paycheck.

"Oh, thank you, Caleb." Bridget throws her arms around him. "You're our hero."

"Let me get your change," he says, digging into his pocket.

"Keep it," I shout. It's the least we can do.

Bridget stands at the door, waving, until his delivery truck rolls out of sight, then closes it, triumphant.

Patty reappears and exhales right in her direction. "Bravo."

"I got us free mozzarella sticks, didn't I?" Bridget says and sashays past.

"By flashing your tits at him." Patty follows.

"All I did was flirt. You should try it some time."

"Guys, guys," I intervene. "C'mon. Dinner's ready."

I set the pizza box down on the dining room table. Malia brings plates and a roll of paper towels from the kitchen. We each drag ooey-gooey slices onto our plates. For a minute, everything is nice and peaceful.

"So Bridget, you let Kyle get past second?" Patty asks, taking a big bite out of her slice.

Of course, it didn't last.

Bridget clucks at the question while pinching a piece of mozzarella from hers.

"Second base is boob, right?" Malia asks, pulling on a long string of melted cheese.

"Yes," says Bridget. She heads to the kitchen for a knife and fork because she's the only human who eats pizza with utensils. "First base is Frenching, second base is—"

"No, it's not," says Patty, helping herself to another slice. She's so athletic, she doesn't have to count calories *or* carbs. "*First* base is boob. Second base is fingering. Third base is—"

"*Second* base is boob," says Malia, licking pepperoni grease off her fingers. "Isn't it?"

"Exactly." Bridget sits back down. "Third base is oral—"

"Bridget! I've been a Fast-Pitch All-Star three years in a row. I know what the bases are."

This is one of those silly fights they will argue to the end of time unless I step in.

"I don't think the bases are really about baseball," I say gingerly. "They're a metaphor for—"

"A meta-*what*?" says Patty. She puts down her pizza and holds up both hands as if stopping traffic. "First base is boob," she says, pointing to her index finger. "Second base is fingering." She points to her middle finger. "Third base is oral." She points to her ring finger. "Home run is all the way."

Malia looks to Bridget, who seems willing to accept this ruling, but I'm wondering why Patty brought all of this up in the first place.

Everyone retreats to the den while I collect all the paper plates and little packets of chili flakes. "Wanna play Boggle?" I call out to steer everyone back into safer territory.

"Let's play Truth or Dare," Patty says with a wicked smile.

"Boggle is better," I beg. Truth or Dare is dangerous.

Malia sits opposite Patty on the couch. Bridget slides onto the recliner. I stuff everything in the trash and hurry back to the den to referee.

"Bridget," says Patty, with a gleam in her eye. "Truth or dare?"

Bridget doesn't flinch. "Truth."

Patty raises a brow. "Have you ever given Kyle a B-J?"

Bridget's face contorts like she just got a big whiff of Brut. "What? No!"

I know I'm supposed to be stopping the escalating tension

between her and Patty, but I can't help asking, "Is it something you actually *blow*? Like a trumpet?"

"No." Malia giggles, her hand over her mouth. "You suck it. And lick."

"Like an Otter Pop," says Patty, who downs the rest of her drink. "Don't be such a virgin."

"My turn," says Bridget. She looks at me and giggles. "Jasmine, truth or dare?"

"Uh, truth," I say. I'm not ding-dong ditching or streaking.

"Who do you have a crush on?" Bridget asks. Her voice vibrates with anticipation.

Patty throws her hands up. "Oh, duh. Mike. Who doesn't know that?"

"I knew it!" Malia says with a clap of her hands.

I haven't admitted anything to anyone yet. "I never said that."

"I'm going again because I answered for you," Patty asserts. "Bridget. What's the furthest you've ever gone with Kyle?"

Bridget squirms.

I should say something. But then Patty will accuse me of taking Bridget's side. I don't *always* take Bridget's side, but we have known each other longer. And we do live on the same street. Still, I've always tried to be a fair arbiter of—

"Right, Jasmine?" says Bridget.

She and Patty are looking at me with wide, wild eyes.

Malia is frozen.

I'm Rip Van Winkle, asleep for a hundred years, with no idea what's going on. "Right . . . what?" I ask.

"Kyle is the lead campaign manager," Bridget boasts. "He could do it without Patty."

"I never said that," I say sharply. How could I have zoned out now, when I'm supposed to be keeping the peace between them?

"Fine then," Patty says. "He can do it without me." She stands up and marches to the sliding glass door.

"Patty!" I scramble to my feet. "I never said that." I glare at Bridget. "Why did you say that?"

Bridget's speech is slow and thick like a warped cassette from the Fanta and Dubonnet. "Because. Patty thinks she's better than everyone with her stupid sports scholarship. 'I know how to win,' blah blah blah. Well, so does Kyle. Kyle knows how to win."

I throw Malia a desperate look and hurry after Patty out the sliding glass door.

The pool light is on. Dad will have a conniption when he realizes he left the heat on, too.

Patty spins around. "Maybe I don't know as much about politics or polls as Kyle, but I know how to win."

"I *know*."

"No matter what *she* says."

She points an accusatory finger at Bridget, who's now barreling toward us. Malia follows.

"Kyle is the brains of the campaign," Bridget slurs. "He's

the one thinking of the stra-tegeries, stra-tat-tegies, whatever and—"

Oh my God! In an instant, Bridget has slipped and fallen into the deep end of the pool.

"Are you okay, are you okay?" I shout, running to the deep end, even though she does have a pool of her own and knows how to swim.

"No," she sputters.

Shit! I never took CPR at the Y over the summer, either, I was too busy watching soap operas and not doing enough to enhance my application, and now my best friend is about to drown, and her and Patty's petty squabbles will seem so silly at her funeral, and Patty is looking at me, ready to dive in and save her—

"My hair's getting all wet," Bridget whines, breast-stroking to the stairs.

Relief rushes through my body. Patty's shoulders relax. Malia bursts out laughing. "Bridget," she says. "We thought you were drowning."

"It's not funny." Bridget wrings the water out of her hair. "I don't even have my suit on."

"Just skinny dip," Patty says. "There are no guys here."

"Um. Yes there are," says Malia.

We all look up to where she's pointing at the back fence.

Kyle and Mike are peering over, a shit-eating grin on Kyle's face.

CHAPTER TEN

MY AIM IS TRUE

Patty and Malia have gone up to Ali's room to watch a movie on that new cable channel. I have to convince Patty I'm on her side, that I need her on my campaign.

Patty is a fighter. It's in her blood. Her ancestors were brawlers. Scottish. Battled the English back in . . . a long time ago. The point is, Hamiltons go down swinging.

Kyle would throw his hands up and walk away if it looked like he couldn't get *a girl* elected. Patty will fight to the death for me. And I'll die if I don't win this election.

At the moment, though, Mike's face is literally inches from mine, and I'm finding it hard to remember anything about my campaign. His hazel eyes are flecked with gold. He smells like Irish Spring.

We're sitting on the floor next to the stereo listening to Elvis Costello's *My Aim Is True*. In my article about how there's really no comparison between the two Elvi, I wrote:

Elvis Costello is one of the greatest singer-songwriters of our generation. Elvis Presley was a Vegas lounge singer who starred in a bunch of B-movies. Mr. Ramos said that was harsh but fair.

Kyle and Bridget are totally making out in the recliner. Patty's right. We can't even have a Kyle-free slumber party.

Oh, wait. Now I remember. This is my third at-bat to talk Mike out of writing an article about Ali in which he defends "student radicals" and mentions me.

"So, um, is your mom a journalist?" I ask, leaning in with what I hope is a coquettish smile. "Does she write for a paper?"

He shakes his head. "But she was friends with Carl Bernstein, that guy who wrote—"

"All the President's Men," we say in unison.

"Jinx." I giggle.

I've been so busy working on my campaign, I haven't even started the book.

He leans back against the stereo cabinet, rests his elbows on his knees. "They went to the same synagogue."

"Oh," I say with more surprise than intended. "You're—"

"Yep." He nods. "Mom's Jewish, my Dad's Catholic."

"Just like me. Dueling cultures, I mean."

He cocks his head and mock appraises me. "Yeah? What are you?"

If my aim were really true, I would admit it.

"Me?" I say with a nervous laugh. "Oh, I'm Persian and

American. I mean Irish American. My mom's Irish. American. And my Dad's . . . Persian."

Majorly convincing.

"My dad was stationed in Iran for a while."

Not only does he pronounce it *Ee-ron,* he knows Persian and Iranian are the same thing. Even though the hostage situation is ruining my campaign, I'm impressed.

"He says it's a shame, what's happening over there."

Talking him out of writing about Ali is not going to be easy. Especially now, when I can feel him looking at me.

"You're beautiful," he says softly.

My first impulse is to say, "You're lying." No one has ever said that to me.

He leans in, as if he's going to kiss me.

The first kiss is so important. The first kiss determines whether you'll have chemistry. Whether he tastes good. Whether he's too soft or too aggressive. Whether—

"I heard you want to interview me." Ali bounds into the living room from the foyer.

Immediately, Mike and I pull apart.

I jump to my feet. "What are you doing home so soon?" I scowl.

Mike jumps up to shake Ali's hand. "Hey, man. I . . ." He looks back and forth between us. "This is your brother?"

"No," I say. Mike looks at me with such sincere confusion, I backtrack. "Yes, he is."

"It's midnight," Ali says. "Dad said I had to be home by midnight or you'd narc on me."

"Hey, man, we gotta go. I have to be home by midnight, too," Mike says to Kyle, who finally comes up for air. He turns back to Ali. "Yeah, interview. Right. How about, like, Tuesday?"

"Right on," says Ali. "I've got a lot to say about the fascist clown running for senior class president against this total *poser.*"

Poser? *Poser?* He's branding me with a scarlet *P,* but I am not a poser. Posers pretend to be something they're not; I'm pretending *not* to be something I am.

And that's strike three. Mike is going to write an article about Ali. If Mike *is* writing an article about Ali, he *cannot* mention me.

"Patty and Malia are in your room," I say, to get rid of him.

Ali must think his wildest fantasies are about to come true and bolts upstairs.

As Kyle and Bridget say their goodbyes, Mike turns to me and half smiles. I can't tell whether he thinks I forgot to tell him about Ali or purposefully hid it from him.

"Trust me, he was a total embarrassment before this whole hostage thing," I say. "But, um . . . can you not mention me? In your article about him?"

Mike's eyes narrow. He draws a breath to answer just as Kyle jangles his keys right in front of Mike's face. "Let's go."

"Oh. Yeah. Sure," Mike says on his way out the door, and I'm left wondering whether he was talking to me or Kyle.

‖‖‖‖‖‖‖‖‖‖‖

Patty is out cold on the floor next to an outlet. Malia is asleep on the couch. I'm on the floor in my sleeping bag next to the recliner. While Bridget's in the bathroom, I've been calculating the evening's pluses and minuses.

On the minus side, Mike now knows Ali is my brother. I'll have to explain why I kept it from him. And I wasn't able to talk him out of writing an article about Ali or mentioning me. Also minus: Patty and Bridget's silly squabbles.

It's like they each want what the other has: Bridget wishes she were talented enough to merit a scholarship, and Patty wishes she could command free mozzarella sticks.

I just want them to get along.

On the plus side, Mike likes me. Also on the plus side, free mozzarella sticks.

Before I arrive at a final tally, Bridget pads back from the bathroom and slips into her sleeping bag. In a harsh whisper, she says, "I'm not hanging out with her anymore. Patty, I mean."

"You can't do that," I blurt.

Like I said, if I take Bridget's side, Patty will quit my campaign. If I take Patty's side, Bridget will make Kyle quit.

"She was just giving you shit," I say. "She's a shit-talker. You said it yourself."

Her eyes flutter as she considers this, fighting to stay

awake. "Is Mike a good kisser?" she asks but falls asleep before I can answer.

|||||||||||||||

Bridget and Malia are still asleep when I'm woken up by voices in the kitchen. I scramble out of my sleeping bag.

Patty's sitting on the kitchen counter looking all chipper while Ali fries up some eggs. "He's so funny," she says as soon as she sees me.

"I was doing my Nixon impression," he brags, which is such a joke. His Nixon impression is worse than the worst Nixon impression. He holds up both hands in peace signs, sinks his head into his shoulders, and says, "I am not a crook."

He slides the fried eggs onto two plates with some slightly burnt toast. "That dude Mike's gonna write quite an exposé. Later." He nods to Patty before heading upstairs to his room, where he'll probably watch as much porn as he can unscramble.

As soon as he's out of earshot, I say, "Patty. You're still on my campaign, right?"

She jumps down from the counter. "I guess. If it's okay with *Bridget*."

"It is." I shush her. "Just don't give her any shit or she'll make Kyle quit."

"Okay, okay," she says, mopping up the yolk with her toast.

We both startle at the furious honking outside. One of her brothers is here to pick her up.

Bridget is still asleep while Patty gathers up her electric blanket and duffel bag and says, as loudly as possible, "Kyle says we campaign hard again next week."

As soon as she closes the door, Malia sits up and rubs her eyes. "Is she scamming on Kyle?" She looks at Bridget like a mama hen watching over her baby chick.

"What? No." I motion her to the kitchen. "She's just mad at Bridget for bailing on us," I say in a low voice. "You know, with Kyle."

Malia glances past me at Bridget, her face creased with concern. "Are you sure?"

"Yes." I lower my voice to a whisper. "She said Kyle is nothing to get a hard-on over."

Just then, there's a light knock on the door, Malia's mom.

"I hope you're right," she murmurs with one last glance at Bridget, who is just now stirring.

The minute she's gone, I turn to Bridget with a big smile and preempt any complaint about Patty. "Where should we go on our first double date?"

Her sleepy eyes widen. "Maybe . . . Farrell's? We could get a Trough."

"Bridget, I'm not eating a Pig's Trough in front of Mike."

I may not eat *anything* in front of Mike but certainly not a twelve-scoop ice-cream sundae with whipped cream and three toppings. Thankfully, this leads to a digression on what color limo to get for prom—royal blue most likely—and Bridget doesn't even mention Patty.

llllllllllllll

All I want to do after my shift at Hot Dog on a Stick is start *All the President's Men* and call Mike to make sure he's not weirded out about Ali. Finally flip through that November issue of *Creem* magazine.

But Auntie's panicking. Evidently, her friend Shahrazad told her President Carter's going to deport all Iranian Americans who aren't citizens. Insult was added to injury when she saw the Tupperware containers still full of rice and ghormeh sabzi.

She's been sitting in the living room smoking cigarette after cigarette.

"Carter's not going to deport everyone," I say, resting my bucket hat on the coffee table.

She waves her hand dismissively. "Government can do anything it want."

It's true in Iran. In Iran, you can be arrested or deported at any time for any reason.

"It's different here," I say. "We have due process."

But in our American Government unit on World War II, we learned there *was* a Japanese American internment camp right here in California because all the Geralds of the world decided people who'd been here for decades—even Japanese

American children who were *born* here—were not "American" enough.

What if she *is* deported, and Grandma Zumideh can't come here ever again, and Dad can't go there, and Ali and I can't visit like Dad promised?

"I go to my room," Auntie says in an anguished voice. I swear, if she were a character in a Victorian romance novel, she'd always be retiring to her fainting couch.

As she passes by, I happen to glance up at the ivy in Mom's macramé hangers. I've forgotten to water them; their leaves are limp and brown, entirely resigned to their fate.

Why is all this responsibility on *my* shoulders? Why am *I* the one sorting out whether Auntie really is in danger of losing her green card? Why am *I* the one Mom asked, "Do you think I should leave your father?" on their last attempt at divorce, and I had to answer, "I don't know, Mom. I'm twelve. But, no." And she didn't.

At NYU, my only responsibility will be to my grades.

⁣|||||||||||||||

Mike calls before I have time to rehearse what to say about Ali. "I'm not saying it's a big deal," he says, "I'm just asking, why didn't you tell me he was your brother?"

"Why would I?" I snap. I mean, we haven't even kissed.

He laughs that laugh that's only for himself. "Because. Mr. Ramos assigned me to write about him. Because he interrupted your campaign kickoff. Because . . ."

He trails off. But I know what he was going to say because we like each other.

"You wouldn't understand," I say, which is what you say when your explanation is weak.

"Try me."

I cluck and exhale and attempt all manner of stall tactics before finally admitting, "With the hostage thing happening in Iran, it's, like, embarrassing to be Iranian. And even more embarrassing to be Ali's sister. He could cost me the election."

He's silent. An air of discomfort as thick as a Stage 4 smog alert settles over us. I knew he wouldn't understand.

"I knew you wouldn't understand."

"No, I do. Sort of. It's just . . . we're Jewish, you know. My mom is. But our name's not. Like, we could pass. My mom tells my sister and me we have a special responsibility to 'claim our heritage.'"

To Claim Our Heritage. Sounds like an Afterschool Special.

"It's not the same," I say. "Israel is not in the news all the time, causing problems for the US." Maybe it is. I don't really follow international news, but anyhow, the point is, Mike is way too honorable for me. "All I'm saying is, it would be better not to emphasize the connection till after the election. You know?"

He's quiet, mulling it over. I can almost see him chewing his lip.

"Mike, in elections, appearances are everything. And my whole admission—my whole *future*—is riding on this election. I mean, what if your sister were totally mortifying?"

At long last, he chuckles. "She is. She's thirteen and still sings the *H.R. Pufnstuf* theme song all the time. They played that show nonstop in Germany."

"See? That could definitely cost you an election." The air of discomfort finally dissipates. "What kind of music did you listen to in Germany?"

Please don't let him say KISS.

"Mostly Armed Forces radio."

An alarmingly vague answer that could include ABBA.

"What's the last album you bought?"

"Um, I guess it was . . ." He laughs nervously.

I hold my breath. I can't date someone who likes Foghat. Or celebrates Rocktober.

"I guess it was . . . Dire Straits."

I exhale. A little.

"Did I pass?" he teases.

"What?" I feign ignorance.

"The test."

I laugh. "Yes."

"I like that you know so much about music," he says. "It's cool. You already know who you are, what you want to do."

I swoon. I'm never keeping another secret from him again.

. . . except for the one about Gerald's playbook.

Or what's inside.

Or the fact that I lied on my application.

But that's not the real me. I'm not a liar. And as soon as this election is over, from here on out, it's nothing but the truth. I swear.

CHAPTER ELEVEN

OH BROTHER

Ten days till Election Day: the day before Thanksgiving. This is the last full week of campaigning since next week is a short week. My schedule is packed with events.

"Every minute counts," says Kyle as we trek toward the field during morning break. "We're now in the persuasion phase of the campaign. By the end of this week, a majority of seniors will have made up their minds. Then it's time to get out the vote." He flips through several pages on his clipboard as we trek toward the field. "Marching band is the biggest undecided voting bloc. You have to win them over."

"Especially since support from the stoners slipped after Gerald gave everyone those lighters," says Patty, who's right in step with him.

I've created a monster. Patty now knows *all about* politics and the finer points of polling.

I'm wearing a mock-up jersey Patty made with an iron-on

decal of an American eagle. "What if marching band doesn't care about a new mascot?"

"That's why there's the free Coke," Patty says, handing me a can.

I nearly twist my ankle on a gopher hole grabbing it from her. "God. I thought beating Gerald would be so much simpler."

"We told you," says Kyle, flipping back two pages, "voters think he's more presidential. Especially the ones worried about the hostages."

Everything is *we* now. They're totally united against me.

"There's nothing Gerald can do about the hostages," I say, as we get closer to the field.

"He's taking a stand against student radicals," says Patty. "That's something."

"It's actually not," I say, trying to keep up with them. "And if Gerald can live in a fantasy land, why am I stopping at free Coke? Why not offer, oh, I don't know, overnight prom on Catalina Island?"

Kyle stops suddenly. "That's a great idea."

I almost bump into him. "No, it's *not*. It's a joke. Just like Gerald thinking there's anything he can do about the hostages."

We step onto the field. There have to be thirty band members tuning up for practice. My stomach churns.

"Platforms are meant to be aspirational," says Kyle. "No one expects you to keep *every* promise. Your job is to get out there and inspire people." With that, he pushes me in front of the Eisenhower High School marching band.

The trumpet players silently tap the valves on their horns while the clarinetists fiddle with their reeds. The drummers in the drumline rock back and forth on their heels.

"You have five minutes," says their student leader, Jonah—who would not share his notes with me in Algebra II last year.

"H-hello," I say over the low hum of their inattention. My throat is so parched, you'd think I had walked through a desert. "Imagine starting the new decade with a new mascot and free Coke every Friday." I dive into my stump speech (as Kyle calls it) with a pageant contestant smile.

Most of the band members are not listening. Jonah is poker-faced.

I hold up the jersey with the ugly, predatory hawk. Talk up the eagle. Brandish the Coke.

The snares ignore me and quietly practice their fills.

Patty and Kyle are on the sidelines with long faces, as if I just fumbled a forty-yard pass.

Dammit. There are no arrows left in my quiver.

Except.

What if . . .

"And my campaign is putting together a proposal for overnight prom on Catalina Island," I shout above the din of their chatter.

Why can't I propose overnight prom on Catalina Island when Gerald is promising to bring the hostages home?

"*Yes,*" Kyle silently mouths.

Everyone pauses. Looks up from their instruments. Jonah's mouth opens.

Crap. Maybe I shouldn't have said it. Maybe—

"Really?" says the lone female trumpeter. "Like, we'd all take the ferry and everything?"

I swallow. My throat is parched. "That's . . . what I'm . . . proposing."

Proposing. Not even promising.

"That'd be *killer,*" Jonah is forced to admit.

Kyle was *so* right about Mike's dad being so wrong! People *do* want empty promises.

"That's why I'm asking you to fly like an eagle with me, Jasmine, for senior class president," I say, with a presidential wave.

A chorus of whoops and cheers erupts. I leave them buzzing about overnight prom.

"That was amazing," Patty says, breathless, catching up to me.

"That's how it's done," Kyle says, falling in step on the other side.

"I think I won them over," I say. I'm *sure* I did. "And I can still win over AV Club. Get me in front of the *Star Wars* guys. I'll dress up as that girl with the cinnamon-bun braids."

"*Hell* yes." Patty high-fives me.

The first bell rings.

Now I know what it must feel like to be a Fast-Pitch All-Star.

He and Patty take off together toward the bungalows. I head in the opposite direction.

I did it. Rallied the troops. Demonstrated leadership ability worthy of second-semester senior class president. Not only am I going to win, I *deserve* to win. I can just see myself at a *Washington Square News* editorial meeting, pitching an interview with Chrissie or my "Where Are All the Punk Chicks?" article.

And no one mentioned the hostages. Maybe it's finally dying down, maybe—

This can't be happening.

Are you kidding me?

It can't be.

On the south wall of the north hall, opposite the lockers, there's a big banner poster that says BOMB IRAN with a graphic of a *bomb* in place of the *O*.

Which Ali is ripping off the wall.

"Pay no attention to this fascist clown, man. The shah's regime was corrupt, in the pocket of the CIA. That's why the students seized the embassy. As soon as the US sends the shah back, they'll let the hostages go."

No matter what I do, or how much progress I make, Ali has to sabotage me. I swear, I'll stab out his eyes with my No. 2 pencil—if he doesn't go blind, at least he'll get lead poisoning.

I start toward him, but before I get there, a junior G.I. Joe gets right in his face. "Hey, traitor. If it's so great in I-ran, why don't you go back on your magic carpet?"

Ali continues ripping down the poster. "You think Aladdin is Iranian? You're an idiot, man."

Junior G.I. Joe flips him off.

"What are you *doing*?" I shriek.

He spins around and holds up Gerald's half-torn sign. "What do you mean, what am I doing? You think this shit can go unanswered?"

"Of course it can, Ali!" I say, with my fingertips to my temple. A migraine is coming on. "It's only high school. It's not even the real world."

He rips the half-torn sign in half again. "If you don't take a stand now, you never will."

"Yes, I will. I will take a stand, I promise. But could you please *sit down* for now?"

"No." He starts to tear down the other half. "We slept through the seventies. It's time to wake up."

"Hey, hey. That's private property," Gerald says, hightailing it toward us with Ellory.

Ali crumples the torn half and throws it at Gerald. "No, it's not. What the hell does 'Bomb Iran' have to do with an election for senior class president anyway?"

"For your information, it's an important plank in my platform. Down with student radicals here and abroad. We're sending a petition to President Carter."

"A petition to *bomb* Iran?" I say. I can't help it. It's ridiculous.

A few more students stop, including the punks, who stand behind Ali.

I should slip away before anyone sees me.

"You're ignorant, man," says Ali, gesturing wildly. "This country was founded by a bunch of radicals who rose up against a tyrannical monarchy, and okay. They became tyrants themselves to all the Native Americans. But that's all the Iranian students are doing: standing up against a tyrannical monarchy."

"Fuck yeah the Pilgrims were radical," Mohawk Punk says, raising his fist.

Too late to slip away. Mike is approaching from the opposite end of the hall.

"All I know is, we don't want I-ran in the hands of Soviet communists like Vietnam," Gerald says, "and then we end up in another endless war."

"Yeah," chime in a couple of junior G.I. Joes who are faced off against the punks.

It's looking like a hallway production of *West Side Story* if the Sharks had pierced eyebrows and the Jets wore camouflage. Mike arrives, making it a dozen or so students gathered in a semicircle around Ali and Gerald, eager spectators just outside the gladiators' ring.

"Iran's got nothing to do with Vietnam," Ali says.

It doesn't.

"It doesn't," Mike says. Out loud.

I'm so torn between rebuking Gerald—Grandma Zumideh would *literally* feel the fallout if Iran were bombed—and distancing myself from Ali, I stand there, mute.

"And this election's got nothing to do with Iran," says Ali.

He starts to tear down the other half of the poster. Gerald grabs his arm. Ali knocks Gerald back. He stumbles. I shriek again. Mike puts a protective arm around my shoulder.

"I'm gonna sue you. I'm gonna sue you," Gerald sputters as Ellory and the junior G.I. Joes help him to his feet.

Next thing I know, Mr. Jackson is bulldozing his way through the crowd. He grasps Ali by the collar. "You're turning into a real rabble-rouser, aren't you?"

"I have a right to free speech." Ali tries to wriggle out of his grasp.

"Not in here, you don't."

"Yes, he does," Mike says, stepping forward.

Mr. Jackson ignores Mike and hustles Ali off to the principal's office. As he does, Ali shouts, "Gerald is a fascist pig! He's the last person you'd want as your senior class president."

Just when I'm appreciating Ali's indirect endorsement of me, Gerald points a finger straight at my face. "My opponent's brother is an I-rain-ian student radical, everyone."

Ellory turns to me. "He's your *brother*?" he asks with exaggerated shock, as if Ali were a serial killer.

I glance at Mike. Honorable Mike, who's urging me, telepathically, to speak up. Defend Ali. Against my better judgment, I say, "So what if he is? So what?"

And immediately regret it. Everyone is looking at me as if I had sprouted that extra limb Flynn is always yapping about.

The final bell rings.

I step forward and quickly backtrack. "I'm *American,* Gerald. A granddaughter of the American Revolution. Irish American. Katie is my middle name."

In fact, I'll go by Jasmine Katie on the ballot to make sure no one knows Ali and I are related.

"A vote for me, Jasmine Katie, is a vote for a new mascot, free Coke Fridays, and . . ." I side-eye Mike. ". . . uh, possibly, overnight prom on Catalina."

After everyone scatters, I turn to Mike, frustrated. "This is why I didn't want to make the connection to Ali until after the election."

"This hostage thing has nothing to do with you," Mike says. He raises a brow. "Overnight prom? Really?"

"Mike, people are not thinking straight right now. They see the hostages blindfolded, and it makes them mad. It makes *me* mad and I'm . . . Iranian," I harshly whisper. "And it's only a prom *proposal.*"

He puts his hand on my waist. "For what it's worth, I think you did the right thing."

The way Mike is willing to speak up and fight for other

people's rights is one of the things I like best about him—even if it is the worst for my campaign.

"Just make sure you don't mention me in that article," I say.

Not even if he calls me Jasmine Katie.

||||||||||||||

After school, I ambush Ali in the kitchen. I've got to stop him from talking about Iranian students till after the election. Begging hasn't worked. Bribing might. "I'll camp out in the parking lot at the Forum overnight, get you tickets to Rush or Pink Floyd. Floor seats."

Camping out at the Forum is major, especially for bands like Rush or Pink Floyd. He knows I'll have to fend off creepy, prog-rock fogies whose Chevy vans are all airbrushed with some combination of psychedelic wizards, doobie-smoking dragons, or flaming unicorns.

"Rush sucks," Ali declares, eating cold rice and a mound of ghormeh sabzi. "Jesus. Gerald is planning a genocidal rally and you're trying to silence *me*?"

I plop my books on the table. "It's not about you. It's about *me* achieving my dream."

He's never on my side anymore. In the pictures of us where it looks like Mom cut my hair with a machete, I'm grinning from ear to ear, proudly balancing him on my lap. He was so cute back then. And gullible. Watching *Dark Shadows* from the hallway, his little hands over his eyes. I would tell him

I was a vampire, flash my incisors, and he did whatever I wanted. And I taught him pig latin. So we could ay-say uck-fay in ront-fay of ad-Day.

We started arguing when Mom and Dad started fighting. With no one around to referee, we battled everything to the death. Even stupid things, like who got the shoe in Monopoly or who got the first banana pancake. Which was a trick. No one wants the first banana pancake, but like I said, he's gullible.

"What do you want?" I throw my hands up. "Money? Weed?"

He stands up and rinses his bowl in the sink. "No. The guys say pot makes us passive."

My mouth opens. "Shit, Ali. Are you doing coke?"

Our cousin, Shayda, was doing a bunch of coke and got down to, like, a size four before she had to go to rehab for drug addiction *and* an eating disorder.

"No. I'm amped. Because the eighties are going to be *radical*, man. You'll see. People are going to rise up. Entrenched corporate power and bureaucracies will fall."

Which sounds about as likely as a Beatles reunion tour.

I trudge up to my room. There's got to be a way to get through to him.

Right when I start my chapter on arousal for psych, it comes to me. Ali is a normal (sort of) young American male. His obsession with the Iranian students can't be stronger than his desire to get laid. If I can get someone to go out with him and tell him his obsession with Iran is a total turnoff, maybe he'll give it up.

Not Patty or Malia. They would be suspect. I don't know any of the junior girls he may have a crush on.

I know: Firuzeh. Ali would *campaign* for Gerald if Firuzeh asked him to. She could definitely get him to stop protesting.

I run downstairs for the cordless, run back up, and dial the emergency number Auntie left when she went away for the weekend. "Hey, Firuzeh. It's Jasmine Zumideh." I lay out my scheme, convey the gravity of the situation—how Ali could ruin my whole future—and offer her twenty bucks if she can get him to stop talking about Iran.

She says she'll call Ali this week and ask if he wants to hang out on Saturday and practice their Farsi.

Yes! He could be neutralized as a threat as early as Sunday.

CHAPTER TWELVE

TOUR DE FORCE

L et's see Patty do *this*," Bridget says with a wide smile, chin tilted up proudly.

She's twisting my hair up in a cinnamon-bun braid for my appearance before the *Star Wars* guys this morning. The white turtleneck I borrowed from her is snug, but with my maxi skirt, looks enough like Princess Leia to impress them—I think. Having never seen *Star Wars*.

I'm sitting on her four-poster bed with the pink netting. Elsie, her golden retriever, has her head in my lap. "There's no way she could," I say.

I need to remind Bridget *she's* my best-est friend.

While she finishes securing the braid with a thousand bobby pins, I glance past the netting at the gaping, white wound on the wall where her Bay City Rollers posters used to be. But, I mean, she was a *sophomore* before I made her tear them down.

"Ow." I wince when she twists too tight.

"Sorry," she says, and relaxes her grip. Her lips purse. "I haven't talked to her since Saturday, you know. Patty," she adds, in case I didn't know.

"Is that why you and Kyle went off-campus for lunch yesterday?"

"Mmmm-hmmm," she says, holding a couple of bobby pins in her mouth. She secures the last one. "That, and Kyle loves the Naugles' bun taco."

I pat the two giant wheels on either side of my head. "Bridget, c'mon. It's our senior year. Let's not waste it fighting."

Honestly, I would say this even if their squabbling didn't imperil my campaign.

"I told her to stop the shit-talking," I say.

I did.

"Can I look now?" I beg.

"Wait." She takes a step back and puts a fingertip to her mouth, Leonardo da Vinci appraising his *Mona Lisa*. "Perfect," she pronounces.

I gently move Elsie aside, stand up, and look at my reflection in Bridget's full-length mirror. The braids *are* perfect.

"And what did Princess Leia do?" Bridget quizzes me while collecting her folder and purse.

"Helped destroy the *Death Star*."

I've done more prep for this than the math section of the SAT.

"Right. And remember, everyone likes R2-D2 better than

C-3PO. But don't say whether you like Han Solo or Luke Skywalker better because no one can agree on that."

"How many times have you seen this movie?"

"Three times with my dad, two times with my little brother." She grabs her keys from the dresser. "I can't wait till cheer is over so we can carpool again."

We haven't had time for just the two of us since she started seeing Kyle. The election hasn't helped. Elsie follows us down the stairs and whines as soon as we walk out the front door.

"Good luck," Bridget calls out and climbs into her sky-blue convertible. "May the Force be with you."

"And also with you," I shout back.

I pop in the back door to grab my purse and keys.

Auntie pauses from cleaning up Ali's breakfast dishes to take in my outfit. "Oh, joonam. This is very nice. Very professional. You have a job interview?"

"Kind of," I say with a kiss on each cheek.

I feel a little silly walking through the halls in this turtleneck and Princess Leia's signature hairstyle. But Kyle said the *Star Wars* guys are meeting in the AV Club room to discuss the release of the newest action figure. This is my opportunity.

They crowd around me as soon as I enter.

"Whoa, you look just like her," a guy with horn-rimmed glasses and a sparse mustache says.

Immediately, they start peppering me with questions.

"Are you glad you helped destroy the *Death Star*?" asks a

guy whose hair feathers more perfectly than mine. "And is Darth Vader really dead?"

"I am and I don't know," I say and point to the next questioner, like it's a press conference.

"Who do you like better: Skywalker or Solo?"

"I like 'em both."

"Are you going to learn to use a lightsaber?"

"Absolutely."

They're eating out of my hands without any mention of a new mascot, free Coke, or my prom proposal.

When the questions get tougher (Why does Luke leave the wampa's cave? How does the Rebel Fleet win at Endor?), I begin my close. "If you love *Star Wars* and Princess Leia as much as I do, I'm asking you to fly like an eagle with me, Jasmine Kat—"

"Zoomba-duh." The guy with horn-rimmed glasses and a sparse mustache suddenly points at me. "I know you. You're that crazy dude's sister."

"Oh yeah, the one who's always talking about oil and I-ran," another says, with a wide-eyed look of wonderment, as if he'd discovered Peter Parker's alter ego.

Which sets off a chain reaction.

"Why should *I* care about *I*-ran?" this guy with a bowl cut says.

"Gerald says if we don't nuke *them*, they'll nuke *us*," announces their leader, who's sporting a thick puka shell necklace.

"My dad says the Middle East is a disaster, but if we don't clean it up, we'll be doing our homework by candlelight 'cause they'll shut off our oil supply," says the dude whose hair feathers more perfectly than mine.

"Guys, guys." I raise my arms to quiet them. "Iran doesn't even have a nuclear weapon," I say with a merry laugh—which I heard Dad say once.

But I'm losing them. After I went to all that trouble for the cinnamon-bun braids.

"Gerald is having a big campaign rally on Monday," Puka Shell adds.

"Right on, man," says the guy with the horn-rimmed glasses. "I'm going."

They all look at me, but not with the same fervor they did before.

"Well, uh, may the Force be with you and please vote for me, Jasmine Katie. Did I mention the free Coke Fridays?"

I hurry out of there and make it to Mr. Ramos's class several minutes late.

Mike motions me to sit next to him. "We're talking about *All the President's Men*," he murmurs.

Which I still haven't started. It's so unlike me. I'm usually first to finish our reading assignments and asking for extra credit. This election has taken up so much of my time.

How did all the *Star Wars* guys know Ali is my brother? Did Gerald do a newsletter about it or start a phone tree? And Gerald is having a *rally*?

"I heard Watergate was actually a plot by the CIA or, you know, an attempted *coup* by the Cubans for the Bay of Pigs," says Flynn.

It's incredible how the wild creatures of his imagination break through the dense thicket of his brain.

"That's not anywhere in the book, Flynn," Mr. Ramos says, shaking his head.

"No, I know," he admits. "But that's what my dad says. And he was right about Kennedy."

They must spend their summers in Loch Ness.

"Okay, what about those of you who have actually *read* the book?" Mr. Ramos holds up his well-worn copy.

"I'm eight chapters in, and Deep Throat is spilling *all* the secrets," Ellory says with a nervous staccato laugh, probably because he just said Deep Throat. Guys get all giggly when they think about that movie or blow jobs in general.

"Sources are crucial," says Mr. Ramos. "Deep Throat was one of Woodward and Bernstein's primary sources. The rest were cabinet officials, who all started backstabbing each other—excuse my French—around this time. Turned on each other and leaked to the press."

"My dad cried when Nixon resigned," Gerald says solemnly. His face hardens. "But the break-in was wrong, and the wrongdoing reached all the way to the top." He looks at me, eyes narrowing with suspicion. "In fact, there's been a break-in tied to a presidential campaign right here at Eisenhower."

Shit. I don't dare say anything. I just sit there and try to look bewildered.

"Really? Care to elaborate?" Mr. Ramos asks.

Gerald leans back and crosses his arms. "Someone stole some very important papers out of my locker."

"How do you know they were stolen?" Mr. Ramos asks with his hand to his chin.

Gerald looks at me. "I just do. But I can tell you this: despite the dirty tricks, my campaign is only getting stronger."

"Because seniors want order restored," says Ellory.

"No, they don't," Mike says with a wink. "They want a new mascot and free Coke."

"And overnight prom," I say, immediately losing steam. "A-a proposal for it, I mean."

"Okay, okay." Mr. Ramos waves his arms to get us back on track. "By this time next week, I expect everyone to have read the book. Moving on." He picks up the *Eisenhower General* weekly binder. "Mike, you on deadline for your free speech article?"

"Yeah, should make this week's edition."

This week's edition? He hasn't even given me a courtesy review of the article to remove any mention of me. Or the election. Or the hostages. Or Iran.

Right when the bell rings, before I can grab him, Mr. Ramos says, "Jasmine, I sent in your letter of rec last week. High praise for your skills as a writer and reporter. Be my first NYU acceptance. Make me proud."

As if there's not enough pressure on me.

"I-I will," I say. I have to catch up to Mike.

"One more thing," he says.

I glance longingly at the door.

"Listen." He leans against his desk in cool teacher mode. "Don't let the hostage thing make you ashamed. To be Iranian."

"Oh, I'm not."

I've only changed my name to Jasmine Katie and disavowed my own brother.

"I felt the same way when I was younger. One of the few Chicanos in a school full of white kids. Every Christmas, we had to bring something for our class party. Of course, I wanted my mom to make sugar cookies like all the other moms. Instead, she made a giant tub of tamales: pork with green chile sauce. Dessert tamales with sweet corn. I was like, 'Mom! Can't you just make sugar cookies?' But now, it's not Christmas without 'em."

He means well, but this would be a better analogy if Mexico had taken a bunch of Texans hostage, which would be *super* embarrassing.

"Yes, thank you, I understand," I say, and hurry out to find Mike, who's waiting right outside the door. "Oh. Hey. Thanks. For defending me in there."

He chuckles. "Gerald would love to think he's at the center of some big Watergate conspiracy."

Wait till Mike finds out Gerald *is* at the center of some big Watergate conspiracy.

"Yeah, uh . . . listen, you're not mentioning me in that article about Ali, are you?"

He shifts his weight. "Well, I mean, I may have mentioned you once, but—"

"Mike, you said you wouldn't."

"I know, I know, but . . ." His brows knit together. "I mean, he *is* your brother. Like, it's a fact. Do you want me to lie?"

My nostrils flare. "Not mentioning me is not *lying.*"

He shifts again. "My dad would call it a sin of omission."

"Well, *I* would call it a courtesy to your"—I was about to say "girlfriend," but it's *way* too soon—"your friend, who's in the midst of a campaign that could determine her whole future."

He chews the inside of his cheek. "I get one last edit before we go to print. I'll red pencil you then."

"Thank you," I say in a tone that doesn't sound at all grateful.

He backs down the hall. "Gotta go, can't be late for fifth period." He turns and jogs toward the double doors.

Good thing I got to him before the article comes—

"I know it was you."

I freeze. Gerald is right behind me.

I adopt a breezy air and turn around. "I have no idea what you're talking about."

He moves close enough for me to see the flurry of dandruff along his side part. "I know it was you who stole my notebook."

I exercise my right to remain silent.

"I'm going to find my Deep Throat. And when I do, you'll either be disqualified as a candidate or the first senior class president ever impeached at Eisenhower High."

|||||||||||||||

He's bluffing. Impeachment is not even a thing at Eisenhower High.

I don't think.

Impeachment would *not* look good on my spring 1980 transcript, even if it does say "senior class president" in the Extracurricular/Awards/Honors section.

I've got to find Patty. I tear through the halls looking for her and almost bump into Bridget.

"How did it go with the *Star Wars* guys?" she says as I back down the hall away from her.

"Fine. I've got to find Patty. I'll talk to you later," I say, turning and taking off.

I finally find her near the bungalows with one of her sporty friends and pull her into the bathroom. After a quick peek under each stall to make sure they're empty, I whisper, "Gerald is onto us."

"No, he's not," Patty says in a regular voice.

"*Shh.* Yes, he is. He said someone broke into his locker and stole his notebook."

She shrugs. "He's bluffing."

"How do you know?"

She considers this. "He can't prove it."

I cock my head. "What if he can?"

She laughs. "He should have had a better lock. Just don't say anything to anyone. *Ever.*"

I catch a glimpse of us in the mirror. Our picture could be plastered across the front page of the school paper, a grainy black-and-white, headline blaring, CANDIDATE ENGAGED IN CLANDESTINE CONVERSATION ABOUT COVER-UP."

"We haven't even used it," she says. "The playbook."

I exhale with disappointment. "All the *Star Wars* guys were asking about Ali. Gerald is getting the word out he's my brother."

"Then we'll get the word out about Gerald," she says with a wicked smile.

"No. No," I say, biting my nail. "We're not doing that."

"Fine," she says. She glances in the mirror and fluffs her hair. "I have to go. I'm meeting with Kyle about GOTV. It means get out the—"

"I *know* what it means."

They're so caught up in winning, they've forgotten about me.

|||||||||||||||||

As soon as I get home, I run upstairs to start a three-way call between me, Patty, and Kyle—I mean, why wasn't I in this GOTV meeting?—when Grandma Jean calls. "Your mom's coming to the phone in a minute," she says. "How are you, honey, and . . ."

5, 4, 3, 2—

". . . how is your Weight Watchers coming along?"

Grandma Jean is physically incapable of getting through a conversation without asking me about Weight Watchers. She hugs me like a warden frisking an inmate, always probing for those few extra pounds.

"Fine," I say and stealthily unwrap a grape Now and Later. "How's Mom?"

"Better. She's seeing an analyst, you know." Her *voice* rolls its eyes. "Your grandfather and I managed to make it through forty-five years without one."

Grandma Jean once threw a crystal ashtray at Grandpa Bob that barely missed his head and smashed into the fireplace. They probably should have seen a counselor.

"Anyway, here's your mother."

The phone rustles. Mom takes the receiver.

"Hi, Mom. What were you doing?" I say, sucking on the Now and Later.

"My TM. Transcendental Meditation."

"What's that?" I fluff my hair in the mirror, all crimped from the cinnamon-bun braids. It does look kind of cool. Could be a prom 'do.

There's a brief pause while she lights up a cigarette. "I go someplace quiet and get comfortable. Then I close my eyes and breathe in and out while repeating my mantra. Karen says it will keep me centered."

She's the one who got Mom interested in Amway and Avon, too.

"Oh. That sounds . . . interesting."

Don't mention Manhattan. Don't mention it.

"Has she been around? Karen?" Mom asks.

"N-no," I say.

Why would Karen, her best friend, come around if she's not here?

There's something Mom's not telling me.

"You're staying there, in Manhattan, aren't you?"

Dammit! Less than a minute in.

"Jasmine, nothing's been decided yet."

I won't know a soul, and Grandma Jean will harangue me about my pretty face if only I would lose those twenty extra pounds.

"Why did you marry him in the first place?" I start pacing, a prosecutor grilling the defendant. "When you knew it wouldn't work."

"Listen, Jasmine," she says, exhaling forcefully, "your dad and I got married when I was twenty. Twenty! I was just a kid who thought 'till death do us part' sounded really romantic. Well, that was before two kids and a job that takes him here, there, and everywhere with who knows who."

Who knows who? I *hate* it when she tells me more than I want to hear. And why can't they just stay together for the sake of the kids like everyone else?

"Whatever. I have to go. I've got a bunch of homework."

As soon as we hang up, instead of starting *All the President's Men,* I collapse on my pillow.

I guess that's it. They're getting divorced. We'll never have another Christmas morning together and will only see Dad over summer vacation.

And everything will be ten times worse if I'm stuck in Manhattan. No, the other one.

CHAPTER THIRTEEN

AYATOLLAH'D YOU SO

K yle says campaign momentum shifts all the time. The trick is to gain momentum, to be on the upswing, right before Election Day. With only a week to go, I have plenty of time to shift momentum back in my favor with a petition for overnight prom in Catalina.

If Gerald can create a bogus petition, so can I.

Mike is waiting for me outside of geometry. Who would have thought I'd like a guy who wears tan cords with a brown, striped velour pullover, but here we are. It looks good on him. I have to smile.

When I get closer, my smile fades.

His lips are tight, his eyes squinty. He holds up a copy of the *Eisenhower General*. "I wanted you to see this. Before—"

I snatch the paper out of his hands. The banner headline reads, AYATOLLAH'D YOU SO.

"It's my profile of Ali," he says, wincing, as if I'm going to slug him.

My eyes dart across the page, scanning for my name.

I just might.

"Mr. Ramos wouldn't let me remove any mention of you," he says, his forehead wrinkling in earnest. "He said that would compromise my journalistic integrity."

"Compromise *you*?" I demand. "What about me?"

The first paragraph reads: *Ali is the brother of Jasmine Zumideh, who's currently running for senior class president. "My dad taught us all this stuff about Iran," says Ali. "As Iranians, my sister and I have to speak up and defend the students because no one else will."*

"He's *congratulating* the Iranian students for taking Americans hostage!"

"I don't think he meant it that way."

I thrust the paper back at him. "It doesn't matter what he *meant*, that's the way everyone will take it."

His head shakes with confusion. "Are you saying no one knew Ali was your brother?"

"Not all five hundred seniors. You think I know every one of them?"

"Well." He shifts uncomfortably. "Maybe you would if you talked to people outside of your little group."

He broke his promise, and now he's judging *me*?

"My '*little group*'?"

He touches my arm with a look of contrition. "I didn't mean it that way."

We're having our first fight, and we haven't even had our first kiss.

I can feel my eyes welling. "You may not care about college admissions because your dad can snap his fingers"—I snap my fingers—"and get you into the Air Force Academy—"

"That's not true," he says with his patented laugh, while carefully folding the paper.

"—but attending NYU is my way out of here."

Two coats of Great Lash sting really bad when you're trying to blink back tears, I learn, as I run down the hall toward the bathroom.

While I stand at the sink dabbing my eyes with the corner of a rolled-up paper towel, Ginny comes out of a stall, leans in to wash her hands, looks at me, and says, "The whole time we've been friends, I never knew you were I-rain-ian," as if I were a zombie or a communist.

I ditch Mr. Ramos's class because I can't stand the thought of Gerald's smug mug for the whole period—or facing Mike. As I walk through the halls, it feels like everyone is staring at me again, just like they did on the first day the hostages were seized—with only a week to go until the election.

||||||||||||||

Patty, Kyle, and I have an emergency huddle after school to figure out how to respond to the article. Kyle says we shouldn't talk here, so we pile into his BMW.

I'm in back, Patty is shotgun. "I'm hungry. Let's drive through somewhere," she says.

Kyle pulls into a Pup 'N' Taco.

While we wait for our turn to order, Patty turns to me and says, "Why didn't you tell Mike not to mention you or say you're I-rain-ian in that article?"

"I did," I snap at her. "Besides, I'm *American*. Irish American. My mom's American."

"Order, please," the cashier says over the scratchy loud-speaker. Their uniforms are so tragic: orange polyester bowling shirts and unflattering trucker caps. I would never work here.

"Is a 'pup' a hot dog or a burger?" Patty asks, peering past Kyle at the menu board. "I want a burger."

"Look," Kyle says in a remarkably calm voice, "it doesn't matter if she is or if she isn't I-rain-ian. What matters is what voters think. It's a burger."

"It's a hot dog," I say at the same time.

"We want them to associate Jasmine with good things, like American eagles and prom. Not bad things, like Ali or I-ran. We'll have one burger and a burrito," he shouts into the speaker. "We have exactly one week till the election. And I have a plan. Jasmine, what do you want?"

By now, I've lost my appetite. Their chili cheese dogs are really good, though.

"Anything else?" asks the disembodied voice.

Right when Kyle says, "No," I say, "A chili cheese dog,"

and the cars behind us honk. "And a chili cheese dog," Kyle shouts then pulls forward.

"What plan? What are we going to do?" I scooch to the middle of the back seat.

"First, you're going to write an op-ed condemning the student radicals in I-ran," says Kyle.

"What?" I cross my arms. "No way. I'm not copying Gerald's platform. I'll write about my proposal for prom instead."

"That'll be five thirty-two," says the girl at the window.

I mean, honestly. Their uniforms are the worst. I hand Kyle my dollar and change.

"Look, Gerald is telling everyone you and Ali sympathize with the I-rain-ian students who took our American heroes hostage," says Kyle. "A prom proposal won't fix that. Second, we're all going to Gerald's rally on Monday."

This makes no sense. "Why would we go to his rally?" I ask.

"To hand out free Coke," he says, as if it's obvious.

I catch a glimpse of Kyle in the rearview. It's clear from the smile on his face he thinks this plan is fiendishly clever. Since he's both fiendish and clever, I don't doubt it.

"And third," Kyle says, "you have to campaign at the dance on Saturday."

"How? By slow-dancing with all the guys?" I harrumph. The only guy I thought I'd be slow-dancing with is Mike, and that's not going to happen now.

Kyle glances at Patty. She takes her cue. "A bunch of seniors will be at the dance Saturday," she says. "The election is the following Wednesday. It's a perfect time to get the word out about Gerald. And his dad."

I lean back with my arms crossed. "I already said I don't want to say the thing about Gerald's dad."

"If you're not on offense, you're on defense," Patty says. She turns around to face me.

Kyle does the same. "We want seniors to think of crime and prison when they think of Gerald, not the hostages."

They have these inappropriately excited looks on their faces, like parents who've just gotten their kids a chess set for Christmas.

"We can't," I say, but my resistance is weakening, especially if a majority of seniors are associating me with Ali and "I-ran."

"Don't take the curve ball out of your repertoire," Patty warns.

I need a minute to think.

Senior class president–elect. That's what I wrote on my application. How could NYU ever admit me if I can't even get my own story straight?

I really don't want to do this. Gerald will be mortified when it gets back to him. But they're right. He's left me no choice. If Gerald is going to talk shit about me, I *have* to talk shit about him. I mean, if you dump pig's blood on Carrie's head, she's going to release telekinetic holy hell, right?

Kyle hands me my chili cheese dog.

Shit. They put onions on it.

I choke them down without saying anything.

Then, as soon as we get back to school, I grab Ginny, pull her aside, and whisper, "Oh my God. Did you hear the rumor about Gerald's dad?"

||||||||||||||

On the drive home, all I can think about is the shit-talk I told Ginny about Gerald's dad. As soon as the words came out of my mouth, I wished I could have inhaled them back in. Honestly, I don't care whether Gerald's dad is in prison. It's got nothing to do with senior class president.

But neither do the hostages.

I need some peace and quiet to figure out what to do next.

When I come through the back door, Ali and Auntie are in the kitchen laughing and dancing, speaking Farsi. Persian music is *blasting*.

"What are you doing?" I have to shout to be heard.

"Celebrating," Auntie Minah says. "This is Googoosh, the Iranian Barbra Streisand. They release thirteen hostages today! I think the crisis is over. And your father will be home for Thanksgiving."

Once again, Ali is all jangly. "And Mike's exposé came out today. It was *radical*."

"No, it wasn't! Why did you mention me? I—oh my God."

I make a beeline for the stereo in the living room and punch stop on the cassette player. "She's even worse than the *American* Barbra Streisand."

Ali and Auntie follow me in.

"What's your problem, man?"

"Nothing," I say crossly.

Auntie says, "I'm sorry you don't like the music, joonam. I forget you don't speak the Farsi."

Between the article and my argument with Mike—and all the unwanted onions on my chili cheese dog—I lose it. "Farsi. *Farsi.* Not 'the' Farsi. We don't use the article 'the' in English, okay? It's just Farsi. You know why I don't speak it? Because it's totally embarrassing to be Iranian right now. I wish I was *normal,* like everyone else."

"You're ashamed to be Iranian," Ali says. He puts a protective arm around Auntie. "But you know what? Iranians should be ashamed of you."

Auntie Minah's face crumples. "Is this true? You are ashamed?"

I run upstairs without answering. I have to get ready for work.

And Auntie would be upset by my answer.

IIIIIIIIIIIIII

My shift at Hot Dog on a Stick will be the respite I need from the emotional turmoil of the election. There's something about the aroma of deep-fried party batter. If they had a Scratch & Sniff for happiness, it would smell like party batter. And hand-stomping the lemonade can be super cathartic. I'll have time to think about what to do next.

Mike hasn't called by the time I leave for my shift. Who knows if he'll even be at the dance on Saturday?

Row after row of palm trees sprout out of concrete center islands on my drive in. They stay evergreen till their fronds shrivel up and dry. A dingy, fall haze hangs just above the horizon. I have to get the hell out of here.

When I get to the mall, every other column throughout the lower level has been wrapped with giant yellow ribbons. A banner that reads IN SUPPORT OF OUR HOSTAGES, WHO ARE REALLY OUR HEROES is draped across the overhang above the escalator.

There is just no escaping it.

Why did the students have to seize the embassy *right* when I decide to run for senior class president? I could have waged a clean campaign instead of rolling around in the mud with Kyle and Patty.

This day will be redeemed if Sam Goody has any copies of the new Specials record. Every time I stop by, it's sold out.

Of course, they don't. However, in addition to the hundred thousand copies of ABBA's *Greatest Hits Vol. 2*, they do have a VHS tape of *All the President's Men*. Now I won't have to read the book. I don't have time.

I get to work with minutes to spare and punch in.

Donna's already there, dipping dogs. "Do you want to dip the cheese or stomp lemonade?"

"Lemonade."

"I'll take the register."

She dips the last dog and wipes her hands while I pick up the hand stomper.

"Did you see all the yellow ribbons?" Donna asks. "They're for our hostages."

"I know," I say, stomping the lemons with particular gusto.

She opens the register and counts the dollar bills. "My dad says Carter should invade I-ran."

"Maybe Carter should make your dad secretary of state," I snap.

She throws me a dirty look that mutates into a manufactured smile when a harried mom and her daughter approach.

The rest of my shift is a disaster. I burn a batch of cheese sticks and spill a tray of lemonade on a poor, unsuspecting family of four.

But the cherry on top of this shit sundae is when Fake Burt Reynolds stops by at the end of the night. He leans against the counter while I close out the register. "You see all the yellow ribbons?"

Donna hands me his mall employee courtesy cup of lemonade and goes back to cleanup.

"They're really cool," I say, jamming the straw into his cup. "Here."

He takes a sip. "Those students, they're like animals, man. Have you seen 'em? They're all hairy, like apes."

Meanwhile, his five o'clock shadow must show up by noon.

"They're not even civilized." He props himself on the counter, resting on his forearms. "That's why there's always war over there. Israel. Lebanon. Kaddafi. The Arabs. I'm telling you, there will *never* be peace in the Middle East."

I will not take the bait.

He takes a big gulp and burps. "If I ever see one of those I-rain-ian dudes on the street—"

"Oh my God!" I finally explode. "Do you really think the students are representative of all Iranians? Do you? Do you think all the Irish are like the IRA, or all Italians are in the Mafia, or, or the Mansons are representative of all *families*?"

"*Jasmine,*" Donna reprimands me as if Fake Burt Reynolds were a real customer.

He backs away with his hands in the air. "Sorry, man. Didn't mean to *offend* you," he says sarcastically, letting me know that was exactly his intent.

Donna throws her hands up. "Why are you so mad? We don't talk to customers like that."

"He's not a customer, and they don't talk to *me* like that. I—I quit!" I shout. With that, I storm out, but not before landing one final glancing blow: "And you know what? Your wedge cut is *super* unflattering."

I walk through the mall with my head held high and my bucket hat on the break room floor. I'm not taking shit from ignorant idiots anymore. And that'll show Donna she's not the boss of me.

||||||||||||||

When I get home, Auntie's standing over a frying pan in the kitchen. The frying pan sizzles. She is still simmering.

I wish I could make her understand what it's like to be a half 'n' half right now, when our countries hate each other, when it feels like my two halves add up to a misshapen whole.

Really quietly, I sit down at the kitchen table. "Amme Minah, I—"

Before I can finish my sentence, she tosses a hard, dry, overcooked patty onto my plate. "Here," she says. "I make a hamburger for you. American." She pulls open the refrigerator door and pulls out a bunch of leftovers. "Every night I cook, make Persian food with the rice, the khoresht. No one ever says, 'Thank you, Amme Minah.'"

I can't believe I yelled at her the way I did. She learned an entirely new language Dad says is twice as hard as Farsi. Meanwhile, I haven't listened to one of those cassettes.

In a really small voice, I say, "Thank you, Amme Minah."

Too little, too late. She waves her hand at me and retreats to the guest room while I pick at my broiled hamburger in stony silence. Until the phone rings.

It's Grandma Zumideh. I barely get out a "Hello," before

she starts wailing and crying in Farsi. She is terrified, all alone in Iran. I keep repeating, "I know, Maman. I know."

Even without understanding much of what she's saying, I know I feel exactly the same way.

CHAPTER FOURTEEN

RUMOURS

I'm sitting at the dining room table opposite Ali, finishing up my second serving of toasted sangak and feta with walnuts and drizzled honey as penance for the way I behaved yesterday.

He emerges from behind his *New York Times* and gestures to my plate. "That doesn't make up for it, you know."

I glare at him and carry my plate to the sink where Auntie is wiping the countertops in Mom's bright orange rubber gloves. "Kheili mamnoon, Amme Minah," I say. "Delicious, as usual."

"You are welcome, glad you like it." She's still frosty.

I put my hand on her shoulder. "And I'm happy about those thirteen hostages."

I mean it. The sooner this crisis is over, the better it is for everyone.

Auntie puts her hand on my hand. "Thank you, joonam."

At least this big breakfast has left me ready to power through the next six days of campaigning.

As I pull into the parking lot and walk past all the various voting blocs—the surfers in their VW bugs, the skaters and stoners with their Toyota trucks, the jocks revving up their Trans Ams, and even the junior G.I. Joes in their dads' Buick sedans—I remind myself: Gerald's platform is *weak*. Dress code. Pledge of Allegiance. I can't let him make it about the hostages. Even if—

Holy.

Shit.

When I round the corner in the north hall, there are at least a hundred Gerald Thomas placards plastered all over the walls with VOTE GERALD THOMAS in big, bold type and underneath, in smaller type, BRING THE HOSTAGES HOME.

There's a traffic jam as everyone stops to read them. Convincing seniors this election is about a dress code is not going to be easy. But then—

"That dude's dad is in jail," a male voice says.

My head swivels. Two guys I recognize from marching band stand behind me, staring at the placards.

"Yeah, for, like, kidnapping or something," the other one says.

They continue down the hall.

Kidnapping?

Kyle is swimming upstream through the sea of students,

fixated on the placards. "How the hell did Gerald get these up so fast?"

"Kyle." I drop my voice. "People are saying Gerald's dad is a kidnapper."

"I know," Kyle says. "It's a counterattack. Gerald says your brother is a student radical, you say his dad's a kidnapper."

"Shh." I lean in. "I'm sure his dad is not in prison for *kidnapping*. It's probably something boring like tax fraud."

He studies Gerald's placard. "Yeah, kidnapping is better for us."

I rear back. "How is kidnapping 'better' for us?"

He points to the placard. "He can't say he supports the hostages when his own father is a kidnapper."

"He is not a kidnapper!" I accidentally shout.

Everyone turns and looks at me.

"We don't know that." Kyle continues down the hall. "And with the election less than a week away, don't take the curve ball out of your repertoire."

Dammit. There's nothing I can do about it now.

Mike is waiting for me in front of geometry again, and that persistent butterfly flutters around in my chest like it's the first day of spring. I know he was trying to do the right thing with his article about Ali, but if he tells me he's doing a cover story on Gerald and his campaign, I'll deck him.

He starts toward me. "Hey. I'm really sorry about the article. I saw all of Gerald's stupid signs. I didn't mean to do anything that would hurt you or your campaign."

"I . . . I'm sorry I got so mad."

He looks down and back up again with his long lashes and the dimple in his chin. "So, um . . . you still going to the dance on Saturday?"

The butterfly takes flight. "Yes, yeah. For sure. Of course."

The bell rings.

"Right on. I'll see you in Mr. Ramos's." He takes off down the hall.

"See you then," I call after him when, suddenly, my stomach cramps. It'll be hard enough to campaign and flirt with Mike at the dance. Now I have to make sure Mr. Maddeningly Decent doesn't hear the rumor about Gerald.

‖‖‖‖‖‖‖‖‖‖‖

"Oh, Jasmine," Auntie says as soon as I walk through the door. "Your father is on the phone."

I set down my books and grab the cordless from her. I haven't talked to him in two days. He has to make Ali stop embarrassing me.

"Hi, Dad. How's your trip going?" I say, heading upstairs.

"Fine, honey, how are you?"

"Fine." My tone is purposefully unconvincing.

"Everything okay?"

I close the door to my room. "I'm running for senior class president and Ali has been, like, super embarrassing."

He sighs. "You always say that."

I flop on my bed. "But, Dad, this time he really is."

Irritation creeps into his voice. "What has he done now?"

I better make this good. I sit up. "Well, the hostages are on the news constantly. In the paper, on TV. Everyone at school is anti-Iranian. Ali keeps making a big scene out of defending the Iranian students."

"Just ignore him," he says.

I stand up, impassioned. "Dad, in elections, appearances are everything. I want voters to associate me with good things, like American eagles and overnight prom. Not Ali or Iran."

Immediately, I wish I hadn't said "or Iran." He's been here for more than twenty-five years, but when he visits Grandma Zumideh in Tehran, he still says, "I'm going home." It must have been so hard for him to come here. He was barely older than I am now. As one of the only Iranian immigrants on the campus of Kansas State University, he must have stuck out like a snowman on the Venice Beach boardwalk.

He always said we would visit "one day soon." After Ali and I graduated from high school. Take us to the Bazaar, the mosques, Golestan Palace—all the places pictured in *Persia: Bridge of Turquoise*. Who knows if we'll ever go now?

"I'm sorry. I didn't mean that. I just mean Ali. Until the election is over."

He lets out a little exhale of frustration. "Okay. I'll talk to him."

Right before we hang up, I suddenly remember—

"Dad, my opponent is Gerald Thomas. You worked with his dad, right?"

After a surprised silence, he says, "I did."

I glance up at the dolls on my pink scalloped shelves. "Is he, um, in prison?"

"Where did you hear *that*?"

I squirm. "It's a—a rumor going around school."

I *know* I started it, but how else am I going to find out the truth?

He clears his throat. "He was . . . he was arrested for embezzling from the company."

Whoa! Kyle and Patty were right. Gerald's dad *is* a criminal. And Gerald is a total hypocrite.

"But he did it for his son," Dad hurriedly adds. "The one who came back from Vietnam. He needed so many surgeries, prosthetics. Insurance wouldn't cover all of it—not even the VA."

And now I feel like throwing up.

"Jasmine? Are you still there?"

"Uh, yeah. Yeah."

"You keep that confidential, okay?"

"I will," I say, because how *could* I say, "Sorry, Dad. Too late."

‖‖‖‖‖‖‖‖‖‖‖

Bridget riffles through my closet looking for the exact, perfect outfit for me to wear to the dance while trying to convince me there's no way I could lose the election. "Kyle told me to call all my friends from catechism. Catholics won the White House for John F. Kennedy, you know."

All I can think about is the stupid rumor I started about

Gerald's dad, especially now that I know the truth. When Mike finds out, he won't be mad at me. Just disappointed. Once again, I didn't think this all the way through.

I distract myself by leafing through Bridget's *Seventeen* magazine. All the models have big, blue eyes and strawberry-blond hair piled up in loose buns, their heart-shaped faces framed by wispy tendrils. Not one "ethnic beauty." I toss the magazine aside.

"What about this?" Bridget pulls out a cream-colored cowl neck and my suede maxi skirt.

I shake my head. "I wore that on Wednesday."

"Or this?" She holds up my satin warm-up jacket.

I shake my head. I really don't want to go. I want to tell her about Gerald's dad. Confess my sin. Negotiate a penance.

She flops down next to me on the bed. Her brows knit together as if she's solving a difficult math problem. "I know. Wear your striped tube top under that white eyelet blouse. With your Candies. And curl your hair. You can borrow my curling iron."

"I wish you were going." I bite my nail.

She bats it away from my mouth. "It's Granny's seventy-fifth. We have a reservation at Knott's Chicken Dinner. I'm not missing fried chicken and boysenberry pie for a dance. Unless it's prom. Besides, Kyle said you guys are there to campaign. Malia will be there."

"She's in Carson with her cousins." I defy her and chew on my middle nail. "Why can't I go to Knott's with you?"

Bridget play-punches me in the arm. "Because. You have to campaign. And you are going to totally make out with Mike. Call me as soon as you get home."

She leaves and, after I spray my hair with enough Aqua Net to ignite my scalp if anyone flicks a Bic within five feet of me, I head downstairs. There's no getting past Auntie Minah without an inspection. She's watching TV. I button up my blouse and throw on a shawl-collar sweater.

"Joonam, why you wear this?" she asks as if I'm Bad Sandy from *Grease,* when Sandy was only trying to fit in.

"I'm going to a dance," I say.

She frowns. "If you are going to a dance, why you don't wear a nice dress or pantsuit?"

Because I'm not running for Congress or hosting the nightly news.

"It's fine, Auntie." I wrap the sweater tighter around me. "This is what everyone is wearing."

She pulls the afghan around her legs. "Be home by midnight. Please."

I don't argue. She'll be asleep by the time I get home, having drifted off during *The Iran Crisis—America Held Hostage: Day Fourteen.*

|||||||||||||

The minute I park the car, I'm overcome by a wave of self-consciousness. My tube top could slip, or I could fall to my death in these Candies, which would serve me right.

A bunch of kids are smoking outside. The chaperones can only cover so much territory. I pay the two-dollar cover charge and get my hand stamped. Inside, it's crowded and sweaty. The disco ball is spinning, along with the DJ.

I make my way through the crowd, scanning for Patty or Kyle or Mike. Gerald is over at the bleachers huddling with some AV Club members.

A bolt of guilt strikes my chest. His brother lost his leg fighting in Vietnam. His dad was only trying to help him.

I have to find Patty and tell her, we *have* to stop the rumor I started.

I head for the bathroom—Patty and Ginny are probably pouring Bacardi into their Cokes at this very moment—when Patty grabs me from behind and shouts in my ear, "I've been telling everyone Gerald's dad is in . . . What happened to your hair?"

She reeks of Jack Daniel's and is wearing more makeup than I've ever seen.

"Nothing. Curling iron. Patty, about the whisper campaign."

"It's working!" she whoops. "I've been telling everyone about it."

She's drunk.

I lean over and whisper-shout in her ear. "You don't know the whole story. His dad—"

"I know Gerald got my brother kicked out, that's all I need to know," she shout-laughs.

"I know, but—"

"Go find Mike." She giggles and pushes me. "I'm gonna get some more punch." She gestures in a vague direction. "And find Kyle." She stumbles away with a Cheshire grin.

Find Kyle. The way she says it. An alarm bell goes off in my head.

Oh, God! Malia was right. Patty *is* scamming on Kyle. No wonder they've been spending so much time alone together on my campaign.

I have to stop her from doing something she'll regret.

As soon as I start after Patty, I find myself face-to-face with Mike—and just as a total make-out slow song is starting.

"Hey," Mike says. He's wearing Levi's and a plaid button-down. Adorably dressed-up.

Don't get sidetracked.

"Hey," I say, looking past him to keep track of Patty.

He leans in and says, "I like your hair."

My heart double-Dutches. The curl must have relaxed. But I can't lose sight of Patty.

"You grew," he says, grinning down at my Candies. He gestures to the dance floor with a shy smile. "You wanna . . . ?"

I manage to nod, but inside, I'm freaking out. I have a vague recollection there's something I'm supposed to be doing about Patty.

Oh right. The rumor about Gerald's dad.

One dance. One slow dance, then I'll find her.

Mike takes my hand and leads me to a dark little oasis on the edge of the dance floor. His arms slip around my waist. Instinctively, I suck it in. I clasp my arms around his neck and rest my head on his shoulder. The lyrics are super romantic, all about longing to love him just for a night, kissing and hugging him and holding him tight.

After a few turns, Mike leans back. I look up. Almost in slow motion, he leans down. His lips graze mine. The rest of the world falls away. I put my hand to his cheek. He is *such* a good kisser. Not like Curtis: a cobra striking its prey, his tongue darting aggressively in and out of my mouth. Mike gently swirls his tongue around mine murmuring, "Mmm." He tastes like cherry Life Savers, an intoxicating mix along with the Irish Spring.

Then suddenly, the song takes an ominous turn. The reasons are not about kissing or hugging or holding anyone tight but about illusions and charades.

At that moment, I catch sight of something across the dance floor. I squint to focus.

It's a dodgeball to the gut.

There, in a dark corner of the bleachers, Kyle is making out with Patty. In fact, he's rounding second base and sliding into third—I think, who made up this meaningless metaphor?

I must look like I've seen Bigfoot. Mike glances over in that direction and back at me. His forehead creases with concern. I break away and barrel toward them.

Mike grabs my arm. "Oh, hey, this might not be the time to—"

I jerk it away and stride across the gym, walk right up to Kyle and Patty and stand in front of them with my arms folded.

They don't notice me.

"What are you doing?" I shout.

Kyle jumps up. "Oh! You . . . we . . . you're not going to tell Bridget, are you?"

"No." I cross my arms.

His face flickers with relief.

"You are."

He drapes an arm around my shoulder and pulls me aside. "Jasmine. We've been working really closely on your campaign. Studying Gerald's playbook, coming up with the whisper campaign about his dad, which is working, by the way."

I pull away. "You don't understand. I don't want it to work, I want it to stop."

"And we're gearing up our whole GOTV campaign. With the race this close, it'll all come down to turnout, you know."

"No. *No.* You're not doing anything else till you tell everyone to stop spreading that rumor and come clean to Bridget."

Kyle's half-assed smile barely conceals a smirk. "Listen, I'm gonna take Patty home. We'll talk Monday. Before we hand out Coke at Gerald's rally—also my idea."

"No, Kyle. Wait. Stop."

He pauses.

"I . . . you're leaving me no choice. I *have* to tell Bridget."

Suddenly, Patty is abreast of him. "If you tell her, we're done with your campaign."

She sobered up quickly.

"And maybe we'll get the vote out for Gerald," Kyle casually threatens. "Do you want that?"

Of course I don't want that. But I don't want Kyle cheating on Bridget with Patty, either.

The thing is, we're MAD. Something we learned about in US History: Mutually Assured Destruction. The reason the United States and the Soviet Union would never nuke each other. If they destroy us, we'll destroy them right back. If I tell on them, they'll blow up my campaign.

"No," I say in the tiniest voice, after which Kyle takes Patty's hand and flagrantly leads her out the back double doors, right past Gerald, whose face is stark white.

"What am I going to do?" I ask, semi-hysterical when Mike walks up. "What do I tell Bridget?"

He gives this real thought. "Well, you could tell her the truth."

"I can't tell her the truth," I snap. Duh, Mike.

"Why not?"

"Because." My hand is to my forehead. "She'll be mad at me."

He looks as if he's tuning in to a radio station that's all static. "Wait, why would she be mad at *you*?"

It's starting to bug me how little insight Mike has into women.

"Because. She knows I always secretly wished she and Kyle would break up."

His face bunches up into a ball of confusion.

"I gotta go," I say. I've got to get home and think about what I'm supposed to tell Bridget when she's getting ready to make our prom-night dinner reservation and book our limo.

But with the race this close, it *will* come down to turnout, and I don't have a "GOTV operation" in place.

Dammit.

The minute I spin around, Gerald is right in front of me, his face as red as a tomato. "You're telling everyone my dad is in prison? For *kidnapping*?"

"That wasn't me," I sputter. "I—I didn't say he was in prison for kidnapping."

The flimsiest technicality, I know.

He takes a step closer. "You don't deserve to represent the senior class and I'm going to make sure everyone knows it."

A sick feeling starts in the pit of my stomach, snakes its way up to my heart, then burns the back of my throat—as if I had swallowed poison. I blink furiously to hold the flood of tears that release themselves as I run to my car.

CHAPTER FIFTEEN

RUNNIN' WITH THE DEVIL

The drive home is a blur. I might have run a stop sign. Or two. I almost twist my ankle teetering to the front door and nearly chuck one of these stupid Candies through the front window.

Ali is lounging on the couch watching *Saturday Night Live*. "How was the dance?"

I throw my purse on the coffee table and collapse in the recliner. "Terrible."

He snorts. "Disco sucks."

Ew. The air smells overwhelmingly of Jovan Musk.

"Why are you all dressed up?" I glare at him.

"Because." He sits up and drapes his arm across the couch. "I took the hottest chick at Lincoln High to see *The Rose*."

I *totally* forgot about Firuzeh. "Did you talk to her? What did she say?"

If he has anything less than a total change of heart about the hostages, I want my twenty bucks back.

His face puckers like he's eaten a lemon. "Of course we talked. What is wrong with you?"

"Nothing." I exhale deeply. "Except . . . Kyle is a snake. And I'm an idiot."

And Patty is a shit-talker. I knew all this before I made them my campaign managers. How could Patty have been taken in by him?

"What'd he do?"

I cannot believe I'm actually tempted to tell Ali. "Nothing," I finally say.

"Dad called," Ali says, turning his attention back to the TV. "He'll be home for Thanksgiving."

"I heard." I drag myself out of the recliner and trudge upstairs.

I sit on the bed, cordless phone in hand, and start to dial Bridget's number a bunch of times. Where do I begin once she answers? Do I ask about the chicken dinner? Or do I open with my big news—that Mike is a great kisser? I can't just come out and say, "Kyle was making out with Patty," can I?

To make matters worse, there *is* a dark corner of my heart that always secretly wished they would break up. I mean, everyone knows how hard it is when your boyfriend breaks up with you. No one tells you how hard it is when your best friend abandons you. Especially for someone as undeserving as Kyle.

But not this way.

Tomorrow marks four days till the election. Only three more days of campaigning. And Patty and Kyle have complicated everything. Now I understand why cover-ups are always accompanying crimes. Why, oh why, did I let them talk me into spreading rumors about Gerald's dad? And making campaign promises I can never deliver? And pretending I don't know Ali?

After running through several doomed scenarios of an imagined conversation with Bridget, I sink down into my pillow and fall asleep clutching the cordless.

||||||||||||||

I don't have to worry about what to tell Bridget for long. The next morning, she's jumping on my bed and squealing, "You didn't call me last night. How was it?"

I rouse myself out of a dead sleep and mumble something incoherent.

"Did you make out with Mike?"

Majorly groggy, I can't help smiling.

She squeals again. "Tell me everything!"

I rub my eyes covered in Great Lash flakes. "We didn't *totally* make out."

"I knew it." She settles in, cross-legged, chin in hands. "Is he a good kisser?"

It's hard to suppress my excitement.

"I *knew* it. Did Kyle dance with anyone? I wouldn't care if he did."

Everything comes rushing back: Patty and Kyle in the bleachers. The illusions, the charades. It's a moment of truth.

I never lie to Bridget. "I love your hair," I told her in sixth grade when she got a shag haircut, but that's about it. She'll find out, eventually. And the first thing she'll ask is, why didn't I tell her sooner? I won't have a good explanation.

But if I tell her the truth, Patty and Kyle will dump me and campaign for Gerald, and they can't. Not this close to the election. Not before Gerald's big rally. And anyway, if I do tell her the truth, she may not believe me. I know Bridget. It will be better if Kyle confesses. Repents. Asks for forgiveness. Begs if he has to.

At long last, I say, "No, he didn't. Dance. With anyone." At least it's not a lie. "Have you talked to him?" I try to affect good cheer, but the wobble in my voice gives me away.

"Not yet. I called him this morning. His mom said he got in late. Had to drive some friend home who was drunk."

He's a real hero, that Kyle.

"C'mon." She grabs my hand. "Let's go to Norm's. You can tell me everything over a steak and eggs breakfast."

I pull my hand away. "I . . . I have so much homework."

She looks at me strangely, as if she can see right through this gossamer fiction. But then she pops up and flips her hair. "Okay," she says, playfully punching me on the arm. "Call me later." Right before she's out the door she turns back and says, "We are so getting a limo for prom."

I feel gross. I need a shower.

The minute I've got the towel around me, the phone rings.
I rush for the hallway. Maybe it's Patty, saying she had too
much to drink, last night was a momentary lapse of judgment, it will never happen again.

"Um, hi, Jasmine."

It's Firuzeh. Her voice drips with apology.

I'm in no mood for manners. "What happened with Ali?"

"Well, we went to see *The Rose*—"

"I know," I say abruptly. "Did our plan work?"

There's a long pause during which Firuzeh must be able
to hear my teeth grind.

"He told me all this stuff about Iran I never knew. Stuff
my mom and dad don't talk about."

Shit.

"Like, did you know the United States staged a coup
against that democratically elected prime minister in the fifties? For the oil. And the CIA trained the shah's secret police."

"Firuzeh," I interrupt. "I want my twenty bucks back."

⫶⫶⫶⫶⫶⫶⫶⫶⫶⫶⫶⫶

At the beginning of the year, I wanted senior year to last forever. To savor all the "lasts." Our last first day at Eisenhower.
Our last homecoming. Our last winter formal, and so on.

Now, I want it all over as fast as possible.

Maybe I will have left a mess, but I can't worry about that
right now. I have to watch *All the President's Men* for Mr. Ramos's class. The house is quiet. Auntie is in her room.

I'll try and talk some sense into Patty when I see her at school tomorrow.

I pop in the VHS tape and settle into the recliner. We were supposed to read the book, but the movie is just the book come to life.

Dammit. The doorbell. I grab my Tab and head for the foyer.

It's Karen. Mom's friend Karen.

She's wearing oversized white sunglasses and wide, white palazzo pants with a navy polyester shirt and skinny bow tie. She dresses like she's always at work, even on weekends.

"Oh, my mom's not here," I say. "She's still in Kansas with Grandma Jean."

She peers in with a hungry smile. "I know, honey. Is your dad around? He was coming back for Thanksgiving, right?"

How does she know that?

"Um, no. He's not back yet."

"I was just checking to see if he needed anything. Or you kids," she quickly adds. "Tell him I stopped by when you see him," she says, and sashays down the front walk.

In an instant, I'm flashing back to junior year, when I was home sick with the flu but dragged myself downstairs so my soap operas could keep me company. Mom was at her Girl Friday job even though it was a Tuesday.

Dad had come home at noon, which was odd, but I was too weak and fevered to ask why. A rap at the door woke me out of my half sleep. I heard voices murmuring.

Whenever I have a fever, my vision gets all weird, as if I'm looking through a fish-eye lens. I thought I was hallucinating when I saw Dad and Karen go to his office. Which seemed impossible because Mom was gone.

Could she be "who knows who"? The reason Mom never left her room and cried for five days straight before she and Dad separated. She couldn't be.

"Hey."

I've been standing there with the door open, and now Bridget is coming right toward me.

"What are you doing here?" I say, with a level of alarm appropriate for a masked intruder.

"Just came to see what you're doing," she says, brushing by me.

I follow her into the den. "Uh, watching a movie."

Smile, smile, smile. Make it convincing.

"Whatcha watching?" She plops on the sofa.

All the President's Men. I have to get rid of her. "We have to watch it for journalism. It's *super* boring."

"I'll watch it with you," she says, and grabs Auntie's afghan.

"You probably won't like it."

She lets out a little laugh. "God. Do you want me to go?"

I hesitate. "No, no. I just . . . I don't know if you'll like it is all."

"Let's see," she says, wrapping the afghan around her shoulders.

At least we don't have to talk much, and I don't have to look her in the eye.

I quickly press play on the remote and focus on the TV. In the first scene, the Watergate burglars break into the Democratic National Headquarters and steal information Nixon will use against them in the next election.

God. We're as bad as the Watergate burglars.

Woodward and Bernstein make calls, cultivate sources, edit copy, and argue with their editor.

When Bernstein mentions the Watergate Hotel, Bridget says, "Should we get a hotel room for prom night? You know, even if it's not overnight in Catalina."

In a really forceful voice I go, "No! We're not going to Catalina, and you're not going to prom with Kyle. He's a snake who's cheating on you with Patty."

Unfortunately, that's only the voice inside my head, which can't seem to make its way out of my mouth.

"I guess. If my dad will let me," I say weakly.

I try to concentrate on the movie, but it's hard with Bridget sitting inches away from me. How will Kyle and Patty act tomorrow, and how am I supposed to act around them?

And why the hell was Karen here asking about Dad?

By the time I tune back in, Woodward and Bernstein are closing in on Nixon's chief of staff, and Bridget is fidgeting.

I feel like I'm on a balcony, really high up, and thinking, what if I jumped? Not a death wish or anything, just a dangerous impulse. That's what it's like. I need to tell her. I should just tell her. But my survival instinct is stronger.

The movie ends with Nixon getting sworn in for his second term while Woodward and Bernstein type away at *The Washington Post*. The credits show how everyone got caught and Nixon eventually resigned in disgrace.

While I put the VHS tape back in its sleeve, Bridget says, "I know. What about Knott's Chicken Dinner for our first double date?"

I can't think about whether I'd be willing to eat fried chicken in front of Mike—the finger licking could go really wrong—without envisioning all of us at a table where me, Mike, and Kyle are in on this awful secret.

"Yeah, maybe."

She casts me a sideways glance. Typically, we'd be talking a mile a minute about when we should go, who should drive, what we should wear, and whether we should try to sneak into Knott's Berry Farm afterward.

Her eyes narrow with suspicion. "What's wrong?"

My heart leaps into my chest. I almost choke on it. "W-with what?"

She un-reclines the recliner. "With you? You've been acting strange lately."

"N-no I haven't, it's just the election," I squeak.

She leans forward. "No, it's not. It's not 'just' the election. You've been avoiding me."

My face feels hot and prickly, like the time I accidentally

sprinkled cayenne pepper in my hot chocolate instead of cinnamon. "It *is* the election. And admissions. You know, I'm
worried. About the early decision thing." I go on and on like
liars do. "Have you, um, applied to State yet?"

"I'm not good at school like you," she says with surprising
intensity. "You're smart and you can write. Mr. Ramos believes in you."

Wow. Bridget has never envied me anything. Ever. It's
unnatural, it literally violates the natural order of things. Like
pigs flying.

Or anyone cheating on her.

"You're smart," I say. I stay on the floor and hug my knees
to my chest because I don't deserve the couch.

She crosses her arms and cocks her head. "Then why
didn't you ask *me* to be on your campaign instead of Patty?"

"I . . . I . . ."

Don't have a good answer for that question and certainly
can't ask Bridget to join my campaign now.

"She volunteered. Kyle said he knew all about the finer
points of polling."

Her mouth starts to quiver. "Is Patty, like, your new best
friend now?"

"What? No."

"You're always talking to her, always huddled in secret
meetings."

This is what I get for trying to make Bridget *and* Patty
think they're my best-est friends.

My face flushes with guilt and embarrassment. I want to tell Bridget the truth. The whole truth. The words pile up in my mouth, ready to spill out, if only I would let them.

"We're just, um, strategizing. It's almost over," I assure her, "and everything will go back to the way it was."

She is clearly as unconvinced of this as I am.

What *will* it look like when this is all over? Best-case scenario: I win the election. Kyle confesses. Bridget breaks up with him. Patty realizes she made a big mistake, and we're all best friends again.

Right.

And the hostages are rescued, Mom and Dad get back together, and we all live happily ever after. And pigs fly.

This is how it happens. A little white lie here, a major compromise there, and before you know it, you're basically Judas. But there's no sympathy for the devil. God, I hate that song. The Rolling Stones suck. They do. Mick Jagger is creepy. His voice is leering and sneering, and I *knew* I shouldn't have made Patty and Kyle my campaign managers.

||||||||||||||

In my dream last night, Kyle and Patty were throwing rotten eggs and tomatoes at Gerald during his campaign rally. I tried to stop them, but my mouth was full of Coke, and I couldn't speak.

I should have called Patty yesterday to talk about Kyle. I don't know what to say. Patty has a defiant streak. If I tell her she *has* to stop seeing Kyle, she'll only want to see him more.

When I get downstairs, Auntie is on the phone. Ali's eating breakfast.

Before I can make my escape without a serving of sangak and feta, Auntie covers the receiver with her hand. "Joonam, can you take me to the immigration office today?"

"Auntie, I can't today," I say, gathering up my folder and keys. "I have a thing after school."

She throws up her hands. "Then I take a taxi."

"Can I take you tomorrow?"

She waves her hand to silence me. Her attorney must be back on the line.

After I load up the car with cups and Coke, I turn back to Ali. "The election is in two days. Remember, Dad said you can't do anything to embarrass me."

"Oh, I won't embarrass you," he says. But his tone is cocky. A little smile plays at his lips.

"Seriously, Ali."

If only baring my incisors at him still worked.

||||||||||||||

I put on Bowie's *Young Americans* and listen to it on the way to school.

Like I wrote in my failed Aspiring Young Journalists article: *Bowie is the master of reinvention. He started out as a folk singer—like Bob Dylan—then became the glam-rock demi-god,*

Ziggy Stardust. Added lightning bolt face paint to his fire-engine-red mullet and morphed into Aladdin Sane. Then shed all those theatrics for the cool simplicity of the Thin White Duke.

Well, I'm shedding my skin, too. Becoming a whole new me since no one will have known the old me at NYU. Slim, confident, Irish American Jasmine Katie, whose integrity *will be* unimpeachable.

Therefore, I will definitely tell Bridget about Patty and Kyle.

Right after the election.

It's in two days. What difference will it make if Bridget finds out now versus one minute after the election is over?

Kyle is waiting for me near my locker. He keeps glancing around, nervously wiping the edge of his mouth with his thumb and forefinger. The minute he sees me, he sprints toward me. "Did you tell her?"

I push past him to my locker. "No. I told you, you have to. And you have to stop seeing Patty." I spin the dial on the lock.

He stands next to me, eyes darting around, as if Bridget is going to burst out from behind a trash can. "Jasmine, we all do things. Questionable things. But if no one finds out, it doesn't really matter. It's like, a tree falls in a forest, right?"

"Kyle. I saw the tree fall. *Mike* saw the tree fall. But if the tree never falls in the forest again . . ." I raise my eyebrows hoping he'll get it.

He doesn't.

"Listen. The election is on Wednesday. My snapshot poll shows Gerald gaining ground with the rockers ever since you said Rush sucks—"

"—they *do*—"

"—which is why we have to focus on the only thing that matters now: *winning*. And keeping everything, you know"—he puts his fingertips to his lips—"*quiet*."

I shove my gym clothes in my locker and slam it shut. The moral high ground I was on has turned to quicksand. I push past him again.

He scrambles after me. "Oh, I forgot to tell you: my mom has a voter file from when she was PTA president sophomore year: the names and numbers of every single senior for our Get Out the Vote effort. See you at morning break," he says, peeling off toward the south hall.

It's going to be hard to talk Patty and Kyle into doing the right thing when I can't even talk myself into it.

I could call admissions if I don't win. Apologize profusely. Say there was a mix-up at the ballot box. Or I could be going to all this trouble to win the election and still not get accepted.

All I have to do is keep my mouth shut for two more days and win, and I could be the first-ever senior from Eisenhower High accepted to New York University.

I accelerated the truth on my application. Now all I have to do is slow it down.

CHAPTER SIXTEEN

GOING SOLO

During our usual morning break on the quad, Bridget and Malia are the only two who don't know Kyle cheated on Bridget with Patty. We're sitting in a circle, with Kyle directly across from Patty, who keeps trying to catch his eye.

Mike is sideways glancing at me, but what am I supposed to say?

"What's everybody doing for Thanksgiving?" Malia asks, oblivious.

Equally oblivious, Bridget says, "We're going to Granny's. What about you, babe?"

"We're, uh, going to my uncle's," says Kyle, obviously not oblivious. He casts Patty a furtive glance. Bridget nudges him. "Tell them the story of how your dad left you and your brother at the club that first Thanksgiving after your parents got divorced." She turns to us. "He paid a waitress fifty bucks to check on them while he and his new girlfriend played golf.

Kyle and his brother ate Thanksgiving dinner *by themselves.*
The waitress made them plates from the buffet." She laughs
at the absurdity.

Malia looks at Kyle as if he were an abandoned puppy.
"That's terrible," she says.

It *is* terrible. I didn't know Kyle's parents were divorced.

He manages a little half smile that's fake. "It wasn't so
bad," he says, unconvincingly.

Mike, who does *not* have the best poker face, keeps looking
at Patty, then Bridget, then Kyle with a big, furrowed brow.

"What about you, Mike?" I say to distract him. "What are
you doing for Thanksgiving?"

His face relaxes into a smile. "This will be our first American Thanksgiving in a long time." He leans back on his
hands. "My mom's making turkey and oyster stuffing—my
dad's from Massachusetts," he says, as if anything could explain oyster stuffing. "And pecan pie for dessert. What about
you?" He brushes my hand.

"Me? I . . ." I draw a breath.

I'm not telling Mr. All-American we may have eggplant
stew and saffron rice with yogurt and cucumbers, plus rosewater ice cream for dessert. Not yet. It's just too weird.

"Um, we're going out. What about you, Patty?" I push my
voice into a higher register to simulate merriment and involve
her in the conversation.

"We're going to my grandma's," she says, picking at a
blade of grass.

Kyle finally catches her eye. "Don't forget about Gerald's rally today after school."

"Why do you want us to go again?" Mike asks. "Seems weird."

"We're piggybacking on Gerald's event," says Kyle. "Handing out free Coke."

"You're not going to do anything mean to him, are you?" Bridget says to me, as if I'm the criminal mastermind.

"All we're doing is handing out free Coke," I say. My face burns as I say it. It *is* weird.

Mike leans forward. "I'll be there covering it for the paper."

Which I wish he would have mentioned to me earlier.

"Hey, did you guys hear that rumor about Gerald's dad?" Malia asks in a hushed tone. "You know, that he's in . . . jail."

"I don't believe it," Mike says with a dismissive shake of his head.

"Me neither," I say, eyeing Patty and Kyle. "I'm *sure* it's not true."

"We have no way of knowing whether it's true or not," Kyle says.

He is such a good liar.

"Who cares if it is?" Mike asks.

"Yeah, who *cares*?" I say, glaring at Kyle.

"*I* do." Patty has finally come alive. "He narc'd on my brother while his own dad was in prison. I care."

Thankfully, the bell rings.

Malia puts her hand on my arm and silently mouths, "Wait."

"You coming?" Mike asks.

My voice cracks. "In a minute."

I already know what she's going to say.

Sure enough, as soon as everyone scatters, Malia whispers, "Did you see Patty?"

"What about her?" I widen my eyes to foster the impression I have no idea what Malia is talking about.

"The way she was looking at Kyle." She glances around. "I heard another rumor. From Ginny. About Patty and Kyle. They were totally making out at the dance."

I literally gulp, like you see in cartoons. "Ginny has gossip on everyone," I say. "Who knows how much of it is true?"

Now I know what "web of lies" means. A new strand is created every time I open my mouth.

Malia gets that maternal look in her eye again. "If Kyle *is* cheating on Bridget with Patty, what would we do?"

Nothing until the election is over, the voice inside my head shouts.

"It's probably gossip," I say. "We shouldn't say anything until we know for sure."

She glances past me in Patty's direction. "Was she the one who told you to change your name to 'Jasmine Katie'?"

My chest grows warm with embarrassment. "Well, no. That was my idea."

She crosses her arms. "Why?"

"Why?" I cross mine. "I thought your mom said to keep my head down."

"She never told us to pretend we're not Black. We *can't*," she says pointedly.

"Malia, there's a whole TV show devoted to the hostage crisis. *Every night.*"

"Whatever," she says with a shrug. "I'll talk to Ginny again. Make sure she saw what she said she saw."

"Fine," I say.

"Fine," she says, and we head our separate ways.

Great. If Ginny is spreading a rumor about Patty and Kyle, it's going to get back to Bridget. It's only a matter of time. I've got to tell her, even if it means she—

Wait a minute.

If Ginny is spreading the rumor about Patty and Kyle, that means it *will* get back to Bridget. If it gets back to Bridget, then I don't have to tell her. I don't have to be the bearer of bad news or see her face twist or watch the tears stream down her face while pretending I didn't know.

But I will *for sure* be there to support her when she finds out. Listen to her and lend a shoulder to cry on, because that's what best friends are for.

ıllııllıllıll

Mr. Ramos is in the midst of our final discussion of *All the President's Men* by the time I get to class. Good thing I watched the VHS last night.

"Everything okay?" Mike whispers when I sit down next to him.

"Yeah, girl stuff," I say, knowing he won't ask follow-up questions on a topic that could include menstruation.

"Haldeman and Ehrlichman were forced to resign after Woodward and Bernstein exposed their role in the Watergate cover-up," says Ellory.

"Exactly. That was the summer of 'seventy-three," says Mr. Ramos.

Summer of '73. The movie only went up to Nixon's second inauguration in 1972. The book must have covered a lot more.

"That was when the backstabbing was in full glory," Mr. Ramos says with a nostalgic smile.

"And all of them were found guilty," Mike says. "Haldeman, Ehrlichman, Mitchell, Colson. All of them."

"The main thing," Gerald says, looking right at me, "is they didn't get away with it even though they thought they would."

Maybe it's a coincidence, but Mr. Ramos turns to me. "What about you, Jasmine? What did you learn about investigative reporting from *All the President's Men*?"

Unfortunately, I never finished my paper because Kyle and Patty ruined my concentration, but I rapidly replay the movie in my mind.

"Well, when Deep Throat tells Woodward and Bernstein to 'follow the money,' I think that's a pretty important principle of investigative reporting. Especially in corruption cases."

Mr. Ramos gets this weird look on his face: a half smile from the nose down and a frown from above. "'Follow the money,' huh?"

Mike casts me a sideways glance.

"Um, yes," I say.

"That *is* what happens," Mr. Ramos says, slowly nodding his head. "In the movie. Not in the book. Did you read the book?"

"I . . . I started it," I stammer like an idiot. How was I supposed to know the movie is different from the book?

He turns to the rest of the class. "As you've heard me say over and over, integrity is the most important quality a good journalist can possess. Unassailable, unimpeachable integrity. If I ask whether you've read the book and you haven't, cop to it."

Mike flashes what's meant to be a sympathetic smile, but his lips purse with judgment like Grandma Jean's.

My shoulders sneak up on my ears as I sink down in my seat.

The minute the bell rings, I hurry out of class without waiting for Mike. He catches up to me in the hall anyway. "'Follow the money.' How did you pick the one line that's in the movie but not in the book?"

I hardly slow down. "Looks like you're the only one with unimpeachable integrity around here." You can hear the bite in my voice.

He steps in front of me and brushes my arm. "Hey, are

you going to tell Bridget about Kyle and Patty? The first rule of covert operations is that someone always leaks."

I can't tell him I'm going to let Ginny spill the beans. But I try to make him understand.

"Mike, she may never forgive me when she knows that I knew."

His forehead wrinkles. "But . . . *you* know that you know."

"I *know*," I say, irritation creeping in. "Don't worry. The truth will come out. I promise."

He nods thoughtfully and backs down the hall. "Okay, then. See you at the rally."

The truth *will* come out. Does it really matter if it's from me?

ıııııııııııııı

Patty and I are setting up a table at the back of the quad before Gerald's rally. Malia and Bridget are rounding up seniors. Mike should be on his way.

Kyle is late.

We barely say one word to each other even as we stand side by side, filling red Solo cups with Coke. It's one of those unseasonably warm November days, sunny and seventy-eight. We forgot ice, and the lukewarm Coke is already going flat.

At the opposite end of the quad, Gerald and Ellory huddle near a microphone and amp they set up just inside the concrete circle.

Mr. Jackson is already patrolling the perimeter.

If I'm not going to be the one to tell Bridget about Kyle and Patty, I can at least try and persuade Patty to do the right thing. My voice is low and my mouth tight. "Patty, I'm sure you had a . . . a momentary lapse in judgment Saturday night."

She pretends to concentrate on the Coke.

"Is this just you getting back at Bridget for all the times she bailed on us?"

"You don't understand." Her voice quavers. "I really like him."

Her voice never quavers.

"He doesn't even like her anymore," she says. "He told me he doesn't want to hurt her feelings by breaking up with her."

She *cannot* be falling for that line.

"Patty, you can't be falling for that line."

Her face momentarily crumples then smooths itself over. "It's not 'a line.' As long as no one says anything, it'll be fine."

"No, it's *not* fine," I say in my harshest whisper yet, as our first senior approaches. "Even if no one says anything, you and Kyle are *not* fine."

"Right on with the free Taco Bell at lunch, man," this dude with a bunch of curls, wearing pink OP shorts and a Sex Wax T-shirt, says. "You got my vote."

"Thank you," I say crisply, handing him his Coke.

He raises his red cup. "Unless the other guy's doing Del Taco."

A line is forming. We'll talk about it later.

We get into a rhythm.

"Thanks, vote Jasmine Katie, for senior class president. Fly like an eagle with Jasmine, for senior class president." I pour cup after cup after cup.

I hate to admit it, but Kyle was right. This *is* a smart strategy. And I never would have thought of it on my own.

Right then, Ellory says something to Gerald. They glare at me and Patty.

This skater dude with long hair and bloodshot eyes who reeks of weed is next in line. He steps up and asks, "What's the difference between you and that other dude anyway?"

"Well, Gerald will make you cut your hair, and you might not be able to wear Hawaiian shirts ever again." I hand him his cup of Coke. "I'm promising a cool new mascot and free Coke on Fridays, *plus* putting together a proposal for overnight prom."

"Right on." He ambles off.

"That's not Gerald's platform and you know it," Ellory says, snatching a cup of lukewarm Coke out of my hands. "Figures you would try to hijack his rally."

"It's not that much of an exaggeration. And I *am* promising free Coke and a new mascot, plus a, a prom . . . proposal."

His face brightens like a kid who's found himself in Santa's lap. "There's one campaign promise you can't keep: new mascot."

"Says who?"

"The bylaws. Only the administration can change it in consultation with the PTA. Probably should have checked before you made it the centerpiece of your campaign," he says, grabbing an extra Coke for Gerald on his way back.

I deflate. "Great. I can see the headline now: NEW PRESIDENT'S AMERICAN EAGLE SHOT DOWN."

"Don't worry about it," Kyle says, materializing next to Patty. "It's just a campaign promise. Won't matter by the time you're elected."

"Everything all set?" Patty murmurs to him.

"What? What's all set?" I ask.

Before he can answer, there's awful screeching from feedback on the mic. Ellory scrambles to fix it.

"Testing. One-two. Is this on?" Gerald taps the mic.

By now, about thirty seniors of all stripes have clustered in the quad: junior G.I. Joes, jocks, cheerleaders, AV Club and marching band members, skaters and stoners. Most everyone is sipping lukewarm Coke from a red Solo cup. Like one big school-sanctioned keg party.

Right then, Malia returns. "Bridget's coming. She's in the bathroom."

"I'm Gerald Thomas and I'm running for senior class president," Gerald booms.

Several seniors cheer. The stoners hold up their American flag lighters. It's unbelievable. Gerald has developed a real following.

"For the past decade, hippies have let everything go to pot."

"Yeah," this stoner dude roars.

A hippie chick in bell bottoms and a peasant blouse—her name is Clover or Cloud or something—throws him a dirty look.

Gerald holds up his index finger. "That's why I'm running to restore order: bring back the dress code, reinstitute the Pledge of Allegiance, that sort of thing."

The junior G.I. Joes whistle.

From the middle of the crowd, Mohawk Punk shouts, "The fascist machine has made you a moron, man."

Oddly, Ali and Safety Pin Punk are nowhere in sight.

Mike finally shows up and stands next to me, pen and notebook in hand. "Ready for some front-page news."

"Make sure to mention the free Coke courtesy of Jasmine Katie," I say.

"Will do."

"And I say, down with student radicals who are ruining this country here and abroad," Gerald says, raising his fist.

Another larger-than-expected cheer.

"My brother is a Vietnam vet who—"

"Baby killer," yells Clover or Cloud or whatever her name is.

Even from a distance, I can see Gerald's eyes burn with fury.

He runs his fingers through his thinning hair. "My

brother is a Vietnam veteran who was *spit* on when he came home. He lost his leg fighting for this country."

Oh shit. I forgot to remind Patty and Kyle not to say anything about Gerald's dad.

"The student radicals who defend our enemies," he gestures to me, "like my opponent Jasmine Zumideh's brother, threaten our whole American way of life."

I *knew* he would try to make Ali my running mate.

"If I win, we'll amend the student handbook to ban disruptive behavior. And I'm sending our petition to President Carter to do whatever is necessary to bring those hostages home. All that pacifist talks about is the energy crisis. Well, here's a crisis he can actually do something about."

The junior G.I. Joes start chanting, "Bomb. Iran. Bomb. Iran!" And the crowd joins in. Ellory beams.

My stomach is sinking, I'm thinking Gerald could actually win this thing. And, depressingly, my fellow seniors can be whipped into an anti-Iranian mob in an instant.

"Jesus," Mike says.

Just when I think it can't get any crazier, a buzz erupts. Several seniors scattered throughout the crowd—a skater here, a jock there—shout even louder than the chants, but it's hard to make out what they're saying. Everyone is glancing around, trying to figure it out.

"What are they saying?" Malia asks, her face scrunched with confusion.

Mike looks to me. I have no idea what's happening.

And then it becomes clear: ping-ponging around the crowd—so no one person will get caught—are shouts of "guilty," "your dad is guilty," and "busted."

The shouts spread like wildfire.

"Oh my God," Malia says, covering her mouth.

Gerald's eyes dart around, trying to identify the source of the shouts.

I look at Patty and Kyle in disbelief.

Slowly, Gerald's smile fades as he realizes what's being said. "It's not true. That's a lie!"

And Kyle is sporting that shit-eating grin again.

Even from the opposite end of the quad, I can see the panic on Gerald's face.

"Make it stop," I yell at Kyle.

But the shouts, which Mr. Jackson is powerless to police, continue.

Ellory scrambles to the mic. Mike looks to me, searching.

"Kyle. Make it *stop*."

"Hey! *Hey*," Ellory yells into the mic.

We all turn.

"It's no surprise Gerald's opponent is desperate enough to hijack his rally." He raises his cup. "Because her campaign promises are as empty as this cup of lukewarm Coke."

A laugh ripples through the crowd. My face turns as red as the Solo cup he holds up.

"If that's the kind of 'leader' you want, then vote for 'Jasmine Katie.'"

My shoulders creep up to my ears.

"If not, vote for your next senior class president, Gerald Thomas." He grabs Gerald's hand and holds it above his head as if he had just won the heavyweight title.

Everyone cheers.

"I've got to get a quote for my article," Mike says and takes off with his notebook.

As soon as he does, I whirl around to face Patty and Kyle. "Did you do this?" I demand. Of course it was them. Of course Kyle, who is both fiendish *and* clever, was never simply going to hand out free Coke.

Kyle motions me to keep my voice down. "A little harmless disruption to throw him off his game. I told you, we were down in the polls."

Patty leaps to Kyle's defense. "Gerald is only getting what he deserves."

That's it. I'm sick of all the dirty tricks and the crimes and the cover-ups that I should have put a stop to long ago. "Forget it. I can do this myself. You're *fired*."

Kyle rears back in surprise, as if I had blasted him with an air gun. "Are you serious?"

Naturally, at that moment, Bridget walks up, all smiles. "What'd I miss?"

"*Everything*," I say.

And right when I'm about to tell her the truth about Kyle

and Patty, punk music comes *blasting* over the school's PA.
It's the Clash. Bellowing about how they're so bo-o-ored with
the USA, followed by a scratchy voice that says, "Hey, everyone. It's Ali on pirate radio."

CHAPTER SEVENTEEN

EMERGENCY BROADCAST SYSTEM

Somehow, Ali has commandeered the school's PA system. Everyone is looking around for the source of this disembodied voice.

"This country was founded by a bunch of 'radicals' like us who stood up to King George."

Ali doesn't know not to shout into the microphone—like, that's the point of a microphone—so his voice sounds all distorted. But he's got everyone's attention.

Safety Pin Punk is in the background shouting, "Oh man, you did it, you did it."

I stand there frozen. Mohawk Punk now has the shit-eating grin. Mr. Jackson makes a beeline for the administration office.

"This election for senior class president is between a fascist clown and a total poser."

"I'll kill him," I yell, and take off running.

From the opposite end of the quad, Mike follows.

There's muffled pounding over the loudspeaker, which must be the school secretary at the door. Why the janitor doesn't immediately intervene with his set of five thousand keys is not clear.

"American democracy is a joke, man. Especially this election, which I encourage everyone to *boycott* on Wednesday and—oh shit!"

Apparently, Mr. Jackson burst in. "You're in big trouble, mister," he says before the mic gets cut off.

By the time I get to the admin office and find Ali, he's in the hallway surrounded by Mohawk Punk, Safety Pin Punk, and a bunch of other kids, including Clover.

"Jackson said a week of detention, man, but it was worth it," Ali says to his admirers.

I push through the crowd and shove Ali so hard he almost falls down.

Mike is right behind me.

The punks go, "Whoa, whoa."

Clover grabs my arm. "No need for violence, man."

"Shut up, Clover," I say and jerk it away.

"My name is Cloud, Jasmine," she says.

Ali regains his footing and starts laughing. *Laughing.* "Don't get all brutal, man. I have a right to free speech, you know. You should try it sometime. Stand up for us."

Before I know it, tears are streaming down my face—and I totally forgot to wear Ultra Lash. "Why are you doing this to me, Ali? The election is in two days. Can't you shut up until then?"

"Because. We're making a statement. And why do you care? You already submitted your application. What does it matter if you win or not?"

I feel sick. Caught in a web of lies, both the spider *and* the fly.

"We're gonna make an even bigger stink on Election Day," he cackles.

"What does that mean?" Mike asks.

"You'll see," Ali says with a gleam in his eye, "but you're gonna want to cover it for the paper."

He and the punks skip off down the hall, high-fiving each other, while his admirers follow along like lemmings. Cloud brings up the rear.

Mike is staring at me, chewing his lip.

"What?" I ask, wiping my eyes.

"You didn't . . . know about what was going to happen to Gerald today, did you?"

Now, the Watergate defendants were all charged with conspiracy, which means two or more people entering into an agreement to commit a crime. Even if one of the defendants doesn't participate in all of the criminal acts, she's still guilty of the larger conspiracy.

"What? No. No, I didn't," I say.

The tiniest tilt of his head makes me think he doesn't believe me.

"What about Kyle and Patty?"

"I fired them."

His eyebrows arch up. "You fired Kyle and Patty?"

"*Yes,*" I say as if he's been interrogating me for hours.

"Oh. Well . . . cool. You did the right thing," he says emphatically.

If Mike's admission to the Air Force Academy hinged on him winning this election, he might not be so righteous.

Suddenly, Mr. Jackson's voice booms, "Miss Zoom-buh-doom."

We both startle.

"Y-yes, sir?" I reply.

"Report to the principal's office tomorrow morning at oh-eight-hundred hours."

I close my eyes.

"That means eight a.m.," Mike says quietly.

"I *know*," I say and take off running down the hall.

||||||||||||

When I get home, all I want to do is go upstairs and collapse on my bed, but Auntie Minah is in the living room pacing back and forth with her hand to her forehead, mumbling in Farsi.

From what I can make out, the United States is now *suing* Iran—who knows how—and she's worried the students will do something crazy in retaliation. Plus, she wasn't able to get to the immigration office today and is anxious they're going to revoke her green card.

She reaches for one of her Camels and lights it up with a shaky hand. "Why won't the United States send the shah back? Then the students are happy, they let the hostages go."

This is the last thing I need right now. But since I could use a cup myself, I do the only thing I can and offer to make tea.

"Yes, joonam, please," she says. "Chai would be good. Merci, kheili mamnoon."

Making Persian tea the right way as Auntie has taught me—boiling water in a kettle and steeping the loose, black leaves in a teapot instead of using a tea bag—gives me time to think.

If Principal Crankovitch asks, I'll tell him I had nothing to do with what happened at Gerald's rally. If I have to, I'll ratfuck Patty and Kyle. Good thing I fired them.

Although.

If Ali and the punks are going to make "a stink" on Election Day, maybe I shouldn't have fired them.

No. I should have. I just have to figure out how to stop Ali on my own.

When water whistles in the kettle, I pour it over the loose tea leaves in the teapot, pop in a cardamom pod, cover, and steep. The cardamom fills the air with a faintly spicy, nutty fragrance.

What about . . . laxative in Ali's morning coffee? He'd be in the bathroom all day.

Or I could crush up one of Mom's sleeping pills and

sprinkle it in his dinner the night before. He'd sleep through the election.

God. He's turning me into a suspect on *Columbo*.

After the tea leaves steep for about five minutes, I pour a small amount of the dark, brown liquid into the tiny gold-rimmed demitasse cups, add hot water, and place each cup on a saucer. I put nabat—this saffron-flavored rock candy—on the side of each saucer like Auntie does and grab some napkins and dates on my way back in.

"Merci, kheili mamnoon," Auntie says as she takes her cup.

We sit in the living room quietly sipping our tea. For a few minutes, it's almost as if there are no hostages. Or Kyle and Patty. Or Gerald.

"I wish I could take you to Iran. Your father always says you are not old enough, but now . . ." Her eyes grow red and moist. "Maybe you never see Isfahan and Naqsh-e Jahan Square. Maman was born there. The Baq-e Eram, oh, joonam, the most beautiful garden in Shiraz. You'll never see where your father and I grew up in Tehran. This is part of you."

The only way I may be able to see Iran now is in Dad's coffee table book.

"Will Grandma Zumideh still be able to come here?"

"I don't know. Already travel is very difficult for her."

Suddenly, tears are streaming down my cheeks like rain on a windshield. I had always thought somehow, someday, she would come back. Or we would go there.

"Oh man, that was awesome!"

Naturally, Ali has to interrupt this poignant moment by bursting through the front door so full of himself, I'm surprised his head fit.

I lean forward to set down my tea (harder than you would think in a dome chair). "No, it wasn't. Wait till Dad hears you got a whole week's worth of detention."

"He'll be proud of me for standing up for us," he says, tossing his books on the coffee table.

I manage to hoist myself out of the dome chair. "No, he won't."

Ali pops a date in his mouth. "Yes, he will."

Now we're standing face-to-face.

"No, he won't."

"Yes, he will."

We're deep into several rounds of no, he won't/yes, he will when Auntie Minah shouts, "*Stop.* Why are you always fighting? Your father would be very upset to see you like this."

Which is not true; Dad always sees us like this.

I point to Ali. "Because he won't shut up."

He points back. "Because she's a total hypocrite."

"In case you haven't noticed, everyone is mad at Iranians right now, Ali. You can't blame me for not wanting to announce it on the *CBS Evening News*."

He steals the nabat candy from my saucer. "This is the time to stand up, when everyone is putting us down."

"Not if you're trying to win an election; that's my nabat."
I swat his hand.

He tosses it back. "You already sent in your application,
so what?"

Auntie closes her eyes. "Ali-jon, your father asked you to
do as your sister says."

He pops another date in his mouth. "Dad said not to say
anything about her and I won't."

"Thank you, Ali-jon." Auntie Minah sits back and sips
her tea.

Ali gallops upstairs.

Now Auntie is the gullible one. Ali would never surrender
that quickly.

"I . . . I have a bunch of homework, excuse me."

I run upstairs to my room. Cue the sad trombone reprise.
I should have known better. A shit-talker and a snake. Now,
here I am, the election is the day after tomorrow, Ali is plotting
to blow it up, I may have unwittingly stirred up a sympathy
vote for my opponent, and I totally betrayed my best friend.
Plus, I have to go to the principal's office in the morning.

The phone rings. I don't budge.

"It's for you," Ali says. He comes to my doorway with the
cordless.

I snatch it from him. "What have I told you about barging
in on me?" I shut the door in his face. As soon as I put the
phone to my ear—

"Are you going to tell Bridget now? Because if you tell Bridget, I'll tell Gerald about the playbook, how you started the rumor about his dad."

Kyle and Patty are not even my campaign managers anymore, and I *still* can't tell Bridget.

"No," I say flatly. "I'm not telling Bridget."

Hopefully, Ginny will do it for me.

We sit there in stubborn silence for a minute.

Finally, in a small voice Patty says, "You really don't want me on your campaign?"

I hesitate. I can hear the hurt in her voice. "This wasn't the way I thought things would work out, but . . . I can do it myself."

As mad as I am at her for complicating everything, I can't help but feel sad. We'll never be the Three Musketeers again.

"Fine, whatever," she says and hangs up.

I've barely hung up when the phone rings again. It's Bridget.

"I'm super mad at Kyle for what happened to Gerald," she says. "It was so mean. Everyone was talking about it after you left."

"What did Kyle . . . say?"

He better not have implicated me.

"He said he told everyone to *boo* Gerald, but it got out of hand."

"Yeah. Out of hand. For sure."

Everything has gotten out of hand.

I could confess. Right now. Not wait for Ginny to tell

Bridget the truth. I *should* confess. But do I really have to sink my college admission over a guy Bridget will have forgotten by our ten-year reunion? Especially when she'll find out about Patty and Kyle soon enough.

"He said I have to help deliver the jocks," Bridget says, her voice full of pride.

She's always been *my* cheerleader. If I had just asked Bridget to persuade every male voter, I'd be better off than I am now, with only one full day to go till the election.

One day. And I'm my own campaign manager. Me. I need a plan. Strategies and tactics, as Kyle would say.

"Yeah, um, the jocks are a really important voting bloc. Listen, Bridget, I've gotta go. I have to work on my campaign."

We hang up. I stare up at the ceiling.

At least no one at NYU will ever know I waged a dirty tricks campaign and betrayed my heritage *and* my best friend to get elected.

No one, that is, except me.

||||||||||||||

The election is tomorrow. It's the last day to campaign. Fourth quarter with minutes to go in the game. Patty would have tackled the opposition for me. Kyle was calling all the plays. *I'm* the quarterback now. I've got the ball, it's all on me. And I have to get across the goal line without fumbling—but I have to start the day in the principal's office. No wonder I feel nauseated.

The *click* of the school secretary's nails as she types and the *thwack* of the carriage return create a distracting hum while I sit in the administration office waiting for Principal Cranko-vitch. Somehow, she manages to answer the phone between thwacks and, every so often, sneak a puff from her cigarette.

The big hand on the wall clock moves in precise, jerky motions from one second to the next. 7:42 a.m. I'd like some time to campaign before first period.

What will my punishment be? Detention? Paddling? He can't punish me if there's no proof of a crime. *It wasn't me* is not even a lie.

"The principal will see you now," the secretary says. She leads me to a door on the far side of the building with a PRIN-CIPAL CRANKOVITCH nameplate. The guys at the engraving factory must have had a good laugh at that one.

My breath starts to grow shallow and, oh no, please don't let me—

Hiccup.

"Miss Zoom-buh-dah." Principal Crankovitch gestures to one of two chairs across from his large L-shaped executive desk. No one gave much thought to the haphazard arrange-ment of framed US maps and college certificates on his walls.

I swallow as hard as I can to stop the—*hiccup*—before sitting on the edge of my seat.

He leans back in his executive chair. His striped tie doesn't go with his short-sleeved button-down shirt. "We worked hard to keep the matter of Gerald's father confidential." He makes a pyramid with his fingertips. "Sensitive family matters have no place in a campaign for senior class president."

"Y-yes, sir. I agree, sir. It—*hiccup*—wasn't me, sir. I didn't start it."

I only lit the match that ignited it when I whispered in Ginny's ear.

He glances at my file. "I see here you've applied to NYU."

I nod enthusiastically. "Yes—*hiccup*—sir."

"These kinds of shenanigans would not reflect well on your transcript, now, would they?"

My shoulders hunch. "No, sir. Like I said, it wasn't me, sir."

He taps his fingertips together. "Even if it wasn't you, you have a responsibility to speak out against anyone advocating in this manner on your behalf. Do you understand?"

I hiccup. And nod again.

He rises. "All right. I'll be keeping an eye on you, young lady."

Great. Now I'm under surveillance.

"Yes, sir."

When I stand up, I gulp hard. My hiccups finally disappear. As he walks me to the door, I can't help asking, "Are you going to talk to Gerald about the things he's been saying about me?"

He adjusts his glasses. "What has he been saying?"

"'Bomb Iran.' Innocent people would be hurt."

"And what does that have to do with you?"

Clearly, he does not read the *Eisenhower General*.

"Well, I'm, I . . ."

Have been going around saying I'm *not* Iranian.

I exhale. "Nothing, sir. Thank you, sir."

||||||||||||||

As soon as I walk out the double doors of the admin building, Kyle is waiting for me, clipboard in hand. I don't want to hear any of his campaign jargon or his stupid poll results.

He trails me to the quad. "Okay, final results of my last snapshot poll: Gerald will carry ROTC and the AV Club," he says. "You've got the skaters and stoners, but half of them won't vote. Bridget and Malia will deliver the cheerleaders and the drill team. The battle is over marching band and the jocks. I can activate our Get Out the Vote effort with one phone call."

"I told you, I'm doing things my way now." I sound more resolute than I feel.

"Just trying to help. Don't forget that, no matter what happens."

He's so desperate for me not to tell Bridget about Patty. Wait till he finds out about Ginny.

I head toward the quad. It's a sprint to the finish. I can do this.

For starters, no more empty campaign promises. Just tell the truth about Gerald. He wants to reinstitute the dress code. He does! A vote for him is a vote for tyranny. Like I said from the start. I should have—

Crap. If it's a sprint to the finish, Gerald has gotten out of the starting blocks before I've even gotten to the track.

"Get your free donuts. Free donuts for seniors," Gerald shouts like a carnival barker in front of boxes and boxes of Winchell's donuts piled high on a table behind him. "Get 'em before they're gone."

He's *bribing* voters. With donuts.

Why didn't I think of that?

Kyle would have thought of that.

Students swarm like honeybees to a hive with less than twenty-four hours till seniors start voting. Why did I pick *now* to make my integrity unimpeachable?

Ali casually saunters up with a cinnamon cruller. "Did you get one? They have bear claws."

My mouth drops open. "Are you kidding? What happened to 'Gerald is a fascist clown'?"

"He is. But if he's giving away free donuts . . ." He walks away, shouting, "This election stinks, boycott the election," with a face full of crumbs.

Fine. Whatever. Gerald is handing out donuts today, I'll hand out something tomorrow. On Election Day. Something sweet and all-American, like . . . Hostess apple pies. I'll pick up a couple cartons tonight at Fedco.

But I can't let Gerald have the spotlight to himself. I set down my folder and purse, march in front of his booth, and shout, "Go ahead. Enjoy your donut today. But tomorrow, vote for me, Jasmine Katie, senior class president."

This is so embarrassing. I hate calling attention to myself. My one and only appearance in the talent show was a bust. Bridget, Ginny, and I danced to Tom Jones's "She's a Lady" in fourth grade. Ginny's mom choreographed the whole thing and stuck me in the back. If I accidentally moved center stage, she'd say, "Can you get back there, behind Ginny, honey?"

"Don't be bamboozled by a bear claw. You'll be stuck in your Sunday best *at school*!"

A smattering of students with maple bars, glazed, and chocolate-covered sprinkles (my favorite) pause, while Gerald scrambles out from behind his table.

"A vote for Gerald is a vote for tyranny, *that's* what he's proposing," I shout.

Suddenly, Gerald is next to me. "Jasmine Katie is a fraud. That's not even her real name."

"Wh—Yes, it is! Katie is my middle name." I gesture wildly toward him. "And Gerald is the fraud. There's nothing he can do about the hostages, no matter what he says."

The first bell rings, but Gerald and I stay there, side by side, shouting.

"She *would* say that since her brother is an Iranian student radical. And she can't change the mascot. We checked."

"Gerald wants to reinstate the Pledge of Allegiance. What's next, prayer in school?"

"Hippies have no respect for God or country—"

"—I have respect for freedom of speech, unlike you who . . ."

I stop midsentence and squint. A cacophony of pounding hammers is coming from the direction of the theater. A bunch of students must be helping the shop teacher build set flats.

"You want to tear down everything we've built in this great nation," Gerald huffs.

Set flat. They're building set flats.

For the fall production of *Fiddler on the Roof.*

Oh my God.

That's *it.*

Forget marching band and jocks, *drama nerds* are the totally overlooked demographic in this election! There have to be thirty seniors in the company between the cast, crew, and extras. Why didn't I think of them until now?

They've been hiding out in the theater rehearsing. Gerald must have overlooked them, too.

If I can lock up their votes, I can start planning my inauguration speech.

I'll crash their rehearsal after school.

"I've gotta go, Gerald," I say and race off to class before he gets the same idea.

CHAPTER EIGHTEEN

AMERICAN AS APPLE PIE

A pop quiz on fetishism spares me the painful necessity of talking to Bridget. If Kyle and Patty were forced to wear a scarlet *A* to symbolize their moral failure, I should be wearing a big *C* for "complicit" to symbolize mine.

"Jasmine. What are you doing?" Bridget leans over and whispers after the quiz.

What am I doing? My mouth opens. What am I doing? Compromising myself to win an election. Denying my heritage. Betraying you.

"What am I doing about . . . what?" I whisper back.

"Thanksgiving. You said you were going out? Where are you going?"

Thanksgiving. She's only asking about Thanksgiving.

This is our first Thanksgiving without Mom. Auntie Minah's not making turkey and stuffing, that's for sure. But I'm not sure what constitutes a Persian Thanksgiving dinner.

"Uh, Marie Callender's," I say.

"Luck out." She nudges me with her elbow. "Bring me back a slice of lemon meringue."

If only that were adequate restitution.

"Time," calls Mr. Maller. "Fetishes, fetishism. Pass 'em up."

He's sporting white bell-bottomed jeans with a wide leather belt and a paisley-patterned, polyester button-up, out of which sprouts a tuft of graying chest hair. By the time he makes it into this decade, we'll already be on to the next.

I sprint away from Bridget on the bell—"Gotta go, important campaign stuff"—and spend the entire lunch period canvassing for votes. I find the rockers under the old oak (lamenting the fact that Styx released a ballad) and apologize for my comments about Rush.

"They were totally taken out of context," I say. "Everyone *knows* Neil Peart is, like, the greatest rock drummer *ever*."

If we were stranded on a desert island, Rush fans would rhapsodize about Neil Peart before gathering coconuts or starting a fire. You have to admire their commitment.

"And Geddy Lee. Oh my God, that voice."

He's *their* Barbra Streisand.

The rockers, skaters, and stoners promise to vote for me—except for one dude who thinks we're electing the actual President of the United States. "I'm voting for Carter, man," he says.

I wrap up and head to Mr. Ramos's class early so I can apologize for the whole book-versus-movie thing.

He's not here.

But Gerald is. Already in his seat. Glowering at me. The corners of his mouth droop, a marionette whose puppeteer is pulling them down with invisible string.

I enter quickly and take a seat, do my best to avoid his gaze, which is more of a withering stare.

"You don't know anything about me or my family, you know," he says in a low voice.

"I know, Gerald. It wasn't me who—"

"There you are." Mike ambles in. "Missed you at lunch." He sets his books down on the desk next to mine and eases into his seat while Gerald maintains his death stare. "Missed everybody, in fact. It was just me and Malia. Did you know her dad was a colonel in the army?"

"Uh, yeah."

Kyle must have taken Bridget off-campus so she wouldn't find out I fired him. Patty was probably with her sporty friends.

"Where were you?" He brushes my forearm with his fingertips.

"Oh, uh, campaigning."

"How'd it go?" he says with a big smile.

I glance at Gerald. "Great."

Ellory follows Flynn in and Xeroxes Gerald's death stare.

"What's news, everybody?" Mr. Ramos bounds in, tosses his keys and papers on his desk.

"Everything okay with the principal?" Mike whispers.

I nod. I'm not telling him about the surveillance.

Mr. Ramos wades into the semicircle. "Before we begin," he says, rubbing his chin, "I heard about what happened yesterday at your rally, Gerald. Whoever started it, totally uncool."

"And it's not true," he says, eyes still fixated on me.

It wasn't my fault, I want to shout. The cigarette I carelessly tossed aside may have started the brush fire, but it wasn't my fault.

"For the record, it's the obligation of every legitimate journalist"—he glances at me—"and politician not to traffic in rumor or innuendo."

Mike squeezes my hand supportively as a wave of guilt breaks against the rapidly eroding shore of my conscience.

"Like, the mob did *not* kill JFK. Neither did Jackie Kennedy."

"Far as we *know*," says Flynn, who is wearing his ELVIS IS ALIVE T-shirt. Mr. Ramos gestures around the semicircle. "Maybe one of our ace reporters will get to the bottom of who started it. The truth always comes out."

Flynn's arms start flailing wildly. "*C'mon*, man. This is all small-time bullshit. Who cares about a high school election when people are sprouting extra *limbs* and shit in Pittsburgh from all the, you know, Three Mile Island nuclear waste. But you're not gonna hear about it in the corporate media *New York Times*."

Mr. Ramos chuckles. "You're more likely to hear about that in the *Daily Bugle* than the Gray Lady. Where are you getting this so-called information, Flynn?"

"Over my CB, man. A community of like-minded truth seekers. My handle is Zapruder."

Mr. Ramos turns to Gerald. "And Gerald, I understand your anger over the hostages, but as journalists—or politicians—we can't let xenophobia or anti-Iranian bias creep into our thinking."

I would pile on if I hadn't made such a show of denouncing my heritage.

"Whatever happens tomorrow, did you both run campaigns you can be proud of?"

Mike looks at me. I glance at Gerald.

"Yes," Gerald says confidently.

"Yes," I say a beat later, much less so.

For the rest of class, I zone out and chew my nail. *The truth always comes out.* That has to be one of those maxims like "nice guys finish first" or "good guys always win" people wish were true but isn't.

I can't think about that right now. The minute the bell rings, I have to get to the theater.

⁞⁞⁞⁞⁞⁞⁞⁞⁞⁞

Ali is hanging out with the punks on the quad, plotting, as I make my way to the theater.

They should be on *my* side. *I* liked punk before Ali. I wrote about Elvis Costello and the Clash. Saw Adam and the Ants at an all-ages club.

Mohawk Punk has the nerve to sneer at me, "You know American democracy stinks, right?"

Ali snickers.

Drama nerds notwithstanding, I do need a plan to defuse their stink bomb, whatever that means. Ali is the ringleader. The punks won't know what to do without him.

If I were a character in an Agatha Christie novel, I'd slip him some arsenic. Not enough to *poison* him poison him. Just, like, *lightly* poison him. Enough to miss a day of school.

For now, though, I've got to win over the drama nerds with talk of Tevye and Golde.

The theater reeks of fresh paint. A handful of students are helping the shop teacher attach wheels to the base of the set flats.

A group of about twenty students—must be the cast—mill around the stage talking and laughing. Oh! There's Nancy Munson, this girl who went to Roosevelt Junior High.

The drama teacher is nowhere in sight. Which means I have at least a few minutes to make my appeal.

I sidle up to the apron of the stage. "Um, hi," I say. My voice is shaky.

They don't hear me.

"Hi, excuse me," I say, much louder.

They all pause and turn. Turns out, you can get stage fright down here, too.

"Hi, Nancy," I say, as brightly as possible.

She looks at me as if I had rushed the stage during "Sunrise, Sunset."

I forge ahead. "My name is Jasmine Katie and I'm running for senior class president."

Nancy frowns. "I thought your name was Jasmine Zumideh."

"Oh. It is. That. Too." I laugh nervously. "But it's Jasmine Katie on the ballot. I wanted to tell you how excited I am about your production of *Fiddler on the Roof.* My mom took me to see it when I was ten, she plays the cast album all the time."

"Really?" says this guy whose short stature is offset by his big attitude.

He was in my AP History class. I can't remember his name.

"What's your favorite number?"

He must be Tevye. He thinks I'm bluffing. He's expecting me to say "If I Were a Rich Man" because that's what everyone would say.

I stare him down. "'Now I Have Everything.' When Perchik asks Hodel to marry him. Or 'Miracle of Miracles.' After Tevye agrees to let Motel marry Tzeitel."

A murmur of approval ripples through the cast. I quickly make my pitch. "The election is tomorrow morning, in place of first period. I know you're all busy, but—"

"Wait a minute." AP History steps forward, puts his forearm to his forehead to block the light, and stares down at me.

"Aren't you the one whose brother has something to do with those hostages?"

"What? No!"

Nancy raises a brow.

"I . . . I mean, yes. He is. My brother. He has *nothing* to do with the hostages, I swear. He just wants you to understand the context."

AP History makes a skeptical "pfft" sound.

"But . . . but that's not the point. The point is, Gerald wants to reinstitute a dress code, which means"—I quickly scan the crowd—"no rainbow suspenders for you," I gesture to a dude wearing them, "or happy-face T-shirts for you." I point to Nancy. "And he's going to reinstate the Pledge of Allegiance, till next thing you know, he's banning your production of *Godspell*!"

They all rear back in horror.

"Because that's what people who want 'order' want," I say in a soft voice for dramatic effect. "To control things. To control *you*."

I'm winning them over. I can feel it.

"I can't wait for your opening night. I'd like to review it for the school paper."

"You never have before," Nancy says with more hurt than anger.

I haven't. Mike is right. I really haven't ventured outside my little circle.

"I know. And I'm sorry for that. But I'll see about setting

up a regular theater review column from now on. Do I have your support?"

After the longest five seconds of my life, AP History finally nods his approval. "Yeah."

"Yeah." Everyone else follows suit.

"Tell everyone, all your friends. And break a leg." I smile and wave on my way out.

I did it! Identified an overlooked demographic and won them over. Even if only half the drama nerds vote, that could be enough to swing the election in my favor. I'm going straight to Fedco to get those cartons of Hostess apple pies.

⁞⁞⁞⁞⁞⁞⁞⁞⁞⁞⁞⁞

"What is all this, joonam?" Auntie asks, as I lug six cartons of Hostess apple pies through the back door. She shakes off Mom's hideous oven mitts to help me carry them in.

"Some sweet treats I bought to hand out during the election tomorrow," I say.

"To bribe voters." Ali snorts from his perch at the kitchen table where his AP History homework is spread out. "Apple pies. Fitting. 'The revolution is not an apple that falls when it is ripe. You have to make it fall.'"

It seemed impossible, but he's now more pretentious than ever.

Auntie takes one look at the garish, bright green-and-white packaging and grimaces. "Why you don't ask me to help you? I could make the zoolbia and bamieh."

"They're fine," I say, giving her a kiss on each cheek. I inhale the tahchin Auntie's just taken out of the oven, this rice cake with yogurt, saffron, egg, and chicken. "Smells delicious, Amme." I wish I had more time for her to teach me how to cook.

I organize my cartons into two piles. Six cartons of fruit pies with six pies each. Not enough for every voter, but if I can get the early word out, hopefully I can—

"Oh, joonam, this came for you today," Auntie says offhandedly.

She's holding up a big manila envelope.

Oh my God.

Is it . . . ?

She hands it to me.

It is.

I freeze. I want to open it, but I don't want to open it. I'm scared.

"It's from the university," Auntie says, as if I don't know.

A wave of dizziness comes over me, but I shake it off, take a deep breath, close my eyes, and rip open the envelope.

Oh my God.

Oh my God!

OH MY GOD!

I start jumping up and down. "I did it! I got in! I got in!"

I got into NYU!

I'm shrieking and crying, and Auntie Minah is shrieking

and crying, we're both jumping up and down with joy. "I'm so proud of you, joonam," Auntie gushes.

Ali barely looks up from his book to grunt, "I get Mom's car when you go."

He can't knock me off my cloud. "I got in," I squeal and run upstairs, take out the entire contents of the envelope, and spread it out on my bed. There's a letter of acceptance, a brochure about campus housing, and a bunch of other papers about the counseling center, meal plans, etc.

Mr. Ramos was right. Early decision *was* a leg up. Senior class president–elect *worked*. It showed leadership. I could make editor of the *Washington Square News*.

Oh my God. I got in!

What will my roommate be like? Will I join a sorority—hell no, I'm not joining a sorority—what about campus dining?

I'm floating, absolutely floating.

A single, chilling sentence in the letter of acceptance sends me crashing down to earth:

> *Your place as an incoming freshman in the Class of 1984 is contingent upon the receipt of your spring 1980 transcript and the maintenance of your grades, disciplinary record, and extracurricular activities.*

Extracurricular activities. My spring 1980 transcript *must* say "senior class president" or . . . what? My admission will be revoked?

Shit. The election is tomorrow. And Ali is going to make a stink.

Make a stink. What does that even mean? He can't literally mean stink bombs, can he? He does love them. More than sparklers and butterflies and whatever else was in the Red Devil Family Pak of fireworks we used to get every Fourth of July. They smell so gross. That would keep a bunch of seniors from voting, for sure.

He probably means *make* a stink. Protest. Disrupt. First period is only fifty minutes. If he pulls another stunt like he did on Monday, ten to fifteen minutes could be consumed in chaos, costing me who knows how many votes.

If he were the reason I lost the election, I would kill him. But by then it would be too late. I'd already be calling admissions. I have to stop him *before* he makes a stink.

Now I see why Nixon authorized the Watergate break-in.

The problem is that laxatives, sleeping pills, arsenic—okay, not arsenic—are too risky. He could get really sick, and it's not like I want to hurt him. I just need someone to keep him quiet for me now that *I got in.*

||||||||||||

"What do you mean 'keep him quiet'?" Patty's voice is full of suspicion.

There's no one else to turn to.

I have the cordless in hand, pacing. "Keep him, like, occupied during first period when everyone is voting."

"How?" she demands.

"I don't know," I say.

I don't want to know.

"What if I—"

"Don't tell me!"

That way I can honestly say I didn't know. But now that I got in, I can't let him jeopardize my acceptance.

"And you won't tell Bridget about me and Kyle? *Ever?*"

Honestly, why is it my responsibility? I'm not the one cheating on her. And *I got in.*

". . . no," I croak.

My dolls look at me with utter disillusionment from their perch on my pink scalloped shelves. I don't blame them.

"But Patty, the election is almost over," I plead. "Maybe you and Kyle are like Sandy and Danny in *Grease.* Like summer lovers. Now that summer is over—"

"It's not summer," she says flatly. "And they stayed together."

"You know what I mean." I exhale. "Besides, you're going off to Cal Poly, he's going to Notre Dame. If you break it off now, it'll be better. For everyone."

She's quiet.

I pause. Maybe I've persuaded her. Maybe she *will* break it off with Kyle. Maybe—

"We can't, like, hurt Ali, right?"

"What? No! Of course you can't hurt him." I turn the

dolls around on my pink scalloped shelves so they won't stare at me. I don't care. I got in.

"Okay, okay. We'll pick him up in the parking lot before first period."

Uh-oh. I shift uneasily. "What do you mean 'we'?"

"Not Kyle," she says, irritated.

"Okay, um . . . thank you."

We hang up.

I'm Mr. Ramos's first student *ever* accepted to NYU. Ali is not going to ruin it. If he were a better brother, one who wanted the best for me, I wouldn't have to do this.

Bridget! I have to tell Bridget.

I can't tell Bridget. I don't want to talk to her until the election is over.

I'm bursting to tell someone besides Auntie and Ali.

I could call Mom.

I pick the phone back up but stop mid-dial. What if she asks about Karen? *Nope, haven't seen her, Mom,* I could say.

I *am* a journalist. I'll tell her the facts, just the facts: *Karen was here. She left.*

Grandma Jean answers.

"That's awful far away from everyone," she says when I tell her my news. "Especially when we have a perfectly fine university right here."

"NYU has a great undergrad program for journalism, Grandma."

"I know, I know." She sighs. "But it sure would be nice if you were here."

Poor Grandma Jean. I forget she's probably lonely, too.

"Well, anyway, honey, congratulations. Here's your mom."

"I got into NYU," I say as soon as Mom comes on the line.

"Congratulations, honey," Mom says with genuine excitement for the first time in a long time. Her Bic lighter clicks. A quick, deep inhale is followed by a long exhale. "I remember how happy I was when I got into Oberlin."

"Oberlin? You never told me that." This is, like, major, breaking news. I want to hear all about it. I settle onto my bed. "I thought you met Dad at Kansas State."

"I did. But I got into Oberlin first."

"Why didn't you go there?"

Another long exhale. "Your grandfather wouldn't pay the private school tuition when we had 'a perfectly fine university' right here."

Poor Mom. I don't know what I'd do if Dad wouldn't pay for NYU. "What was your major?"

"Business admin at KSU. English at Oberlin."

I sit up. "Mom, the Oberlin English department is super competitive." I would have applied there except Oberlin doesn't have a journalism department. Or a music scene. Chrissie Hynde had the good sense to get out of Akron when she could. "How did you get in?"

"Oh, I don't know. A few short stories I had written, I guess."

A few short stories. Mom was a *writer*? Wow. She had an ambition beyond her Mrs. degree.

"What were they about?"

"Oh, nothing. They were silly."

And now I'm dying to read them. Were they swooning romances or fanciful adventures whose characters lived lives she could only dream of?

"I probably threw them away."

The combination of embarrassment and wistfulness in her voice makes me choke up. She had dreams. Ambitions. And she abandoned them all for us.

But her regret is a big NO EXIT sign off a dusty, two-lane highway in Manhattan, Kansas, or a five-lane freeway in Bumfuck. She may have missed her opportunity for reinvention, but I'm not missing mine.

CHAPTER NINETEEN

THE PRICE OF DEMOCRACY

This is it. Election Day. I wake up with a ton of nervous energy, a swarm of bumblebees buzzing through my veins. It's weird that days like these are not heralded by some sort of signal: the trill of a trumpet or maybe a foghorn.

I totter down the stairs in my Candies. They're not the most practical, but I want to look my best. Ali is at the kitchen table casually eating his sangak and feta as if he weren't planning to blow up the election. I don't even give him the satisfaction of asking him not to interfere since Patty is going to stop him. I gave her all the details of his morning routine.

Auntie's on the phone, pacing back and forth with the cordless. She keeps putting her hand to her forehead and saying, "Yes. Yes. I understand."

As I start to gather up my boxes of all-American Hostess apple pies, she covers the phone with her hand. "Joonam, I *have* to go to the immigration office today. Please, can you take me?"

I pause. "Today? Auntie, I can't. It's the election."

Literally, my date with destiny.

"If I had a car, I would take you, Amme," says Ali.

He's such a kiss-up.

"Can we go Monday?"

"My attorney says *today*."

Today, of all days.

"After school?"

"I take a taxi," she says, waving her hand at me.

"I'm so sorry, Auntie," I say on my way out.

I'm a terrible niece, but the immigration office is more than an hour's drive away, and my entire future rests on what happens between now and the final bell at 8:55 a.m.

||||||||||||||

The day is gray. In Bumfuck, fog doesn't curl seductively around landmarks or drape itself across the landscape, it just hangs there making the sky look flat and dingy. Still, walking through the parking lot balancing six cartons of apple pies—while wearing my Candies—I'm hopeful. Ali won't make a stink, I've got the drama nerds on my side, and *I got in.*

Volunteers have set up a table for me near our polling place—the gym. I tape a handmade VOTE FOR JASMINE KATIE placard to the front and unpack the first couple cartons of apple pies.

Several junior G.I. Joes wearing their JROTC uniforms pass by. I follow them and peer around the corner at Gerald's table laid out with a bunch of mini American flags.

There's nothing more I can do now. The only way I could be more patriotic than Gerald is to have shown up in an American eagle costume.

I check my watch. Ten minutes till eight. Patty must have nabbed Ali by now. An olive pit of worry settles into my stomach. But it's for his own good. When he hijacked the PA system, he got a week's worth of detention. He could have gotten suspended, or even expelled, for "making a stink" if I hadn't enlisted Patty to stop him.

I finish laying out my apple pies with a few minutes to spare when Mr. Ramos comes striding across the basketball court in my direction.

Oh no. He *is* an investigative journalist. He could have found out about the dirty tricks I pulled on Gerald and want to recall my letter of recommendation.

"Jasmine." He nods, surveying the apple pies. "Price of democracy, I guess."

He knows something. My mouth shapes itself into a smile, but my lips twitch.

He picks up an apple pie, turns it over. "This contest between you and Gerald got a little . . . heated."

"It did." I brace myself. He's going to bust me.

He puts the apple pie down. "Well. I hope it puts one of you over the top with NYU."

"Oh, um, I got in," I say. "I just found out last night."

"You got in?" He rubs his chin.

He knows something. My chest tightens.

"Oh man, right *on*. You did it. My first NYU acceptance. I'm so proud of you."

He doesn't know anything!

"It's all because of you," I gush. "Early decision, your letter of recommendation."

"Aw, you would've gotten in anyway." He literally pats me on the back. "You did it by staying true to yourself. Wrote about Bowie when I told you to write about wrong-doing."

My heart sinks. I haven't, actually. Stayed true to myself.

"See you in class. Good luck today," he says, and strides back across the basketball court.

Right away, voters start streaming in and out of the gym. Malia and two drill team girls—Laurie and Lori—come running over. "We just voted for you."

"Then you all get apple pies," I say with overbaked enthusiasm.

Laurie and Lori tear into theirs. Malia declines hers. She has a big audition next week.

She gestures to my handmade VOTE FOR JASMINE KATIE placard and teases, "You going back to Jasmine Zumideh after this is all over?"

"Yes," I say with an embarrassed laugh. "I know. I shouldn't have changed it. But guess what?" I say, and then contain my excitement because maybe I shouldn't be broadcasting this in case I don't win the election. "I got into NYU."

"You got in?" She squeals and throws her arms around me. "Congratulations!"

Feeling like a total fraud has really marred this moment. I could pull Malia aside, tell her the whole story: about the application, the playbook, the whisper campaign. And Kyle and Patty. She would be sympathetic. Malia *has* to get into USC.

"Malia, there's something I have to—"

"Hey, Jasmine," Lori interrupts, crumpling her apple pie wrapper. "In your first act as president can you legalize senior ditch day?"

"Oh, um, yeah. Sure."

Actually, that would have been a good plank in my platform. Too bad I'm getting the hang of this whole election thing now that it's over.

"You were saying?" Malia looks at me with her big, expectant brown eyes.

There's no way to unravel all the tangles right now.

"Uh, if I don't see you, have a great Thanksgiving."

"You, too," she shouts, and they all run off.

A steady stream of surfers and skaters and several cheerleaders stop by for their pies, plus the entire lead cast of *Fiddler on the Roof.* Early returns look encouraging.

After the first rush, Gerald has the nerve to amble over. "Our table's been mobbed."

He's trying to head-fake me.

"Mine, too." I pick up a pie. "Everyone who voted for me gets one of these."

He glances at the growing pile of empty wrappers. "Don't think my administration will forget about all the dirty tricks. You should be ashamed of the way you campaigned."

"*I* should be ashamed? Ha. That's rich." Which is the first time I've ever gotten to say that. "Do you even know what 'bomb Iran' means? My grandmother lives there, all my dad's relatives. Millions of innocent people would *die.*"

"Why didn't you stand up and say that instead of spreading rumors about my dad, *Jasmine Katie?*"

It's so cutting, so true, a knife to the gut.

"Be-because I—"

"Hi, guys."

We both startle when Bridget walks up.

Gerald spins on his heels and heads back to his table. As a parting shot, he says, "I wonder what NYU would do if they knew the truth about you."

"What's that supposed to mean?" Bridget asks, arms folded, sneering at him on my behalf.

"Nothing. He's trying to throw me off my game."

But I could see him calling admissions, telling them I stole his campaign materials and started a vicious rumor about his dad.

That's if I win. If I lose, *I* have to make the call and admit I lied.

"He's just mad because I, um, I got in," I say in a muted

tone. Somehow, I know not to throw the confetti around Bridget.

"You got in," she says with the approximation of a smile. "That's great."

It's not great. For her. It's so much easier to leave than to be the one left behind.

And yet, she's still here to support me.

Before I get knocked down and held under by a tidal wave of guilt, I remind myself, whatever the penance, it will be worth it when I'm on the masthead of *Creem* magazine.

"I'm here to deliver the jocks and AV Club, so give me those apple pies." She picks up one of the cartons and heads for the entrance to the gym. "Hey, boys. Cast your vote for Jasmine, then come and get it."

She's swarmed immediately.

The wave still hits.

Just then, Mike shows up and spies the apple pies. "Did you save one for me?"

"Here," I say glumly, handing him one. "The price of democracy."

He rips off the wrapper and takes a bite. "I thought your brother was planning a protest." He notices my frown. "Don't worry. The article won't come out till after the election."

Now I can't look *him* in the eye. And what *is* Patty doing with Ali? I glance over Mike's shoulder to avoid his gaze, and—

Wait . . . is that . . .

It can't be.

It has to be a mirage.

But it isn't.

"Joonam, joonam."

It's Auntie Minah, traipsing across the basketball court toward the gym, carrying two big Tupperware containers. A taxi idles in the faculty lot behind her.

Mike breaks into a big grin. "Is that your aunt?" He gallops toward her. "Hello, ma'am. I'm Mike. Can I help you with that?"

My face is matchstick red. Why does he have to be such a goddamned Boy Scout?

"Yes, please. Thank you, Mike," Auntie says. "I am Jasmine's Amme Minah."

She's wearing a silk paisley scarf and her oversized Jackie-O sunglasses. She gestures to the Tupperware container. "I forget, joonam. I make the zoolbia and bamieh for you to hand out to your friends. So they vote for you."

There is no way I'm handing out zoolbia and bamieh.

"Oh, uh, thank you, Auntie," I say, taking the containers from her.

"Amme, joonam. Speak the Farsi. Please."

I'm dying inside.

"Oh man, my favorite," says Mike.

Auntie removes her scarf and glasses. "You like the zoolbia and bamieh?"

Mike takes the lid off the containers. I stop myself from putting them back on.

"My dad was stationed in Iran for a while and my mom's best friend, Mrs. Khavari, used to make them."

"You are very nice boy, Mike," she says, taking his hand. "Joonam, he is very nice boy."

"He is," I say, and it's true. He is *nice*—who else would help Auntie carry her containers and get excited about zoolbia and bamieh?—but I wish she would leave before someone says something mean about her.

"Here." She gestures to the containers. "Take one."

Mike looks like a kid in a candy store, selecting the best Persian pastry.

"Where is Ali?" Auntie asks, looking around.

I glance around nervously. "He's around here . . . somewhere."

"I was just going to find him," Mike says, bamieh in hand.

She puts her sunglasses back on. "Tell him his amme was here. A taxi is waiting to take me to the immigration office."

Mike cocks his head at me. If this were *his* aunt, he would surely drive her to the immigration office. But then he probably helps his mom with the dishes and wears his I HEART GRANDMA sweatshirt even when she's not around.

"Amme, wait," I call after her. "I'll take you. As soon as voting is over. You can write me a note to get out of school for the rest of the day."

"Thank you, joonam. Thank you." She fishes a ten-dollar bill out of her wallet. "Mike, can you please pay the taxi, tell him I stay here?"

"Yes, ma'am. I will. Nice to meet you." He turns to me and salutes. "See you later, Madame President."

He passes the punks on his way to the taxi. They're pacing back and forth, no doubt wondering, where is Ali? Not making a stink, that's where.

But what did Patty do with him? The olive pit turns into a peach pit.

Before I dwell on what happened to Ali, the dude with a bunch of curls and pink OP shorts and his friends walk up to our table. "All right, we voted for you. Don't we get an apple pie or something?"

Bridget took the last carton. The rest are empty.

"We, we ran out," I stammer.

Auntie springs into action. "That's why I bring the zoolbia and bamieh," she says, beaming and pointing to the Tupperware containers.

Too late to stop her.

She hands one to each of them. "Is like a donut."

They regard the zoolbia and bamieh suspiciously. They're going to spit it out. And Auntie will be crushed. Why did she have to come?

The dude with curls takes a tiny nibble of a little round bamieh then pops the whole thing in his mouth. "Oh man, it is," he says. "Can I have another one?"

"Yes," says Auntie. "I bring enough for everyone."

To my surprise, the zoolbia and bamieh go like gangbusters. She hands them out to a steady stream of seniors, including a bunch of marching band members. I start to relax. A little.

"Ew, what are those?"

Ginny has suddenly appeared, peering into Auntie's Tupperware container.

"Would you like to try? Is delicious," says Auntie.

"Er, no thank you." She grimaces.

She moves toward me, eyes darting around. "I voted for you," she says. "But you know your campaign manager is totally cheating on Bridget. With Patty."

"I . . . I heard that rumor," I squeak. "Are you sure?"

Her head bobs emphatically. "I saw them at the dance. *Someone's* got to tell her," she says, glancing in Bridget's direction.

Yeah. *You* were supposed to.

We watch Bridget surrounded by her admirers, laughing, flirting.

"I'll tell her," I say, coming to the unavoidable conclusion.

Just let me get through this election first.

Ginny stops to give Bridget a hug on her way to class, eyeing me as she does.

Bridget heads back to our table with her empty carton. "Hi, Auntie Minah. What are you doing here?" she asks with a bright smile.

"I help Jasmine to win the president." Auntie puts the lid back on her Tupperware container. "Zoolbia and bamieh are all gone," she says with a triumphant smile.

Bridget sets down the empty carton. "Me, too. I had the jocks eating out of my hand. How much longer?"

I glance at my watch. "Less than a minute to go."

Mike comes back around the corner with a frown on his face. "I can't find him anywhere."

"Who?" Bridget asks. "Kyle? He and Patty are 'getting out the vote.'"

"No, Ali. I heard he was planning a protest. I'm supposed to cover it for the paper." He looks over in the direction of the punks. Mike is smart. He knows something is amiss. He might have asked more questions if the bell hadn't finally rung, and—

Oh my God . . . the bell rang. The bell rang! That means it's over! The election is finally over. We won't find out who wins till Monday, but it's over. Thank God.

Bridget whoops. Auntie throws her arms around me. "I am so proud of you, Jasmine-joon. You are going to win the president and you got into university."

"You got in?" Mike asks with a cocked head.

"I did," I say with a weak smile. "Yesterday. In all the excitement, I didn't get the chance to call you."

He throws his arms around me. "Oh man, that's great."

Why do I feel like I want to cry?

"I called everyone from catechism last night like I promised, so you'll get the Catholic vote," Bridget boasts.

Of course she did.

"Don't worry, you're going to win. Bye, Auntie," she says with a little wave.

Mike squeezes my arm. "Call me when you get back from the immigration office." He shakes his head. "Wonder what happened to your brother."

The peach pit is now the size of an avocado pit.

Everyone scatters while Auntie helps me clean up the mess.

The mess I've made is much bigger than the couple dozen Hostess apple pie wrappers littered across the quad. Bridget will be heartbroken when she learns the truth about Kyle. She and Patty may never speak to each other again.

And I could still lose on Monday.

All I can do now is stuff everything into the overflowing waste can, clamp down the lid, and leave the mess for someone else to clean up.

CHAPTER TWENTY

IMMIGRANT SONG

We're stuck in traffic on the 405 freeway, inching our way down the pass that separates the Valley from the Westside. The four lanes of traffic down below are a cabbage patch of cars rooted in the pavement.

"What if there is a problem with my green card?" Auntie frets.

"Dad will help you sort it out," I say distractedly.

All I can think about are the election results and what to do about Bridget.

"When is your mother coming back?" Auntie Minah asks, lips pursed into the same straight line of disapproval as when Grandma Jean talks about Dad.

There's an accident up ahead, flashing lights.

"She may stay in Kansas. With my grandma."

Auntie huffs, folds her arms.

She's been here a month. She must be ready to go back home, to her job, her routine.

"My birthday's next month, Auntie. I'll be eighteen. Ali and I won't need another adult around anymore. You can go back to San Francisco. Oh, and we have to stop by school after we're done for you to sign me out. Otherwise, they'll mark me as truant." And I don't need a "truant" on my transcript.

She doesn't hear a word I said.

"I am not like your mother and father," she says, staring straight ahead. "I never leave you and Ali all alone."

A wave wells up in my chest. It's true.

Ali. He must be back at school by now.

||||||||||||||

"Look at this," Auntie cries as we inch down Wilshire Blvd. There are hundreds of protesters outside the Federal Building. "Don't talk to anyone," she says. "We go straight to the second floor."

I make my way into the parking lot and lean out the driver's side window to grab a ticket from the attendant. The car behind me honks.

"Why is he honking? Why are you honking?" Auntie yells out the passenger window.

Tensions are running high.

We circle the lot twice and find a cramped space between a Datsun 240Z and a Trans Am. My door barely opens. I in-

hale to climb out. Immediately, Auntie reaches for my hand.
"Stay with me, joonam."

I haven't been around this many Persian people in my life.
There are a bunch of different protesters. One group holds up
signs that say, IRANIANS FOR FREEDOM and WE WANT DE-
MOCRACY. Other signs say, USA STAY AWAY and THE SHAH IS
A WAR CRIMINAL. Some are in Farsi. A group of American
counterprotesters wave signs that say, LET THEM GO and DROP
THE BOMB ON IRAN.

That's not fair. Persians are American, too. If I were covering this for the school paper, I would have to describe them
as mostly *white* American protesters, who just don't understand.

Auntie maneuvers her way through the crowd, never letting go of my hand. My head is down. I simply follow her
feet. Suddenly, she drops my hand. My head snaps up.

"Shahrazad, what are you doing here?"

"Salaam, Minah-joon, Jasmine-joon. Haal-e shoma chetowr-e?" Shahrazad shouts above the din.

"Hi, Jasmine. How are you?" Firuzeh shouts, giving me a
kiss on each cheek.

The house could be on fire, everyone evacuating, and
Persians would still stop to exchange pleasantries.

"Fine, thank you, Shahrazad, Firuzeh. How are you?" I
shout back.

"Are you here to protest?" Firuzeh asks excitedly.

"No. For Auntie's green card. You're *protesting*?"

"Yeah. You really should talk to your brother about everything that's going on," Firuzeh says, leaning in. "He totally opened my eyes."

God. What did Patty do to stop him from making a stink?

"You come back after you are done, Minah-joon." Shahrazad grabs her hand. "We have tea somewhere."

"I'm sorry, Shahrazad. Jasmine has to go back to school. Another time."

We all kiss each other on each cheek again and Auntie and I head inside.

|||||||||||||

The immigration office is all institutional green. The waiting room is filled with Iranians, men with thick, dark hair and women in chadors. You can feel the frayed nerves.

We find two seats together and wait. The minutes tick by.

Maybe Patty dropped him off at the park. Maybe she took him out to breakfast. All I said was to keep him occupied.

"Miss Zumba-day?" a clerk holding a clipboard finally calls out.

Auntie gathers up her purse and rises. I do the same.

"Zumideh. I am Minah Zumideh," she says, extending her hand.

"She your daughter?" The clerk nods to me.

Auntie wraps her arm around my shoulder. "My niece. I take care of her and her brother while her father is gone."

Apparently, Mom does not exist.

The clerk motions for us to follow her down a long hall into a small office. She hands Auntie's case file to an agent and gestures to the two chairs across from the agent's desk.

"This is Agent Rubino."

We sit. The clerk leaves and shuts the door.

Agent Rubino is wearing a frilly white blouse with a little black bow tie. But she's all business. She leafs through Auntie's file.

"President Carter is going to deport me?" Auntie asks, near tears.

I grab her hand.

"What? No. This has nothing to do with Carter. It looks like you left the country."

Her hand is shaking. I squeeze it.

"Yes. For a few months last year. I go back to Iran. My maman was sick. My mother. When she is better, I come back to the United States. I tell this to my attorney."

"Well," Agent Rubino says, finally looking up at her, "you should have gotten a returning resident visa before you came back. You may have jeopardized your permanent resident status."

Auntie gasps.

"What does that mean?" I lean forward. "Would she have to go back to Iran?"

"Possibly. You'll have to call your attorney and figure out why he didn't file form I-131." She tosses the file on her desk as if that's that.

"You can't do that," I say before my brain can stop me.

"Excuse me?"

"Joonam," Auntie says harshly.

"No. You can't do that." I stand up, gesturing wildly toward the window. "Have you seen the news? It's chaos in Iran."

She exhales and clasps her hands in front of her. "I understand, but—"

"Do you? Do you really? Do you understand Iran is in total chaos right now because the *United States* and, and, Britain and Russia before that are always interfering for the oil?"

"That may very well be, but—"

"They propped up corrupt governments. I mean, the CIA helped stage a *coup* in 1953."

Auntie's eyes are two big saucers.

I have no idea where this is all coming from.

Yes, I do.

"There's a reason everyone is protesting right outside your door."

Agent Rubino sits back. "Nice speech, but . . . there's nothing I can do." She turns to Auntie. "If your attorney filed the proper paperwork, it might be a clerical error. You'll need to call him." She flashes us an impatient smile. "Anything else I can help you with?"

"No," I say sharply, rise, and usher Auntie out with my hand on her shoulder. "Don't worry, Dad will help sort everything out," I say as we make our way down the stairs. "Remember, he works in defense. He can pull some strings."

"What if he can't?" Auntie's voice is full of fear.

"He *will*," I promise.

He better.

When we get outside, the crowd has thinned out. We find Shahrazad and Firuzeh on our way back to the car.

"What happened?" Shahrazad asks with the same look of fear that's on Auntie's face.

"Maybe I have to go back to Iran," Auntie says, fanning her eyes so her mascara won't run.

"No, you won't," I say to her. "No, she won't," I say to them. "Her attorney has to file some form, that's all."

"You should have seen Jasmine." Auntie wipes her eye. "She made a speech in there, stood up for Iranian people."

"You *did*?" says Firuzeh, wide-eyed.

"I did."

As soon as we get back to school, I *have* to find Ali.

"We go for tea now," says Shahrazad. "There's a Persian restaurant a few miles away."

"I'd like that," I say. I really would. "But I have to get back to school. Another time?"

Firuzeh smiles at me. "Another time. My treat."

We fly over the 405 on the way back since we're going against traffic. I pull into the faculty lot. There are a few empty spaces and, besides, school is almost over. Auntie dons her sunglasses and scarf and follows me to the administration building.

Out of the corner of my eye, way across the quad, I catch sight of Mohawk Punk and Safety Pin Punk. Without Ali.

Without Ali. It's the end of the day. Where is he?

The avocado pit has grown into an underripe avocado.

I open the double doors. Auntie approaches the front desk. "My aunt didn't sign me out, so she's here to do it now." I keep glancing back through the front window for any sign of Ali.

"Reason for your absence?" the school secretary asks.

"Family emergency."

Auntie signs my excused absence form just as the final bell rings.

When we exit the administration building, I do a sweep of the quad. Ali has US government in the bungalows. Patty will be coming from home ec in the north hall. I'll position myself at the far end of the quad and catch at least one of them as they cross to the parking lot.

"Auntie, stay here." I gesture to the double doors. "I'll be back in a minute."

Just as I head to the far end of the quad, Safety Pin Punk and Mohawk Punk sprint across the field. "There you are, man! Where you been?"

Ali comes staggering around the corner of the gym, yelling, "I was held hostage! I was held hostage!"

Immediately, the avocado sinks to the bottom of my stomach. *Hostage?*

"Ali!" Auntie cries and dashes toward him.

I run after her, eyes darting around frantically for Patty.

She grabs him by the shoulders. "Ali, what happened?"

"I was held hostage! In a closet. The janitor just let me out."

A bunch of students stop to watch. There's a collective moment of shock, then several start laughing.

Ali's eyes flash with indignation. "It's not funny. They threw me in. I've been stuck in there for hours."

"Who?" Mike appears out of nowhere.

"I don't know. Two guys I've never seen before."

Oh no. They must be Patty's cousins. Or her older brothers' friends.

Just then, Patty spills out of the north hall, laughing and talking with her sporty friends. She stops short when she sees Ali and the crowd surrounding him.

"Why?" Mike asks, his brow furrowed with concern.

"I have no idea," Ali yells at him. "Probably has something to do with my protests."

I've got to get to Patty before she bolts. Before I can, Mr. Jackson shows up because any group of students standing around after the bell has to be up to no good. Patty's right; he does have a hard-on for detention.

"What's going on here?" he demands.

"Some dudes I've never seen before threw me in a supply closet in the gym," Ali says, still semi-hysterical.

Now Gerald is charging toward us with the junior G.I. Joes. As if he needs another dirty trick to uncover.

I motion wildly for Patty to come over, but she stands there, motionless.

"Wait, wait," says Mr. Jackson. "You don't give a good goddamn about our hostages, our heroes, over there in I-ran, but you're making a stink about being in a closet for a few *hours*?"

"Some idiots throw him in a supply closet and you blame *him*?" Mike shoots back.

Honestly, I'm thinking the same thing. How could he even begin to blame Ali?

"He didn't seem to think holding people hostage was so bad when he caused a ruckus at the election assembly—"

"He stood up for Iranian people," Auntie cuts in.

"—trashing our government. Just like the communists. Rationed grain and cheese is nothing to celebrate compared to aisle after aisle in our beautiful American grocery stores."

"Why are you talking about cheese when we are talking about Ali?" Auntie demands.

"I'm just saying, maybe he brought this on himself."

Auntie, Mr. Jackson, Ali, and Mike go back and forth, talking over each other, as I curse myself for going along with this stupid scheme even though I never said to throw him in a closet.

"Let's see what Principal Crankovitch has to say about this," Mr. Jackson says to Ali.

Ali points to himself in disbelief. "You're arresting *me*?"

"I think this matter should be brought to the principal's attention." He puts his hand on the small of Ali's back and hustles him toward the administration office.

The punks follow, protesting, "That's not fair, man."

"It's not fair!" cries Auntie, who follows the punks.

"It's *not* fair," I say.

"I'm going after them," Mike says.

Shit. I want to go with Ali, but I have to talk to Patty.

"I'll be right there," I call out and take off toward her.

She walks toward me, arms folded.

I lay into her. "You held him *hostage* in a supply closet?"

"He was gonna make a stink about I-ran again and blow up the election," she says. "I kept him quiet, didn't I? What did you think I was going to do? Take him to Denny's?"

"I thought it was one of the possibilities," I whisper-shout. "If anyone finds out . . ."

"They're not gonna find out," says Patty. "Ali never saw me. We thought he'd get out sooner, someone would hear him."

Why, oh why, did I trade the last shred of my integrity for this? I can't even feign outrage.

"Thanks. For nothing," I say and trek back to the administration office.

"It'll be worth it come Monday. You'll see," she calls after me.

Monday. Think about Monday. The election results. How happy I'll be if Principal Crankovitch announces my name for senior class president because *I got in*. It all *will* have been worth it. It—

"I've got my Deep Throat."

Gerald is right in front of me. His eyes are bright, his smile wolfish. I can see his teeth.

He's bluffing. Patty's sure of it.

"Keep chasing your tail, Gerald. It wasn't me."

"I'm going to Principal Crankovitch once I have all my evidence. If you win, prepare to be impeached." He struts away with his chin jutting out.

"That's not even a thing," I call after him. "You can't impeach a senior class president."

Besides, only me, Patty, and Kyle know about the playbook. There's no way they'd tell Gerald. That would only implicate them. He's totally bluffing.

And anyway, Nixon was never actually impeached. He resigned before they could fire him. If I win, I'll never resign.

And he's bluffing.

By the time I get to the administration office, Mike, Auntie, and the punks are all huddled protectively around Ali.

"We told Principal Crankovitch what happened," Mike says solemnly. "He agreed Ali doesn't deserve detention or suspension."

"Are you okay?" I ask Ali, which is like the Symbionese Liberation Army asking Patty Hearst if she's comfortable.

"Yeah." He shrugs. But his face is etched with anxiety.

"Ali-jon, you come home now." Auntie rests her hand on his shoulder. "I make your favorite: homemade doogh." She turns to the punks. "Delicious yogurt soda with mint."

Their faces twist in horror—but it *is* good. Oddly tangy and minty and bubbly.

"We're going to Naugles, I'm starving," Ali says, still shaken. "I'll be home later."

"Are you sure you're okay?" I ask again.

"*Yeah*," he says defensively because, sadly, it's weird that I keep asking.

Auntie kisses him on each cheek. "I'm so happy you are safe, Ali-jon."

Mike follows me and Auntie outside. His brows are all squinchy, his tone angry. "Who would do that to him?"

"I don't know," I say, in a pitch way higher than my natural voice.

"Ali's friends say could be CIA," says Auntie, with her hand to her chest.

"It's not the CIA," I say.

Mike looks as if he's turning something over in his mind. "Well, call you later," he says with a wave of his hand. Not a kiss, not a presidential salute. Not even a real wave.

More like the hand signal for "stop."

||||||||||||||||

As soon as we get home, I belly flop on my bed and lie there. The election is over. Turnout was good. Patty kept Ali quiet. Dad will be here tomorrow for Thanksgiving. I should be elated, but I'm exhausted.

Did I run a campaign I can be proud of?

No. But this whole campaign has been like an elaborate setup of dominos in the shape of a dragon or an intricate spiral. Once the first domino falls, there's no stopping the others.

Mr. Ramos said I was his first-ever student with a shot at acceptance to NYU. Was I not supposed to take it? Am I not supposed to be on that tour bus with Chrissie Hynde? It's not my fault the only way I could get in was by becoming senior class president.

If I don't win. I don't even want to think about it. Stuck in Bumfuck. A bitter bridesmaid for Bridget, telling everyone at our ten-year reunion, oh, I finally got promoted to assistant copywriter. Or married, like Mom, in Manhattan, Kansas, having given up on my dreams to raise two kids too ungrateful to ever thank me for it.

The truth is, I *have* reinvented myself—as someone who would deny her heritage and backstab her best friend. Which means I *have* to get out of here.

I can't face the person I've become.

CHAPTER TWENTY-ONE

THE UGLY AMERICAN

Dad's flight came in late last night. I have to get to him first, before Ali tells him about the "kidnapping" and makes it sound worse than it was. I pad downstairs to his study.

He's murmuring on the phone when I appear in his doorway. Calling it a study makes it sound so grand. There's a banged-up desk with an office telephone and an IBM Selectric I'm not allowed to use, plus a bookshelf with biographies of Winston Churchill and John F. Kennedy, and several books in Farsi.

"Hi, Dad. Happy Thanksgiving," I say, as soon as he hangs up.

He rises and motions me in for a hug and a kiss on each cheek. "Hi, honey."

I linger at his desk. "How was your flight?"

"Good." He sits. "A delay in Denver. There's always a delay in Denver."

I pick up the decorative khatam box on his shelf and run my finger over the inlaid geometric pattern. "Window or aisle seat?"

"Aisle," he says, swiveling back toward his typewriter.

I put the box down. "The election was yesterday," I say, watching him out of the corner of my eye.

He finger-pecks a few words. "That's good. Did you win?"

"We won't find out till Monday." I pick up a small, decorative copper bowl and turn it over in my hands. "Ali made such a ruckus, some idiot threw him in a supply closet," I say, as nonchalantly as possible. "He's going to make it sound like he had it worse than those poor hostages." I push out a two-syllable laugh—"huh-hah"—to emphasize how silly that would be.

Uh-oh. He stops typing and looks up with concern. "Somebody locked Ali in a *closet*?"

I put down the copper bowl. "No, no. Not the principal or anything. A student. It was, like, a stupid prank."

His brows stay stuck together. Shit. He's picturing Ali in that closet.

Now I'm picturing Ali in that closet. He was probably scared, pounding on the door, trying to get out. What the hell was Patty thinking?

What the hell was *I* thinking?

But it's over now. I can't let Dad turn it into a major deal where he asks the school to launch an investigation.

"He's *fine*," I say. "He even went out with his friends last night."

Dad's face fills with relief. "You sure?"

"Ye-es." I stretch the word out, which makes it sound more definite. "No matter what he says."

He grabs the Wite-Out to blot an errant word or letter. "Okay," he says, blowing on the small, chalky patch. "If you're sure."

"I am," I say, my cue to take the win and go.

|||||||||||||

I sit in bed with the phone next to me, debating whether to call Mike.

He and his dad must be watching the Cotton Bowl or the Punch Bowl, or whatever, on their big console TV in their nice, cozy house with a brick fireplace, their golden retriever Rusty—or, no, Sarge—at their feet while his little sister helps Mom in the kitchen. An all-American Norman Rockwell painting come to life.

Meanwhile, we're all in our separate rooms while Auntie makes Cornish hens and fesenjoon with pomegranate relish. We're not from different cultures, we're from different *planets*.

And I like him. I really like him. I pick up the phone to dial, when—

What the hell?

Mike is already on the line.

Talking to *Ali*.

"Then what happened?" he asks.

Shit, shit, shit. I cover the receiver with my hand so they won't hear me hyperventilating.

"After I pounded on the door for what felt like hours, I sat on the floor with *no* idea when anyone would rescue me," Ali says.

I *knew* he would make it sound like he'd had it worse than the hostages.

"Anything else you remember about the guys who threw you in?" Mike asks.

I can just picture him with his pen and notebook. Honestly, he's *worse* than Woodward and Bernstein.

"Mmm . . . no. I told you everything I know," says Ali.

Oh no. How much does he know?

"I'm telling you, it's because I'm speaking out, trying to tell people the truth about Iran."

Ali is actually grandiose enough to believe some shadowy government force abducted him instead of Patty and her goon squad.

"All right, man," says Mike. "Call me if you remember anything else."

Finally, they're wrapping up.

"Hey, is Jasmine around?"

Shit. SHIT. If I hang up now, they'll know I was on the line. Eavesdropping.

"Let me get her. Jasmine," Ali calls up to me.

I freeze. Resist the urge to answer, even to exhale.

"Jasmine," he calls again.

I remain perfectly still, holding my breath.

"I guess she's not here. But I'll tell her you called."

"Thanks," Mike says. "And Happy Thanksgiving."

Oh my God, hang up already.

"You, too, man. I'll call you if I think of anything."

"Right on."

I'm about to asphyxiate.

"Bye."

"Bye."

They hang up. Five seconds longer and I would be lying, dead, on the floor.

I sit back on my bed. Ali is pointing Mike in the wrong direction. If an article comes out, it won't have anything to do with me.

This is an unexpected turn of events for which I am very thankful.

||||||||||||

The table is all set. The Cornish hens and fesenjoon, the saffron rice and pomegranate relish are all laid out, along with sabzi: mint leaves, raw onion, and radishes with flat bread. It's beautiful.

Auntie frowns when I set down my canned cranberry sauce that has retained its perfect cylindrical shape, ridges and all. There's nothing more Thanksgiving than the *thwack* canned cranberry sauce makes when it plops out of the can. But it's definitely the ugly American at this table.

Dad thanks Auntie profusely in Farsi and sits down. Ali follows. All that's missing are Mom and Grandma Jean from the two conspicuously empty chairs.

Last Thanksgiving was when Mom and Dad got into a huge fight right before dinner. Eventually, Mom came to the table and sat in wounded silence; Dad's was more grudging.

"I know it's not traditional, like your grandmother's," Auntie says, "but I hope you like it."

By "traditional" she means boring, conventional, may as well be McDonald's.

"Fesenjoon, yes," Ali says. "Kheili mamnoon, Amme Minah."

"Thank you, Amme," I say, then quickly add, "Kheili mamnoon."

We dig in. The Cornish hen is delicious, more tender than turkey. Pairs perfectly with the canned cranberry. Maybe we'll finally have a peaceful Thanksgiving like the Pilgrims and Native Americans intended. Although, how the Native Americans were supposed to be at peace with people who gave them smallpox-infested blankets is beyond me.

Then Dad turns to Ali and says, "So, why were you thrown in that closet again?"

Or not.

"I told you. For trying to educate people about Iran," Ali says, rolling a slice of onion up in a basil leaf.

"Oh right, like defending the Iranian students is some big public service," I say, and grab a piece of charred flatbread from the basket.

"It is. Everybody's ignorant, Dad. You should hear this joker Gerald. He wants Carter to drop the *bomb* on Iran." He nods toward me. "And she's okay with it."

"No, I'm not," I say, struggling to carve the Cornish hen, which is trickier than it looks. "But who cares what Gerald says?"

Honestly, Ali can blab about Iran all he wants now that the election is over.

Dad takes a big sip of wine and blots his mouth with Mom's cloth napkin, which is really meant for display only. "Your sister said it had nothing to do with Iran. That it was a prank."

Ali looks at me and rears his head back. "How do you know?"

Oh no. I have to convince them I don't. Know. "I don't *know*, you know, I was just saying, it's *probably* a prank."

"This reporter's looking into it," Ali assures Dad, as if Mike's article came from the assignment desk at *The New York Times*.

Right then, the doorbell rings.

"I'll get it," I say, jumping up.

I better be more careful. Even my speculation could give me away.

It's Karen. Again. Mom's friend Karen, standing there on

the porch, holding what looks like a store-bought pumpkin pie.

"What are you doing here? I mean, my mom's still in Kansas with Grandma Jean."

She peers in with that hungry smile. "I know. I brought a pie for you kids and your dad."

Holy shit. She *is* "who knows who," the reason Mom and Dad are semi-divorced. And she's one of Mom's best friends. How could she? And to show up here—on *Thanksgiving*, when we're all supposed to be together as a family.

No way I'm letting her in.

I snatch the pie right out of her hands. "Thank you," I say with excessive politeness. "We're right in the middle of dinner, but I'm sure we'll enjoy it for dessert."

With that, I shut the door in her face. We're not eating her stupid pumpkin pie when Auntie made saffron pudding with rosewater, topped with caramelized pistachios and raisins.

"Who was that?" Dad calls from the dining room.

"No one," I say, crossing through the living room to the kitchen, where I stuff Karen's pumpkin pie underneath all the food scraps and several days' worth of trash.

"My stomach hurts," I say when I reappear in the dining room. "I'm going to lie down for a minute. I'll be back to help you with the dishes, Amme."

I run upstairs. Now that I *know* it's her, am I supposed to tell Mom? *You know how you're always asking about Karen,*

Mom? Well, she was here, but she wasn't looking for you. Why do I have to be the one to break Mom's heart?

I shove the memory of Karen and Dad out of my mind, but it's immediately replaced by an image of Bridget, mascara running down her cheeks like Mom's once she finds out about Kyle and Patty. Why do I have to be the one to break Bridget's heart?

When I go back downstairs to help, Auntie's fishing Karen's pumpkin pie out of the trash. She holds it up in her bright, orange-gloved hand. "Joonam, did you put this in here?"

"Uh, yeah. I did," I say. "I got it at the store, but it's spoiled. So I threw it away."

"Oh, okay," Auntie says and stuffs it back in.

||||||||||||||

It's kind of bittersweet to be missing the big day-after-Thanksgiving sales at the mall today. We were always mobbed. I miss dipping dogs and hand-stomping lemonade. I shouldn't have quit. I need money for food and gas. I'm one step away from applying to Pup 'N' Taco, and orange is my *worst* color.

Honestly, as shift leader, Donna *was* the boss of me. I *really* didn't think that through.

I can't concentrate on my senior project for journalism. Partly because I keep thinking about Karen and Bridget and partly because Ali's music is so loud.

These days, instead of lying on the floor listening to

Emerson, Lake & Palmer or Jethro Tull, he paces back and forth listening to the Sex Pistols and the Ramones. Who knows what he's plotting? Maybe Gerald is right about student radicals.

On Monday, I find out my fate: I'll either be Jasmine Katie, on my way to interviewing Chrissie Hynde. Or I'll have missed the bus altogether.

Turnout was good—I think. Kyle will have the results based on exit-polling already.

Gerald can't be serious about having found his Deep Throat . . . can he? He can't. He's just trying to psych me out.

It's working. What if Mike does figure out it was Patty who "kidnapped" Ali at my request?

I need a distraction. I'll spend the rest of the day cleaning my room. I haven't vacuumed in a month. There are two fossilized Skittles under my bed. I'm tempted to sift through my acceptance packet again, but I can't. Not until my victory is assured.

The phone rings. I make a mad dash for the hallway. Maybe it's Mike.

It's Bridget.

"Hey, hi, hi . . . you," I stammer. "How was your Thanksgiving?"

"Fine. Granny made sweet potato casserole and green bean casserole—which is gross, but you know how she puts crushed Ruffles on top—and cherry and pecan pie. How was yours?"

I pull the phone into my room. "Oh, fine. My aunt made Persian food."

I can't even tell her about Karen without being overcome with guilt about Patty.

"Are you going to Amy Freeman's keg party tomorrow night? You, me, Mike, and Kyle can double-date."

I shift the phone from one ear to the other to stall for a half second. "I . . . I thought you weren't coming home till Sunday."

"My brother has a football game Sunday, so Mom wanted us home Saturday afternoon."

I should tell her. I should just tell her. What could Patty do, sue me?

I glance at my acceptance packet. Patty could still ratfuck me, that's what. Tell Principal Crankovitch I was the mastermind behind the "break-in."

"I have so much homework to catch up on now that the election is over," I say.

"Come on, party pooper," she mock moans.

"No. I really, really do," I say, sharper than intended.

"Okay, okay," she says, slightly wounded. "If you change your mind, call me."

I hang up and sit on the edge of my bed staring ahead. All I want to do now is crawl under the covers and wake up to the happy realization this entire month was a bad dream.

After what may be minutes or hours, Mom calls to ask if Ali and I would come out to Kansas for Christmas vacation. "It'll be a white Christmas," she says, her best sales pitch.

There's no use arguing. We have to go. Grandma Jean will make homemade fudge and caramels and ginger snaps with lemon icing and still remind me about watching my weight.

Right as we're about to hang up, she asks, "Has Karen been around?" Her voice is pinched, as if she's not sure she wants to know the answer.

I should have done a better job preparing for this question. "She's not your friend, Mom," I say, before I can stop myself.

There's a long silence, during which I hold my breath. I mean, I could be wrong about Karen and Dad. The evidence is all circumstantial.

But in this really tiny voice she says, "I know."

||||||||||||

Dad left this morning before Ali and I woke up. I didn't want a big goodbye. I wouldn't have known what to say other than, how could you?

Auntie is in the kitchen making aash-e reshteh, this bean-and-noodle soup, for lunch, and Ali is hanging out with his punk friends. No way am I going to Amy Freeman's keg party. I *have* to finish my punk chicks senior project.

It's so hard to concentrate. Instead of working on my project, I take a nap and watch a VHS of *American Graffiti,* which is super depressing. The lives of teenagers were so carefree in the olden days.

Since it's just me and Auntie for dinner, we order Chinese. Auntie notices the deep furrow across my forehead as I spread plum sauce across my moo shu pancake.

"You are worried about your mother and father, joonam. Their divorce?"

"Um, yeah."

If only it were that simple.

If only Patty's brother hadn't stolen that stupid playbook, I wouldn't have started the rumor about him, and Gerald wouldn't have anything to hold over my head. That playbook is the original sin. And I bet I could have won without it.

We finish our dinner, and I clean up while Auntie makes tea. My fortune cookie reads: *All things are difficult before they are easy.* Which is true. There are so many things I would do differently if I had the chance to do them again.

We settle in to watch a rerun of *The Rockford Files.* This rich guy whose parents are murdered hires Rockford to find the killer. The police think he's the prime suspect, only they have no evidence, therefore they can't arrest him. He offers Rockford twenty thousand dollars to find the real killers, who turn out to be shadowy bad guys.

"Mr. Rockford, he always solves the mystery," Auntie says admiringly.

He does. Which takes the mystery out of it. But just as she's about to turn it to *The Love Boat,* something clicks.

"Wait," I say, which I didn't mean to say out loud.

"What?"

"Nothing."

No evidence.

Oh my God.

No evidence!

If Gerald's stolen playbook is evidence of the crime, all I have to do is get Patty's brother to break into his locker again and put it back. It'll be like it never happened! And if I win on Monday, I won't have to admit I lied on my application. Plus, Gerald can't threaten me with impeachment anymore.

Oh my God.

All things are difficult before they are easy.

It's so simple. I have to get to that keg party and tell Patty.

CHAPTER TWENTY-TWO

KEG PARTY BUST

There are already, like, a billion people at this party. I had to park four blocks away. Amy's house is a one-story ranch on a big corner lot, painted this weird shade of green, like a Shamrock Shake. An old Big Wheel with streamers flowing out of the handlebars is parked on the porch.

I'm going to find Patty, make sure her brother puts Gerald's playbook back first thing Monday morning, then leave.

A bunch of head bangers spill out of the garage and onto the front yard, beer sloshing out of their red, plastic cups, while the cover band plays "Sweet Leaf" because it's, like, constitutionally required. I get a contact high walking around the side yard, where a group of stoners are passing around a bong.

When I finally get to the backyard, Kyle and Bridget are totally making out in a lounge chair by the barbeque. I do *not* want to talk to them right now. All I want is for Patty's brother to put the playbook back. I stand off to the side looking for her.

Ginny is standing by the keg with a group of junior girls when Mike comes through the back gate. Which is weird. I didn't tell him I was coming to the party, and he didn't tell me.

I better pretend I'm here for no other reason than to party.

I dodge and weave around a throng of partygoers to get to him. "Hey," I say, so laid-back I could fall over. "I didn't know you were going to be here."

"Uh, yeah. I didn't know you were going to be here, either." He shifts from side to side. "I, um, I'm here to talk to Ali. And the punks. For my article."

The rug is pulled out from under my stomach.

"They said they saw two guys with Patty in the parking lot they had never seen before. One of them was wearing a KEEP ON TRUCKIN' T-shirt."

My face turns as red hot as the surface of the sun.

Mike continues, "Ali said one of the guys who kidnapped him was wearing a KEEP ON TRUCKIN' T-shirt."

He cannot have cracked the case this fast. Keep a poker face. Keep a poker face.

I contrive a merry laugh. "Mike. He wasn't *kidnapped*. Some jerks threw him in a supply closet. You know Ali's going to turn himself into a big martyr for his followers."

"You didn't know anything about it?" He has this pained look on his face, as if it hurts him even to ask.

A million different possibilities run through my mind while the band murders "Purple Haze."

I could lie and Mike may never find out the truth.

I could lie and Mike might find out the truth, but only after we had broken up. After prom.

I could lie and, if he did find out the truth, still deny I had anything to do with it.

But I am growing weary of lying.

"Mike, I didn't actually *kidnap* him. It was Patty, she . . ." I don't bother to finish.

The look on his face. He's not mad, but he *is* disappointed.

I cross my arms. "You don't know what it's like right now. To be Iranian."

For a split second, he smiles. But it's one of those I-can't-fucking-believe-you-just-said-that imposters.

"Don't know what it's like? Are you kidding? You know my parents were turned down for membership at the Chevy Chase Country Club because of my mom? Have you ever heard of this thing called World War II?"

"Oh my God, yes. Of course. I'm sorry. That's not what I meant. I . . ."

I can't find the words. I'm picturing him writing an exposé of all the dirty tricks I've pulled during this campaign. I'll be suspended, expelled. Arrested, even. My admission will be revoked for sure. Mr. Ramos would lose all faith in me.

I have no choice.

I swallow hard. "Look. My dream is to go to NYU, just

like your dream is to go to the Air Force Academy. I had to win this election to make that happen."

His eyes narrow, like he knows what's coming.

"Just like you need those four credits to graduate." There's no other way out, but that doesn't stop my stomach from turning.

His face turns white.

"I won't say anything if you won't."

Mike's jaw tightens. He's trapped.

Before he can say anything—if he were going to say anything—Bridget drags Kyle over. "Hey! You came," she says. She's had a few beers. She giggles at Mike. "We should totally double-date."

Mike doesn't answer.

And just when it's like, okay, the only guy in the whole world who likes me *and* zoolbia and bamieh will never, *ever* talk to me again—but at least I've averted *total* disaster—Patty comes stumbling over with her gaggle of sporty girls.

"Hey, Jasmine. Mike. Bridget. *Kyle.*"

Which elicits a gale of drunken giggles from the gaggle.

Patty gestures wildly toward Bridget with her cup. "You guys remember Bridget. She's a total Catholic girl goody-goody."

Bridget pulls away from Kyle. "What did you call me?"

Kyle casts Patty a pleading look and pulls Bridget back. "Babe. Come on. She's wasted."

Patty glares at him and snarls at Bridget. "I *said* you're a Catholic girl goody-goody."

Bridget takes another step toward her. "So what if I am?"

They've never fought like this before. Just that one time, during a particularly heated game of Operation, when Bridget got frustrated because she couldn't remove the pencil, and the buzzer kept buzzing, and Patty kept laughing, and Bridget ended up upending the board, which is really unlike Bridget, but just goes to show, she does have her breaking point.

I should get between them. But Patty can throw a punch, and Bridget slaps like nobody's business.

Kyle grabs Bridget's arm to hold her back.

She jerks it away. "Doesn't mean I take shit from sluts like you," Bridget says, and pushes Patty.

This random dude with an Afro says, "All right, chick fight."

Patty pushes back, only she doesn't realize she's still holding her beer cup. It spills all over Bridget's T-shirt. Her *white* T-shirt.

Whereupon Random Afro Dude says, "All right! Wet T-shirt."

Bridget shrieks and pushes Patty again, and Patty *hurls* all over her.

In his running color commentary, Random Afro Dude says, "Oh, man, she blew chunks."

Bridget is squealing, "It's all over me, it's all over me!"

Mike and I stand there in shock while Kyle throws Patty a death stare and hustles Bridget off to the bathroom. Patty watches them go. Her mouth trembles, she's fighting back tears.

The sporty girls pull her away, leaving me and Mike behind in all the confusion. After a long, awkward pause, I force a laugh. "Wow. Patty was so wasted."

He studies me for what feels like forever. Finally, he says, "I thought you were different," turns around, and walks away.

I call after him. "I am! I am. Different."

It's only after he disappears out the back gate the utter irony hits me.

What have I done? It's like I dropped an atomic bomb in the middle of everyone, and the fallout is radiating everywhere: on Patty and Bridget and Kyle and me and Mike. And Gerald.

I fight my way into the house and down a narrow hallway to where Kyle is standing in front of the bathroom door. I give him the same death stare he gave Patty and knock. Bridget opens the door a crack. I enter quickly, close the door, and lock it.

She's at the sink blow-drying her T-shirt. "Oh my God. What is Patty's problem?"

I collapse on the toilet seat. "I . . . she's upset about . . . something." I can't think straight. I've poisoned everything.

She turns off the blow dryer. "Well, forget her. We both know she talks shit about everyone anyway." She brightens.

"What'd Mike say? Should we all go to Bob's Big Boy for a combo?"

Tears stream down my face. "No, no. I don't think so."

Someone pounds on the door. A line must be forming outside.

She turns to look at me. "Why not? What happened?"

I grab several sheets of toilet paper and dab my eyes. "He doesn't like me anymore."

"How do you know?"

"I just do," I say, trying to stifle a sob.

She turns back to the mirror. "Well, forget him. You need to find a good guy. Like Kyle."

I can't help it. "Bridget, Kyle's not a good guy."

There is a moment of stunned silence. Hers and mine. I stand up. Our eyes lock in the mirror.

I hurry out of the bathroom.

The minute I open the door, I tear into Kyle. "I'm sick of this! You have to tell Bridget about you and Patty."

He draws a quick breath, as if he's been punched in the gut.

"What about Patty?" Bridget says.

She is *right* behind me.

I close my eyes. I didn't intend for her to hear me. Not now, not here. Without turning around, I run down the hall and nearly have a head-on collision with a hardcore punker dude. His head is shaved into a Mohawk, he has on an earring and studded leather bracelets and—

"Ali?"

"You did it! It was you," he says, stabbing a finger right at me. "Those dudes who kidnapped me, they did it for you."

There's no point trying to defend myself.

Safety Pin Punk gets right in my face. "I voted for you, man. For the free Coke Fridays. And now you've gone and made a *mockery* of democracy."

Everything is crashing down around me. I push past them. Once I make it to the front door, I make a beeline for my car.

I barely get across the front lawn when Malia walks up the driveway. Before I can even attempt to get her on my side, she says, "I *knew* we should have said something to Bridget."

Then she adds the kicker.

"Ginny is right. You *are* totally two-faced."

I am. The truth is, I liked being the only thing Bridget and Patty had in common. If only I had encouraged them to be better friends on their own, we might not be in this catastrophe.

It's harder than you would think to run and cry, but I manage to dodge the out-of-control Big Wheel and run the whole four blocks to my car, sobbing the entire time.

CHAPTER TWENTY-THREE

HEY JUDAS

In my dream last night, I was on a flight to New York. The entire wing of our plane broke off and everyone was screaming, and people were being sucked out.

The worst part was waking up to all the wreckage I've created.

I drag myself downstairs past ten, eyes all puffy and red from crying. Ali is already home, in the kitchen frying an egg. Honestly, I prefer his puffy hair.

"I just thought of a new Beatles song," he says. "'Hey Judas.'"

I trudge over to the kitchen cabinet, pull out the Cap'n Crunch and a bowl, and stand over the sink to eat it like a human sandbag: heavy, weighted down.

"Don't you care about assholes like Gerald and his anti-Iranian bullshit?" Ali asks, flipping his egg.

I can barely lift my arm to my mouth. "Yes, Ali. But I had to win this election to get into NYU."

Which is the whole problem, because the ends *don't* justify the means.

"When they start rounding us up and putting us in camps, your acceptance will be real comforting."

How selfish I've been.

He slides his egg out of the frying pan and onto his toast. "Dad will be home Tuesday."

I pause mid-crunch. "Why?"

He shrugs. "They have to do some kind of background check on him, like he's an enemy of the state or something." He dumps his frying pan into the sink and brushes past me.

I go back upstairs and sit on my bed. My dolls have all turned their backs on me. They wouldn't even want to go to NYU with me now. I can't look at my acceptance packet. All I can do is think about what I'm going to say to Bridget. Dammit. I should have told her sooner.

I *still* don't know what to say. But I have no choice. The walk across the street is the longest of my life.

Bridget's mom lets me in. Elsie follows me upstairs and scratches excitedly while I stand outside Bridget's bedroom door contemplating whether to turn and run. Elsie whines and scratches so hard, I knock lightly before Bridget opens the door and sees me standing there like an idiot.

"Who is it?" she says in a small, wounded voice.

I open the door a crack and peer in. Elsie bounds past

me and jumps on her bed. Bridget is lying on top of her bedspread in the fetal position, in the same clothes she was wearing last night.

"Can I come in?" My voice catches.

Bridget turns and looks at me. Shrugs. Turns her head away.

I inch my way in and slowly lower myself onto the edge of her bed. Elsie starts thumping her tail. Now that I'm here, I wish I had rehearsed what I was going to say. What comes tumbling out is, "I wanted to tell you. I *told* him to tell you."

Absolutely no reaction. Elsie licks her face.

A lump in your throat is a real thing. It feels like a golf ball. I manage to croak, "Bridget, I'm so sorry I didn't tell you."

She won't look at me. Honestly, I should leave it at that, but the urge to defend myself takes over. Barely audibly, I say, "You always wanted to be with him. This was our senior year. You bailed on us."

She turns to face me. Her cheeks are splotchy, her eyes are redder and puffier than mine. Her face twists and her voice squeaks when she says, "I bailed on *you*? You've been talking about leaving for *two whole years*, since the start of junior year."

Oh my God. She's right. I never stopped to think about how babbling on and on about NYU would make Bridget feel.

She puts her head back in her pillow. "It's like you can't wait to get away from me."

"Can't wait to get away from *you*? Bridget, I can't wait to get away from *me*."

She looks up at me, completely confused.

"NYU was my opportunity to create a whole new me. I'm so sick of the old one."

I feel silly even saying it.

Elsie rests her head next to Bridget's.

"I wish you had told me," she says, voice cracking. "About Kyle. If you had told me, I wouldn't have . . ." Her tone is muffled. She's sobbing, her face buried in her pillow.

"Wouldn't have . . . ?"

My stomach drops from the fifth floor to the first. If I had been a true friend, one whose integrity was unimpeachable, Bridget would not have lost her virginity to a slithering snake of a boyfriend destined to betray her. Instead, she was stranded, alone, on this four-poster bed whose frothy pink netting could not protect her from the dragons I should have stayed to slay.

"Bridget," I squeak, tears running down my face. "I'm so, so sorry. Can you ever forgive me? Please?"

She looks at me with something worse than a death stare—total indifference. "What's the point? You're leaving anyway." Then turns back around and lays her head down.

I sit there for another minute, unsure what to do. Finally, I stand up and slowly inch my way toward the door, close it as quietly as possible, then tumble down the stairs and out the front door without even saying goodbye to Bridget's mom because I can't stop the gusher that's coming.

I have to get out of here. *Now.* As far away as possible. Maybe I'll finish out the year in Manhattan, Kansas. I can't face anyone here.

||||||||||||||

When I get home, Auntie and Ali are standing in front of the television, transfixed. This time, a bunch of *Americans* are burning the *Iranian* flag.

"Pfft. 'Patriotic' Americans are burning the flag," says Ali. He yells at the TV. "Like we care, assholes. It's a *symbol.*"

Dad was so wrong. The hostage crisis is not going to be over anytime soon.

Creases of worry have settled into Auntie's face. Her eyes well up. "They are mad with Iranian people," she says. "But they don't know us. Now, they'll never know us."

She's right. We can feel it. Nothing will ever be the same between our two countries. We stand there, helpless, a sense of quiet doom enveloping the room until the dogs next door— the neighbor's yappy terriers—start barking.

"Be quiet!" Ali shouts.

"I can't watch anymore," Auntie says, and heads for the kitchen. I follow her, unsure what to do while she frantically forages around the pantry. "We have no saffron or black tea or chickpea flour or dried limes."

This doesn't sound like a crisis, but she's acting like it is. The dogs don't help. They keep yipping and yapping.

"Joonam, please. Take me to Persian market. We need the saffron. And eggplant. I need to make the baademjoon. Now."

The last thing I want after my big blowout with Bridget is to drive forty minutes to the nearest Persian market to buy ingredients for eggplant stew, but I grab my keys and yell at the dogs on our way out.

The minute we step outside, it becomes clear why the dogs are barking: our house has been egged and papered. Someone has graffitied BOMB IRAN on our side wall.

Auntie puts her hand to her mouth. "Oh God, joonam. Who do this?"

We've never been egged before.

"Stupid kids who don't know any better," I say, and shout at Ali to come outside.

Auntie stares at the graffiti.

"They want to bomb Iran."

Auntie gasps. I shouldn't have said that.

Ali comes to the front door and steps outside. "What the *hell*?"

"See what your stupid demonstrations did," I nearly spit.

He walks out on the front lawn, surveying the damage. "You're blaming this on *me*?"

"If you hadn't constantly been in everyone's face about Iran."

He turns to me and laughs. "You know what I just realized? You're worse than a poser. You're a *coward*. You can't even stand up to a couple of stupid students, but you think you're going to make some great journalist?" He begins picking up the rolls of toilet paper scattered across the lawn.

His words feel like a slap across the face. And I should know. Lisa Robbins slapped me in third grade when I told her Santa Claus wasn't real. (Mom had just told me, and it seemed like a big scoop.) But he's right. I *am* a coward. I haven't been able to stand up for Iran. Or Bridget.

After the sting subsides, without saying anything, I join him on the lawn pulling down the toilet paper. "Should we call the police?"

"Think they'll care?" He starts for the garage to get the rake and a bucket to clean off the egg. "Don't tell Dad. I'll clean it up."

"I'll help," I say.

Overwhelmed, Auntie heads back inside.

⁞⁞⁞⁞⁞⁞⁞⁞⁞⁞⁞⁞

It took us forever to get all the toilet paper down from the olive tree and for Ali to wash the egg off the garage door. He says the punks will help him repaint the side wall before Dad gets home.

I've been sitting on my bed for hours trying to figure out what to do next.

The first thing is, I've got to stop blaming everyone else.

I mean, I could have made them put Gerald's playbook back and never started the whisper campaign about his dad. I should have told Bridget about Patty and Kyle.

And honestly, the original sin was lying on my application. If I hadn't, I would never have started the whisper campaign about Gerald, betrayed Bridget, or had my own brother kidnapped.

All I wanted was to go to NYU. To interview Chrissie Hynde in the back of her tour bus. Become a great rock journalist and make Mr. Ramos proud. Between the dirty tricks and the cover-ups and the betrayal, I keep saying this is not me, I'm not like this. But I am. This is the person I've become in order to be the person I wanted to be.

The question is, how do I get the old me back?

CHAPTER TWENTY-FOUR

THE RESULTS ARE IN

Mr. Ramos was right. My appreciation of the Beatles has deepened with age.

Last night, I put on *Yesterday and Today* after *Young Americans* and kept listening to "Yesterday" over and over. It was so depressing, I went downstairs and ate an entire can of Pillsbury Supreme Chocolate Frosting. But I'm not worrying about my weight ever again because, even if he never speaks to me, Mike liked me just the way I am. And honestly, I like myself the way I am. Persian women are not meant to be stick thin.

There was something about the lyrics—the shadows hanging over me, the longing for yesterday—that told me exactly what I need to do today.

First, I make an apology mix tape for Bridget including "Suzie Q" by Creedence Clearwater Revival, the first forty-five record I ever bought her; "Joy to the World" by Three Dog Night, playing on a loop at the mall when our parents finally let us go by ourselves; "Crocodile Rock," by Elton John, commemorating our first dance in sixth grade; and "Saturday Night" by the Bay City Rollers because Bridget is a girl who loves the Bay City Rollers, and I have to respect that. I conclude with "Alison" by Elvis Costello—from now on, my aim *is* true.

Next, I drive through McDonald's to get Ali an Egg McMuffin as a peace offering before school. "Don't worry, it's not laced with arsenic or anything," I say as I hand it to him.

He raises an eyebrow. "Prove it."

I take a bite and hand it back.

"Thanks?" he says with a question mark at the end.

On my way to school, I stop at the store and buy a single white rose in a glass vase. If everything goes according to plan, Bridget will accept it and the mix tape, along with my apology.

When I get to school, I go straight to Bridget's locker and put her white rose and mix tape in the center. As soon as I close her locker door, Kyle is standing right there. I've never seen him like this: the confidence drained out of him like a day-old party balloon.

"I really loved her, you know." His skin is pale, with dark, crescent moons under his eyes. "Now I've lost her. She won't talk to me. Do you know what that's like?"

I look at him long and hard. Finally, I say, "Yeah. I do," and continue down the hall to the auditorium for the special assembly to announce the winners of the student council elections.

I hide out backstage while the hall fills up, peering at the audience. Bridget is sitting with Malia. If Malia is finally going to choose sides, I'm glad she's choosing Bridget's.

Mike sits next to Ellory. Mr. Ramos sits in front of them. Patty is with her sporty friends. She keeps sneaking glances in Bridget's direction, but Bridget won't look at her. Mr. Jackson stands guard over Ali and the punks.

Once all the candidates take their seats onstage, I slip into mine. Gerald sits next to me with his arms folded. He won't even look at me.

There's a plan A and a plan B. I know exactly what I'm going to say. I've thought this all the way through. Still, as Principal Crankovitch reads the names of the freshman and sophomore officers, my hands start to sweat. Pits, too.

With the announcement of each class's winners, my breath gets shallower and shallower. *Breathe.* Slowly and steadily. Hiccups will not hijack me today.

Almost there. Jena McCoy is senior class secretary. Jessica Taylor is treasurer. Kitty Gardner is vice president.

Principal Crankovitch returns to the podium after her thank-you speech. "Congratulations, Kitty. Remember, in the event the president cannot fulfill his or her duties, the vice president takes over. Don't think it can't happen. Just ask Chester Arthur or Lyndon Johnson."

Gerald leans over and whispers, "Like if a president is *impeached*," which only makes my conviction stronger.

Principal Crankovitch continues. "And now, for senior class president. The senior class president for the final semester of the 1979–1980 school year is . . ."

I look out at the audience. Bridget isn't smiling, but she's not frowning, either. Mike also has a stone face. It's not like I deserve anything more.

"Jasmine Zoom-bye-ya."

Plan A.

I close my eyes. When I open them, I'm powered by a burst of adrenaline, a sprinter taking off from the starting blocks. I shake Principal Crankovitch's hand and step up to the mic.

"Thank you, Principal Crankovitch, and everyone who voted for me."

I pause. I could leave it at that. Gerald is threatening impeachment, but who knows whether he could prove anything. I could go off to NYU and never look back.

I keep thinking about those lyrics, about yesterday, when all my troubles seemed so far away. When I was the old me.

"I have something I want to say. But first, I need to tell you that I'm . . ."

I look out at the audience, which could turn into an angry mob at any minute.

I lean into the mic. "I'm *Iranian*."

There's a collective gasp.

"There. I said it. Yeah, it's not I-ran, like 'I ran for office and totally compromised myself to win,' but *Ee-ron.* Ee-ron-ian. And it's pronounced Zoom-ee-day. Jasmine Zumideh," I say. And not just with the voice inside my head.

A couple of students start booing. I raise my hand to quiet them.

"No, listen. Please. When this whole hostage thing happened, it was really embarrassing to be Iranian. I felt like I had to hide my identity." I look right at Ali. "But my brother is right. The time to stand up is when everyone is putting you down. This is my brother, Ali, everyone."

Being the ham that he is, he stands up. The punks wolf whistle and drown out another chorus of boos. But Mike's stone face is softening. And Mr. Ramos is nodding supportively.

"It was me who stole Gerald's playbook and started those rumors. That's all they were. Rumors."

People are buzzing now instead of booing.

I turn to Gerald. "Gerald, I am so sorry."

His eyes are still narrow with suspicion.

"It was also me who made sure my brother wouldn't make a stink on Election Day."

Patty's mouth is open, probably expecting me to narc on her.

"And . . ." I lock eyes with Bridget. ". . . betrayed my best friend. Then tried to cover it all up."

It's dead quiet.

"I did all those things because I thought they would help me win. I didn't think about what I would lose in the process. So, effective immediately, I'm officially declining the office of senior class president. I'll still fight for freedom of speech and dress—and stand up for Iranian people—but Gerald Thomas is your new senior class president, everyone."

I motion a stunned Gerald to the podium.

A stoner stands up and shouts, "There go our free Coke Fridays." The dude with pink OP shorts chimes in, "And our Taco Bell Tuesdays."

A completely bewildered Gerald stands at the podium next to me. Luckily, he's speechless, because I have one more thing to say.

"Lastly, someone vandalized our house yesterday. I don't know who, I'm not trying to get anyone in trouble, but I want to start a club. An Iranian American Club, or maybe, like, an International Culture Club where we all try to understand one another better. I invite you, Gerald, as someone who has a complete misunderstanding of Iran and Iranians, to be our first member."

He must be in shock. He nods.

I close with a heartfelt thank-you and take my seat to what sounds like resounding applause but is probably just Mike and Mr. Ramos.

If I hadn't won (plan B), I would have commandeered the microphone like Ali and made my apologies anyway.

I exhale for the first time in what feels like weeks. Hopefully, by tomorrow this will all be yesterday's news.

||||||||||||||

I make a beeline for Bridget after assembly. Malia hovers protectively by her side. Her face is still unreadable.

"Gosh, I'm so glad that's over," I say.

She is silent.

Just as I begin to grow uneasy, she asks, "What about NYU?"

The question creates an opening, even if her tone is flat and emotionless.

"Looks like we'll be going to Cal State together." I swallow nervously. This may be too much too soon. But the very slightest crinkle of her eyes lets me know it will take time, but I may be able to recover what's been lost.

Malia is not as forgiving. She takes her hand. "Come on." They head off to the bathroom.

When I turn around, Mike is standing there, grinning. He picks me up and twirls me around. "I knew it! I knew you were different."

We hold a look. "Mike, I never would have told Mr. Buchanan about the credits, I swear. But I'm sorry, really sorry, for even threatening that. I'll make it up to you with mountains of bamieh and zoolbia, I promise."

Ali and the punks are marching over. I brace myself for Ali to tear into me. I deserve it.

Instead, he says, "That was *punk*, man." Safety Pin Punk and Mohawk Punk nod in agreement. "Yeah," says Safety Pin Punk. "And we're gonna find whoever graffitied your house and beat their asses."

I shake my head emphatically. "I'd rather you come to the first meeting of my International Culture Club and convince people like Gerald why they're wrong."

They shrug. "Yeah, we'd rather beat the asses of whoever graffitied your house."

I'll talk them out of it later.

Beyond them, Patty and her sporty friends are staring at me.

"I'll be right back." As soon as I start toward Patty, she comes toward me. Like we're going to duel. We stand there for a minute not saying anything.

Finally, I say, "Patty, I'm sorry. You campaigned hard. I know you wanted to win."

She won't look directly at me. "Whatever. Thanks, I guess, for not narcing on me."

"If Gerald tries to get any of us in trouble, I'll take full responsibility."

Her eyes grow red and watery. She stares past me. "No one like him has ever liked me," she says softly.

I put my hand on her arm. "He doesn't deserve either of you."

We hold a look. Without answering, she turns and walks back to her sporty friends.

I'm so relieved it's all over, when I walk back to Mike, without thinking, I say, "Wanna go to prom with me?"

His eyebrows rear up. "Sure. If we're still here."

"What?" I don't understand.

"My dad. He might be redeployed to the Middle East."

As if I had any doubt this whole hostage crisis was not some elaborate scheme to throw the election to Gerald.

The bell rings. Mike drapes his arm around my shoulder and walks me to geometry.

〰〰〰〰〰〰

There's this high you get when you finally come clean after weeks and weeks of lying. I'm lighter, almost floating. Mr. Buchanan brings me back down to earth.

As soon as he sees me, he says, "Here to amend your application, I assume." My file is already on his desk. "Looks like you torpedoed your NYU admission." He looks closer at my application. "Zumideh. What kind of name is that anyway?"

I'm so shocked, I almost can't speak. "You . . . you said my name right!"

"When have I ever said it wrong?"

Er, every time.

"It's Iranian."

His head cocks, then starts nodding, like, yes, he's seeing it. He leans back in his chair, clasps his hands around his head. "You know, it took a lot of courage to do what you did."

"Thank you, Mr. Buchanan," I say, unexpectedly choking up.

"I bet you've learned a valuable lesson, young lady," he says, smiling up at President Nixon. "If you're going to go to the trouble of committing those crimes, you must do a better job covering them up."

||||||||||||||

When I get home, Auntie is in the kitchen chopping away. "Salam, joonam. How was school? Did you win your election?"

Her voice is so chipper, I stand there with a frozen smile. "Um, sort of, Amme Minah."

"I talk to my attorney today. It was a big mistake. I go back to Iran for only one month, he accidentally wrote one year. He talked to Immigration. Everything is okay with my green card. And your father will be home tomorrow. I am making the khoresht-e baademjoon."

I quickly set down my purse and folder. "Teach me."

Her face lights up. I grab an apron from the drawer.

"First, you get lamb from the butcher. Then four eggplant and two onion. Yellow, not white."

I throw my arms around her and give her a big kiss on the cheek. She is beautiful. I love that she makes us mounds of Persian food and wants us to be fluent in Farsi and has given us a crash course in All Things Iranian.

"Merci, Amme. Kheili mamnoon."

She wipes away a tear.

"The onion. It make me cry. Now. Can of tomato, whole tomato, not crushed. We are not making spaghetti sauce."

"Yes, Amme." I nod obediently.

"We are making the khoresht," she says with a grand sweep of her arm.

||||||||||||||

It's almost ten o'clock. It's been really hard not to call Bridget. But I know she needs time. I sift through my college admissions folder and dig out the Cal State application. I can complete mine and, when she's ready, help Bridget with hers. It's time for me to be *her* cheerleader.

My NYU acceptance package is still on my desk. It's harder than I would have thought to throw it out. What if I'm tossing away my whole future along with that letter of acceptance and housing and meal plan brochures?

I turn my dolls around so they can encourage me and do it in one, fell swoop. I do it, dump the whole thing in the trash.

The hardest part is over.

And no matter what, I will always be Mr. Ramos's first-ever acceptance to NYU.

I fish the letter of acceptance out of the trash and read it one more time, then slip it into my drawer. No one can ever take that away from me.

CHAPTER TWENTY-FIVE

HEAD OF STATE

Dad got in late today. We all sit down at the dinner table with him while he eats his khoresht-e baadamjoon. He says the background check is not unusual. He has to go through one every few years. "Everything okay here?" he asks.

Ali and Auntie and I exchange knowing glances. "Yes, fine, daadash," Auntie says.

Ali and the punks did a good job painting over the graffiti. We got every single bit of toilet paper down.

He turns to Ali. "Did you do as your sister asked? And what the hell happened to your hair?"

Before Ali can answer, I say, "He did, Dad. And I've decided to stick around here and go to State instead of NYU."

He doesn't need to know about the personal soap opera that went into my decision. He's too wrapped up in his own.

He cocks his head. "You sure? I though you wanted to be on the East Coast. Major in journalism."

My throat catches. "I'll get there. Eventually."

After dinner, when he's in his office, I linger at the door. Finally, he looks up. I'm really not sure how to say it, so I just come out and say it. "Tell Karen . . . not to come here anymore. Okay?"

His face flickers with embarrassment, but he nods and says, "Okay."

⫿⫿⫿⫿⫿⫿⫿⫿⫿⫿⫿⫿

After dinner, I go upstairs to call Mom. Grandma Jean answers. "Your mom is coming home soon, honey."

She *is*? "You mean we're not moving to Manhattan?"

"No."

I try not to whoop with joy.

"She decided it would be too much to uproot you and Ali. Now, you kids be kind to her. Please. She's going to be a bit fragile."

I finally understand why.

"We will, Grandma."

When Mom comes on the phone, she says we can get a place closer to Cal State University. "You won't have to drive so far."

I was going to say we could stay here since Dad is getting an apartment. But she probably wants a fresh start on a Karen-free cul-de-sac.

"Mom. Are you sure you want to come back?"

I mean, if this is her only opportunity for reinvention, Ali and I can tough it out in Manhattan for a couple years.

"I miss you kids. My job is there. It's your home."

Then, to my surprise, she excitedly adds—

"I may take a class at the junior college in the fall. Creative writing."

|||||||||||||

It's lunchtime, one week since I put the white rose and mix tape in Bridget's locker. She's sitting with Malia and Ginny. I'm sitting with Mike. Patty is with her sporty friends. Kyle is probably still nursing his wounds off-campus at the Shakey's all-you-can-eat buffet.

When the bell rings, I tell Mike I'll meet him in class and sidle over to where Bridget is sitting, hoping to catch her before fourth period.

Her jaw is tense, but she still says, "Hey," when I approach.

"Hey," I say.

Malia and Ginny do not say, "Hey." Their newfound status as Bridget's first- and second-best friends stings. But I'm determined to work my way back to number one.

Bridget stands up and faces me. "I got your rose and your mix tape." She nods across the quad to Patty. "Are you still talking to her?"

This will be the worst part. Trying to mend all the fences I tore down.

"Bridget, I don't blame you if you never forgive her. But I threw them together on my campaign. I should have told you about them. And I didn't."

She looks at the ground.

I raise my right hand. "I'll make it up to you, I swear. I'll wash your car every week and help you with your application for State. And I'll never lie to you again, I promise."

Her jaw relaxes. A little. "I heard they have a Delta Zeta chapter at State."

This is a test I'm determined to ace. "Yes! We'll rush together. That'll be so fun."

It's harder than you would think to be 100 percent honest at all times. I *will* rush a sorority if that's what Bridget wants. As penance. The equivalence of five thousand Hail Marys.

"Have you talked to Kyle?" I ask and immediately cringe.

"No."

Figuring out how to talk about what happened will take time.

"Bridget, c'mon," Malia calls out to her as the bell rings.

As Bridget turns to walk away, I say, "Maybe we can go for a double dip after school."

I'm about to kick myself for saying something so pushy when the faintest smile flickers across her face.

||||||||||||||

Even though I had tossed out the invitation, I'm still stunned when I hear the *meep-meep* of Bridget's Karmann Ghia from outside after school. I leap over the coffee table and grab my purse and keys before she changes her mind.

"Fosters Freeze or Baskin-Robbins?" she asks when I climb into the passenger seat.

"Either one," I say, swallowing nervously.

She pulls away from the curb and presses play on her cassette. Instantly, the familiar stomp-clap floods the speakers. "*S-A-T-U-R-D-A-Y . . . night!*"

I have to smile.

"I can't believe you made me take down my Bay City Rollers posters," she says.

"I'll put them back up if you want," I say.

We both laugh. It feels good, almost normal.

We talk about what she might major in at State—fashion merchandising is a strong possibility—and our strategies for getting the best Christmas tan but avoid any mention of Kyle.

I'm determined to follow her lead and talk about him only when she's ready.

|||||||||||||||

Auntie is flying back to San Francisco tonight. Mom will be home tomorrow. She made Mom's favorite for her return: chicken kabobs and rice layered with sour cherries.

Ali has brought her bags downstairs. Dad is jingling his keys, waiting impatiently to drive her to the airport, even though all the rush hour traffic has died down on the 405.

Finally, Auntie comes downstairs, tying her silk paisley scarf.

Suddenly, I get all choked up.

"Doostet daaram, Amme Minah." I fight back the tears. "And kheili mamnoon. Thank you. For everything."

"I love you, too, my dear Jasmine." She takes my face in her hands. "I am so proud of you, joonam. The way you stand up for Iranian people."

It's a losing battle. Tears stream down my face.

She gives Ali a big hug, adjusts her scarf, and follows Dad out the door.

After she's gone, Ali and I stand there for a quiet moment reflecting on these crazy past few weeks.

"Man, I'm going to miss her," he says. He heads for the kitchen. "We haven't eaten this good in years."

"Me, too." I nod, wiping my eyes.

Here I thought we didn't need anyone to take care of us.

‖‖‖‖‖‖‖‖‖‖‖

Mr. Ramos holds up my senior project during class. "Your first-person narrative of the whole election experience, your conflicts as an Iranian American. Best thing you've ever written."

Mike squeezes my hand. The first paragraph reads:

The giant yellow ribbons, they're everywhere: wrapped around every other column of the lower level of the mall to remind shoppers not to forget about the hostages. But while everyone else gets to think only of the hostages, Iranian Americans are forced to think about the students, what drove them to do something so desperate. The truth is, those who want to "round up" Iranians or bomb Iran don't know the whole story. It's my job—as an Iranian American and a journalist—to make sure they do.

Of course, Flynn has to add, "If you were a *real* journalist, you'd be writing about how the hostage crisis was totally engineered by the CIA to turn everyone against I-ran."

Mr. Ramos says we can hold our International Culture Club meetings in his room during lunch once a month. In March, we'll celebrate Persian New Year. Ginny wants to bring kimchi one month—pickled vegetables—and bulgogi (marinated barbecue beef) and talk about how her mom hates *M*A*S*H* because of its unrealistic portrayal of the Korean War. Mike will talk about Passover, this seven-day holiday with special meals and prayer services.

I want Malia's mom to talk about the Watts Riots—right after she gets over Malia deferring her enrollment at USC for a non-speaking role on this new TV show, *The Facts of Life.*

Gerald says he's starting his own club, Young Republicans for Ronald Reagan. Reagan used to be the governor of California. Now he's running against Carter for president. Before he was governor, he was, like, a silent film star.

Everything is finally getting back to normal.

When I get home from school, the January 1980 issue of *Creem* magazine with Joe Jackson on the cover is waiting for me on the kitchen counter.

Shit.

This is going to be harder than I thought.

I throw it in the trash.

‖‖‖‖‖‖‖‖‖‖

The February 1980 issue of *Creem* magazine with Debbie Harry on the cover is waiting for me on the kitchen counter when I get home. Could be good research for my "Where Are All the Punk Chicks?" article.

I hesitate a beat before throwing it in the trash.

Shit. Did I make the biggest mistake of my life?

‖‖‖‖‖‖‖‖‖‖

I talked to Mr. Ramos after class today. He says I didn't make the biggest mistake of my life, that writing samples count more than anything when pitching a magazine like *Creem*. He suggested I intern at *LA Weekly* over the summer to do artist interviews and record reviews.

There are a bunch of clubs we can go to in Hollywood when I turn eighteen. And on KROQ, Rodney Bingenheimer seems to think there's going to be a new, 1980s music scene exploding right here in Los Angeles. If so, I'll have a front-row seat.

The Pretenders—*Pretenders*
Record Review for the *Eisenhower General*
By Jasmine Zumideh

January 5, 1980

It's finally here: the stellar debut record from pop-punkers the Pretenders. Lead singer/songwriter Chrissie Hynde channels Iggy Pop's androgynous swagger under a driving beat and snarling guitars. She doesn't so much sing as command on tracks like "Precious," "The Wait," and "Tattooed Love Boys." But just when you're thinking the album is all propulsive guitar licks and battered drums, Chrissie's tender side takes over on "Up the Neck" and "Kid." "Brass in Pocket," a bouncy, pop tune, would be at home on American Top 40. Bottom line: the Ramones may wanna be sedated, but after listening to this album, I wanna be Chrissie Hynde.

I got my job back at Hot Dog on a Stick! I didn't even have to make out with the assistant manager. He knows I'm super skilled at dipping dogs. And Fake Burt Reynolds got fired for pretending to fellate one of the adult toys.

When I get home from my shift, the March 1980 issue of *Creem* magazine is on the kitchen counter with a bunch of artists on the cover including Graham Parker and Cheap Trick. I hesitate a beat before scooping up the magazine and heading to my room.

Bridget arrives a few minutes later with the latest issue

of *Seventeen*. We lie on the bed flipping through our magazines.

"Oh, um . . . Mike asked me to prom," I tell Bridget. "I mean, he reminded me that I had asked him and said he was accepting."

She doesn't answer.

It's been three months since the election fiasco, and there are still these awkward moments.

"I . . . I guess his dad hasn't been deployed to the Middle East."

"Whatever. Go if you want," she says, never glancing up.

"I'm not going," I say.

She flips her magazine shut and turns to face me. "*What? Why?*"

She *is* Bridget. She can't suddenly pretend she doesn't care about prom.

"I told him I have a date that night." I nudge her with my shoulder. "Remember? We're going to see *The Empire Strikes Back*."

I'll suffer through it. For Bridget.

She flashes me a smile and starts flipping back through her magazine. Super nonchalantly, she says, "Oh, I got accepted to State."

I can't help but squeal.

"Are you still sad? About NYU?" she asks.

"A little. But Mr. Ramos thinks I can succeed anywhere, even as an English major at State."

"Good. 'Cuz you're gonna have to help me with English. And we can rush that sorority together. My mom was a Delta Zeta . . ."

She goes on and on. But I don't mind.

On the days we don't carpool, I'm going to listen to those Learning Language cassettes. Firuzeh is also going to State. I'll be able to speak to her in Farsi.

Best of all, I just found out the Pretenders are playing Perkins Palace in Pasadena this October. Looks like I might be on that tour bus with Chrissie Hynde after all.

ACKNOWLEDGMENTS

This book would not be an actual thing you are holding in your hand (or tablet) without my agent, Laura Bradford, who patiently held mine during the entire submission process. You are truly a superwoman, Laura!

I have been blessed with the platonic ideal of an editor in Alexandra Sehulster, who *gets* me and my words, makes me go deeper and do better, and has been more supportive than a memory foam mattress covered in marshmallow fluff.

And thank you to Alexandra's assistant, Cassidy Graham, who has calmly and capably kept track of all the administrative details surrounding publication.

My gorgeous cover is just as fun, colorful, and chaotic as the events of the book thanks to the awesome talents of designer Olga Grlic and illustrator Petra Braun! Thank you to designer Devan Norman as well for the wonderful interior!

I am spectacularly grateful to the entire Wednesday Books team (I had a whole team!) who put their faith and heroic effort into the marketing and promotion of this book: Rivka Holler, Alexis Neuville, Brant Janeway, and Emily Day, as well as my publicist, Meghan Harrington, who has been a true champion of me and Jasmine.

I am so thankful for the early and continuing support of my dear friends—and best betas in the business—Kitty Schaller, Jena Ellis, Jessica Rose, Benita Shaw, and Carol Pearce.

How lucky I am to have found critique (and commiseration) partners in Lynn Q. Yu, Jason "J Bae" Nadeau, and Randall McCormick.

Additional, early-stage editorial input from Alison Weiss, Ellen Brock, and Roma Panganaban was enormously helpful.

I've inherited my love of words and my Persian half from my dad, Iraj Azimzadeh (whose political instincts I trust above all others'), and my deepening appreciation for Persian food and culture from my wonderful stepmother, Mitra Mohajer.

I am grateful for the unwavering pride my mom, Sharan McNerney, always had in me. I love you, Mom, and hope you can see and celebrate all of this from your perch up there.

Thank you, Grandma Jenny, for instilling a lifelong love of reading by teaching me how after my older sister, Shirin Donoghue (who's read and loved everything I've ever written), went off to kindergarten (I was so jealous!).

To my little bear, Teddy, who's been by my side (or on the couch or on our bed) for every minute of drafting, writing, and revising this book. And finally, I reserve my deepest gratitude for my husband, my very own Prince Charming, Wayne Boyer, and my son, Alec, who remains my proudest achievement.